Trio of
Sorcery

TOR BOOKS BY MERCEDES LACKEY

Firebird
Sacred Ground

DIANA TREGARDE NOVELS

Burning Water
Children of the Night
Jinx High

THE HALFBLOOD CHRONICLES
(written with Andre Norton)

The Elvenbane
Elvenblood
Elvenborn

Trio of Sorcery

MERCEDES LACKEY

TOR®

A TOM DOHERTY ASSOCIATES BOOK

NEW YORK

TRIO OF SORCERY

Copyright © 2010 by Mercedes Lackey

Book design by Ellen Cipriano

A Tor Book
Published by Tom Doherty Associates, LLC
175 Fifth Avenue
New York, NY 10010

www.tor-forge.com

Tor® is a registered trademark of Tom Doherty Associates, LLC.

ISBN 978-0-7653-2851-9

First Edition: November 2010

Printed in the United States of America

0   9   8   7   6   5   4   3   2   1

Dedicated to
Paul Fisher
aka
"Captive Brit"
Computer Wizard
Extraordinaire

Acknowledgments

I would like to acknowledge the invaluable help for "Ghost in the Machine" of game developers Vince "Dark Watcher" D'Amelio and Melissa "War Witch" Bianco of the MMORPG City of Heroes/City of Villians/Going Rogue produced by NCSoft/Paragon Studios (www.cityofheroes .com). They helped me balance the line between "this information will be outdated tomorrow" and "too much hand-waving, smoke, and mirrors" with their invaluable insights into the life and work of a dev and critique of the story.

I would also like to thank the Mission Architect team at the same game for allowing me to put Diana Tregarde as the contact for my Guest Author arc "Mystery on the Boardwalk." Go to www.cityofheroes.com for details and a fourteen-day free trial if you want to see this story in action!

CONTENTS

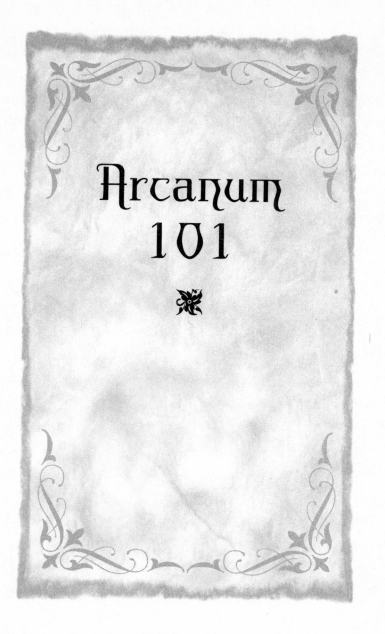

Arcanum 101

This is the first Diana Tregarde story in decades. And in a sense this is the first Diana Tregarde story, period.

It takes place in the early 1970s and it will be hard for anyone younger than thirty to realize what a very different world that was. Computers were the size of buildings. We were still putting men on the moon, but there is more computing power in a common iPhone than there was at all of Cape Kennedy. Watergate was about to happen. Nixon hadn't yet resigned. U.S. soldiers were still fighting and dying in Vietnam. There was no such thing as being "openly gay." There also was no such thing as HIV.

Jimi Hendrix, Janis Joplin, and Brian Jones were all recently dead of various self-indulgences, but John Lennon was still alive.

The only time you saw windmills was on a farm or in Holland.

Gas was twenty-five cents a gallon, threatening to go up to thirty.

No one had ever heard of, much less seen, a Japanese manga.

Britney Spears wasn't even born. Neither was Leonardo DiCaprio.

Stand-up comedians only performed in nightclubs with bad reputations, or in Las Vegas. No one would consider going out for a night of comedy.

There was no MTV. Anytime there was a rock-themed television program, it was an event. There was barely cable TV. Most people made do with three channels and what was not yet called PBS. When you had cable TV, you had a whole twelve channels!

"Portable" music was via a transistor radio.

No one had ever heard of rap. And if anyone had heard a rap song, they would have considered it a quaint offshoot of beat poetry, which was so, so 1950s.

You bought most of your reading material at the drugstore from revolving racks, or digest-size monthly fiction magazines in a small magazine rack, unless you were really lucky and were in a town big enough to actually have a bookstore.

Research meant going to the library and looking things up in books.

So as you read this, if you find yourself thinking, "Well, why didn't they just—" the answer is probably, "Because they didn't have it then."

Enjoy.

As apartments went, it wasn't much; a third-floor studio that had as its main attractions the fact that it was within walking distance of Harvard Square and the University, and that it had a fireplace. If you were a witch, a fireplace was a necessity. Some things just couldn't be done over the stove.

Not to mention that some things would be pretty dangerous without a chimney to carry off the smoke. It worked, she'd seen to that. Hers did, anyway. And she'd had a repairman in to make sure the dampers worked too. No point in sending heat up the chimney when she didn't have a fire going.

She put her back to the simple cast-iron fireplace with its chipped stone hearth and painted wooden mantel and surround and surveyed her tiny sanctuary.

It had no view; in fact, the only window looked right at the brick wall of the building next door. It got next to no

natural light. Both of these reasons were why it was cheap—
or cheaper than the apartments that had more "ambience."
No matter how spartan a place was, you were going to pay
for a place close to the University.

The floors were wood, but that was only because the
place was so old; there were still the remains of gaslight
fixtures in the room. Those floors were scarred and the
varnish was nearly black. The walls had been painted so
many times that the paint was nearly a quarter-inch thick.
The current color was sort of cream. The building dated to
1881, a fact Diana knew because the cornerstone had that
date carved into it. It was a real apartment building though,
not a house carved up into apartments. She was pretty
sure that this flat had been occupied steadily by poor
Harvard students—or possibly poor clerks or poor shop
employees—since the building was new. There was no
"Victorian charm" about this place. It was a plain little
painted box.

Diana Tregarde really didn't care that the place had no
ambience to speak of. What she cared about was the location and that it came unfurnished—which meant she could
move in her own bed and desk and anything else she
could squeeze in—and that it was cheap. She had done the
math, and an apartment close to Harvard and no car was
cheaper than a less expensive apartment farther away plus
the cost of owning and running a car.

She had her double inheritance squirreled away, but

that was going to have to last not only through her college years, but probably for at least a few months beyond, until she figured out how she was going to make a living.

No one was going to pay her to be a practicing witch, after all.

At least with her furniture and the things that she couldn't bear to put into storage in place, the apartment almost looked like home.

Almost, because Memaw wasn't here, and for a while, no place would be home without Memaw in it, and even after a year that was hard to get used to.

She shook off her melancholy. Memaw hadn't been young when she'd had Di's father, and *he* hadn't been young when he and her mother had produced Di. Memaw'd been ninety-three, very tired, very worn-out, aching in every joint and needing a walker or a wheelchair—it wasn't easy raising a budding witch and a probable Guardian—and she had been more than ready to go once Di could fend for herself. It wasn't fair to be unhappy because Memaw had gone on to the Summer Country. But it was so hard. . . . No Memaw to laugh at her mistakes and her jokes, to know exactly what to do when something magical was baffling Di—

You're just feeling sorry for yourself. Stop it.

She took stock of the place that was certainly going to be her home for the next four years, and probably beyond that. Under the window, the battered old rolltop desk that had been Memaw's held her typewriter, and beside the typewriter was the neat paper stack of her current project. In the bookcases on either side of the desk were all the books for all her classes this semester at Harvard.

She couldn't help her smug smile. She was a freshman. She wasn't supposed to be living off-campus, she was supposed to be living in a dormitory. The only freshmen who were allowed to live off-campus were those whose homes were in Cambridge, and who, presumably, were "properly supervised" by adult guardians. It might be 1972, but colleges still took *in loco parentis* seriously.

Well, she was legally an adult with her own means of support (even if it was an inheritance) and no legal guardian, and this apartment was, now, her home. Harvard didn't have rules covering this particular contingency. And after floundering for some time, the University reluctantly gave her off-campus privileges and assigned her to Dudley House, the House for a handful of graduate students and those others who weren't resident in any of the other twelve Houses.

Oh yes, the Houses. Harvard, unlike 99.9 percent of the other colleges and universities in the United States, operated on the English model. After your freshman year, you moved to a House, which had a Junior Common Room and a Senior Common Room and Tutors and . . . well, it all sounded like a Dorothy L. Sayers novel. But that would have been damned inconvenient for a practicing witch, and . . . dangerous too, for the people around Di. She didn't dare have a roommate, didn't dare be in a space where people

could just come waltzing in or would be suspicious of a
locked door.

She sighed. *This is a bloody inconvenient life, if you ask
me,* she thought, not for the first time, and went back to
her survey of her domicile to see if anything could be im-
proved. So, desk flanked by bookcases and the radiator
under the window, which was the west side. On the north,
a kitchenette with a tiny range, sink, and fridge, plus the
doors to her bathroom and closet, with Memaw's huge old
kitchen cupboard in between. Bed on the east wall flanked
by more bookcases, a canopy bed Di had built herself with
the help of a carpenter friend of Memaw's when she was
fourteen and decided that what she wanted for her birthday was a medieval canopy bed with a bookcase headboard
and heavy bedcurtains all around it. Memaw had insisted
it be a bolt-together thing "in case you ever need to take
it somewhere"; at fourteen she hadn't been able to imagine
that contingency, but now she was glad Memaw had insisted. So there it was, looking wildly incongruous in the
otherwise spare space. And on the south, the fireplace,
with her love seat and two comfortable chairs in front of
it, and on either side of it, locked cupboards that held
her . . . supplies. A black-and-white television sat on top
of the lower cupboard, her stereo next to it. The latter was
going to get more use than the former. Right now the radio
in the headboard of the bed was playing; the classical station. Not that Di disliked rock, but she wasn't in the
mood.

The ceilings here were very high. *If I can get the wood in here I can probably build a freestanding loft. That would be good for storage anyway.* As it stood, she'd have to go down to the storage units in the basement if she wanted any significant amount of firewood. Her unit was top to bottom with firewood she'd had loaded into the back end of the moving truck. She'd paid for a full load, so by golly, she made sure she got one.

A huge braided rag rug covered most of the floor. The walls had reproductions of Alphonse Mucha posters. The curtains on the window were from her old bedroom; Memaw's house had been an old Victorian too, and the windows of her old bedroom were just as tall. This was as homey as it was going to get.

She lit some cinnamon incense to give the place a scent, then went to the big cupboard to get out some candles. She'd made them herself, made a huge stock of them one year when she got the bug to try candlemaking. The ones for "public use" were all creamy white and bayberry scented. She'd even gathered the bayberries herself. Memaw had been big on doing everything you could for yourself. Especially when it came to your magic supplies.

After placing the candles around the room, she went to the bookcase to give a quick read to the first chapter of one of her course books. At Harvard you were expected to declare a "concentration" and Di had been torn between something practical, like—oh, law—and something she actually wanted to study. Maybe if Memaw was still alive, she'd have been able to face four years of something she really didn't want to do—

No, probably not. And she knew what Memaw would say. Had said. *"Choose what makes you excited. You can always bag groceries if you have to."*

If she could have, she'd have flung caution to the wind and asked for special studies in magic . . .

Bad idea, Di. Really bad idea.

So she picked the concentration she thought was closest to that: Folklore and Myth. She was by no means an expert in any other belief system than the more-or-less Celtic version Memaw had taught her, and knowing what critters might come out of you from another mythos was a very good idea. Especially for a Guardian. Too bad there wasn't a chance anyone was ever going to hire a Resident Folklorist . . .

But the only other thing that appealed, Fiction Writing, was . . . not an option either. She rather doubted that her professors would approve of the sort of fiction she wanted to write, and the sort they would want her to write would make her open a vein. Literary Fiction—well, from all her research, besides being the sort of thing that she loathed reading, let alone writing, Literary Fiction was not the stuff that put food on the table on any kind of regular basis.

Romance writing, however, did. Reading it, historical romance anyway, had been Di's secret guilty pleasure, shared with Memaw who was an avid Georgette Heyer fan, and Memaw had encouraged her in trying her own hand at it. What was more, Memaw was a good, and picky, critic. Di sometimes wondered if magic wasn't the only thing she'd gotten from her grandmother; many times she had wondered if Memaw herself had cherished the notion of being a writer, but had never gotten the encouragement and excellent critique that she lavished on Di.

She gave a look of longing at the typewriter, but picked up the book instead. Studies first.

It would take a while to get the first book sold, and more time to get to the point where she could make a living at it, and meanwhile, a degree from Harvard was not chopped liver. Once the country got out of that rat-bastard Nixon's recession, which according to *her* prognostications should be about when she graduated, she ought to be able to find *something*. Substitute teacher; a lot of places only required a sub to have a bachelor's degree and not in teaching. Librarian, maybe.

What the heck. I can always work in an occult bookstore.

She buried herself in the first chapter of her textbook, reading and taking notes. But when she was done and had closed the book, she found herself staring into the dark fireplace, pondering.

Because here was the problem. She was a Guardian. She'd been one since she was sixteen, which, Memaw had said, was about the right age for something like that to happen. Job, commitment, vocation, whatever it was . . . no one would ever, ever actually *pay* her to do this. In fact, that was the point. You did this work because it was the right thing to do, not because you were going to be rewarded in any way.

She was pretty sure that her parents had not been Guardians, though Memaw had never said. In fact, though she had only been three when they died, she was pretty sure they hadn't had so much as a hint of magic about them. They had both died when a train derailed and went into Newark Bay in 1958 in a terrible accident that killed forty-six other people. Ironically, the only reason her mother had been on the train was because she had wanted to go into New York City to shop. And there was no great anti-Guardian conspiracy at work in the deaths of her parents, either, just a terrible accident that had taken one or more of the parents of a lot of kids. Ordinary parents, as ordinary as hers.

Intelligent, without a doubt, and they had to have been good people, given Memaw, but utterly ordinary. Nothing in any of their belongings—Memaw had faithfully saved anything she thought Di might want to see one day—gave her any indication that they even suspected Memaw was anything besides a good mother and kind mother-in-law, much less a practicing witch.

Well, men did tend to be oblivious. From all the pictures in the family photo albums, Memaw had been the perfect housewife, even if she had been a single one, what with her husband never coming back from the Normandy invasion. Di could not even begin to imagine how hard it must have been to keep the fact that you were a witch secret from your husband. It was all very amusing in the movies, but in real life it must have made her inclined to tear her hair out.

The room was getting chilly as well as dark, and in accordance with some time-honored agreement among all landlords, the heat was not due to be turned on for a couple of weeks. Another good reason for the fireplace. Di had anticipated this, and laid the fire earlier; now she used the first spell she had ever learned to ignite both the tinder beneath the logs and the wicks of the candles.

"*Fiat ignis,*" she murmured, and pointed her finger at the fireplace, like a gun. The tinder went up with a *whoosh,* and the logs "took" immediately. So did the candlewicks, and the pleasant bayberry scent joined the cinnamon and wood smoke.

She pulled the crocheted afghan she'd gotten at a church sale over her legs and curled up, staring at the flames and thinking. The afghan was warm and soft, and had been made by someone who loved the feel of the yarn in her fingers as she worked. It had, as they said, "good vibes."

She couldn't recall a moment from the time she'd entered Memaw's home to stay that she hadn't known that her grandmother could do magic. She remembered Memaw soothing bumps and bruises with a touch and a murmur of words, remembered Memaw lighting candles and the fireplace, and remembered the teddy bear that Memaw had persuaded a house-spirit to "animate" once when Di was sick. Nothing like singing and dancing, just curling up, cuddling, and crooning. So Memaw must have known that Di had the gift too, and that the best way to teach her was to keep it from being something scary. On the other hand, Di also couldn't remember a time when Memaw hadn't made it very clear that this was something to be kept between the two of them. *"Not everyone can do this, sweetie. Keep it secret so they aren't jealous."* Or, *"The neighbors think we're strange enough, don't say anything about this, okay?"*

She had learned how to keep secrets from a very young age. Probably some child psychologist would make much of that, but she couldn't see that it had harmed her any.

Then again, there weren't a lot of kids who grew up being able to see things that no one else could. Saying "Look at that!" and pointing at the creature that was perfectly clear to *you*, but invisible to everyone else, taught you pretty quickly to keep your mouth shut.

Good thing that most people go, "Oh, what an active imagination!" when you're a little kid, not "Lock her up, she's nuts!"

Not that she could actually *do* magic until she was old enough to realize that it really did matter what the neighbors thought about you. That was the year that the other kids started calling her "Wednesday."

Memaw wasn't big on family photo albums, but they did have one, and now Di could admit that the nickname was apt. There were three photos of her from that year, two of them the mandatory class and school photos, and there she was, a stick-straight, solemn-eyed, dark-haired child with her hair in two equally straight ponytails. And while the teen glamour magazines were showing straight, straight mod hair, either long or short, no one around her town wore their hair like that. The flip was very much the thing, with some teasing on top. Not big hair, like the fifties, but not ironed-flat straight either.

She hated the nickname and she hated Wednesday Addams. But most of all she hated Jimmy Mason, who had first started calling her that.

She sighed and rested her head on her hand, elbow on the arm of the love seat.

She had Memaw cut her hair boyishly short, but nothing would get him to stop. Finally she decided she was going to curse him.

It wasn't hard to get "something" from him. She used her big vocabulary for once, standing where the teachers could see her, but not necessarily hear her, and started taunting him. Finally, as she had known he would do, he flew into a rage and came at her.

She'd been dodging worse things than him for two years at that point (though never, never as bad as the things she encountered once she was a Guardian). She was coming into her magic, and arcane critters smelled that, and scented her youth, and came hunting. She easily dodged him, but while he was windmilling away, trying futilely to hit her, she snatched a tiny handful of hair. He squalled and came at her harder, which was when the teachers finally took notice (or resignedly knew they were

being forced to take notice, they didn't care for her either),
and pulled him off.

She had her prize.

She took it home and began to construct a Curse Doll.
Memaw caught her at it of course, because all manner of
tiny little nasty things started flitting about her the moment she began doing something that dark. Rather than
stop her, though, Memaw just stared her down until she
stopped of her own accord.

Then Memaw told her, in blunt and no uncertain terms,
about the Threefold Law. "Now," she finished. "I don't for a
minute think that boy doesn't deserve a set down. But if you
give more tit than he gave tat, *you* will be getting every bit of
that, times three, right in *your* face. Reckon you want that?"

Now, by this point, she was accustomed to actually
stopping and thinking things through when confronted by
such a question, and it didn't take much thinking to realize that no, she didn't want that. All he'd done was taunt
her. Well, she'd taunted him back, she'd made him furi-
ous, and gotten him in trouble at school for fighting on
top of that. The score was probably even at this point.

But Memaw hadn't let it rest there. "You want to teach
some sprout a lesson, you put the Mirror on him," she continued, an ever-so-slightly malicious smile on her face.
"I'll show you."

So that afternoon she had taken the doll and showed
Di how to cast the Mirror of Consequences on someone.
It was *hard*. It was the hardest spell she had ever done to

that point, even with assistance, and it was still hard, to this day, because you had to be absolutely fair about it, or it wouldn't work, it would be flawed, and the flaws would break it. What it did was to reflect everything that someone did right back at him. So there were immediate consequences to his actions and words, instead of delayed. If he taunted someone, those taunts would be reflected back on him, so that instead of getting the laughs he'd gotten before from calling her Wednesday, people wouldn't find it quite so funny, and would think about the time he'd called them, or a friend, similar names. If he tried to fight, he would lose; either his opponent would suddenly find more strength and skill than he normally had, or an authority figure would take notice and intervene right away. The more he hated, the more he would *be* hated.

But it wasn't all one-way, this Mirror. If he started acting nice to people, that would be reflected too. People would like him more, just for starters.

Now they call that "instant karma," she reflected.

"You've done this before, haven't you?" she'd said to Memaw, who only smirked.

Well, Jimmy got his dose of instant karma when everyone started calling him "Mason Jar." It was a stupid name, it wasn't even that much of an insult except that Jimmy was built like a fireplug. But it got his goat. And when he came at people, the teachers noticed *instantly*. He didn't have any time to taunt her anymore, and without him to keep it going, people stopped calling her Wednesday.

Later that year his dad's job moved them down south, so she had no idea what happened to him. But Memaw had reminded her to take the spell off him, so she did. Reluctantly, but she did. Did he ever learn his lesson? Maybe. Maybe not. Whether he did or not, as Memaw reminded her, was up to *him*, not her.

"You can't make someone change," she'd said. "All you can do is make it uncomfortable for 'em not to. And if you aren't around to supervise, well, better take the heat off before they boil over."

Memaw had let Di read virtually anything she wanted to, from the old grimoires in spidery handwriting to the comic books that she got with her allowance money. And maybe that was the reason why, all those comic books, and the idea that if you had power you had to do something good with it, that she'd done what she had done. She still could not imagine herself saying anything but yes to the question that had been posed to her, the night she turned sixteen.

She didn't remember most of it, actually. Which the few other Guardians she'd spoken to so far had told her was pretty typical. Mostly they all remembered very intense light, the sense that they were being offered enormous power if they only used it to keep ordinary folks safe, and someone or something waiting for an answer. And then the next day . . . well, there it was. Where there had been a little warm glow of magic inside, there was now this— atomic reactor. And there was the certain knowledge that if it was ever used selfishly it would be abruptly taken away. There were no second chances when you were a Guardian. And Di suspected that if you said no, you wouldn't ever remember getting the offer.

Memaw had recognized what had happened to her. The moment that Di came down to breakfast that first morning, Memaw had given her a strange look . . . and from then on treated her not like a teenager, but like an adult who simply didn't have as much experience as she did.

She had shown Di some passages in some of those old grimoires, about how to call the Guardians if you were in trouble. There was even something like it in a Dione Fortune book, although Fortune didn't call them "Guardians," and her ritual was dorky and awkward, if sincere, and *nothing* like the ones the witches used. By that point, of course, Di had known that the ritual itself didn't matter, it was that you knew Guardians existed, and that if you got into occult trouble that you hadn't caused, and you called on them, they'd come.

"But what if what happens is your fault, Memaw?"

"Depends. But everything has consequences, my girl, and those consequences fall harder on those who meddle with magic. Just bear in mind, when you get the Call, you must answer."

Within a week of accepting the power and the job, she had gotten the Call.

That memory was as clear as the one of being offered Guardianship was vague.

The funny thing was she had half expected to be jolted awake in the middle of the night, or to see some ethereal creepy-crawly come smashing through her bedroom window. What happened was much calmer than that. In the middle of the day, a strange woman had come up to the door and knocked. When Memaw answered, the woman had said hesitantly, "They say someone here can help me—"

Then she had seen Di, standing behind Memaw, and nodded. And Di had *known*.

"I can," she said steadily, and stepped forward. And Memaw, who otherwise would have had all manner of questions, simply moved aside.

It had been a matter of a family curse, which Di had never felt was a particularly fair situation, and in this case, where the woman was someone's illegitimate child, the daughter of a man she didn't know, it was particularly unfair. This first time—other Guardians told her the first time was always easy and clear-cut—the solution was simple and straightforward. She offered herself as the woman's Champion, was accepted, and fought a mage-duel with the revenant that kept the curse going. It fell and dissipated, and that was that. Well, not *quite* that simple; it had been one heck of a fight and had required everything she could muster. But she had never had a moment of doubt that, as long as she kept her head, she was going to win.

As "just" a witch, she would never have had the strength to fight off a revenant like that. It probably would have taken an entire coven to take the thing down, and maybe

not even then. Most of the time, if a family curse was involved, all a coven could do was shield one individual
from the effects of the curse; the next appropriate family
member would then find the full curse descending on
him or her. And it was heartbreaking, utterly heartbreaking, to see someone who was the last in a line have to decide whether or not to risk having a child. Not *children*,
because it would be difficult to protect two people from
a powerful, generational curse with the resources of a
single coven; three would be almost impossible. A single
child would be all that a cursed individual would dare to
have. And then that meant that eventually the parent would
have to subject that child not only to the need to protect
itself but the decision of whether or not to have a child of
his or her own. And so on . . .

But no. Di was a Guardian. And if the person in question was truly innocent, and the curse in question entirely unfair, she could end it by ending the thing that
powered it.

Even if . . . as in this case . . . the thing that powered
it was the tattered and bitter remains of the spirit of the
person that had created the curse in the first place.

It had been simple. It had been very clear-cut. The solution was obvious and well within her arsenal of spells. As
other Guardians said, the first time was always clear-cut
and easy in the sense that the solution was obvious. But
easy in the sense that it was effortless? Not even close.

It's raining. Why does it always rain when the shit hits the fan?

And night. It was always night when bad things happened, but that was kind of par for the course. Bad Things liked the night. The few Bad Things that didn't like the night generally preferred the other extreme, burning sun and destructive heat. She didn't think it was likely she was going to run into any ancient Egyptian demons any time soon, so she had better get used to after-hours work.

Mind you, she was having no trouble actually seeing. There was so much lightning that it was like a disco or a rock concert.

It was midnight, she was in the middle of nowhere, and it wasn't just raining, it was bucketing down. If Di hadn't been reasonably sure that some Guardianly immunity from lightning strikes was going to protect her while she was doing Guardian business, she'd have been flat on the ground praying she didn't get hit.

She slogged through knee-high weeds in her toughest (soaked) jeans and the rubber stable boots she was glad Memaw had insisted she wear, with a sledgehammer in one hand and a duffle in the other, making her way by what she could see in the flashes. She was in the barren graveyard of an old farmstead, which itself was nothing more than the stump of an old chimney and a riot of blackberry vines. The graveyard was so old and abandoned that the headstones were all but unreadable, but she didn't need headstones to tell her where her target was. The spell she had cast to allow her to see magic left no doubt as to where she was going. She crossed the line where the old wooden fence had once been, stepped onto the graveyard soil, and paused.

A heavy black miasma hung over the grave she was seeking. She approached it, keeping her shields up against a thick fog that actually resisted her as she pushed her way to the headstone. It couldn't touch her, not through her protections. It kept clear of her by a good three inches, trying to surge forward but not getting past her shields.

Once she reached the grave site itself, she put down the bag of tools she was carrying in her right hand, and shifted the sledgehammer she had been carrying in her left into both hands. It was as heavy a hammer as she could manage to swing. Memaw had suggested it. "Some people would leave the headstone, but since there isn't anyone going to notice out there, I say, be sure." Di had agreed, and together, the two of them had made plans to consecrate it.

Lightning flashed as she swung the sledgehammer grimly over her head, and thunder boomed just as she hit the stone.

She didn't think it was coincidence.

When the flash and boom repeated with each of the next three blows, she became sure that it wasn't coincidence—

and given the surge of energy she felt each time she hit the headstone, she was also sure that whatever was in control of the lightning was also on her side. She wasn't a weakling . . . but she wasn't all that strong either, and the granite headstone shouldn't be shattering the way it was, like a Hollywood rock in a movie about chain gangs. With exactly nine blows, the marker was obliterated, no piece any larger than a quarter.

Di reached into her bag and pulled out the shaker jar of consecrated salt. Ordinary salt would do, according to the grimoire, but as Memaw said, why take chances? Sheltering the jar from the rain so the salt wouldn't clump and clog the holes in the top, she shook the jar vigorously and coated the fragments and rubble of the headstone with the salt.

Nothing happened when she did that, but she hadn't expected anything to. The real fight was about to start.

She was soaked to the skin despite her raincoat, her hair was plastered flat to her head, and it was a good thing she'd tied it back hard or she'd never have been able to see. The miasma roiled in protest, rising up in waves that threatened, but did not actually wash over her. Dear gods, it was freezing—much colder than it should have been. It was a cold she knew; she'd felt it before around ghosts. What was new was the fury she felt directed against her, like a blizzard wind, ice-edged and lethal.

She put the sealed jar back down in her bag. She was going to need it again in a while. Then she took out the shovel.

Bloody hell, I don't know why they didn't issue me with a little Guardian ditchdigger while they were giving me the rest of it. . . .

This time there were no timed rumblings in the heavens when she took the first shovelful. Once again, though, it was as surprisingly easy to dig as it had been to shatter the headstone. This wasn't like moving heavy soil loaded with rain, it was more like shoveling sand at the beach. Maybe they weren't giving her a little work crew of her own, but at least they were helping. Whoever *they* were.

The rain pounded on her head and the black fog circled her, hating her, but still unable to touch her. Di figured that since no one had come after this thing before, and it had never encountered opposition, it wasn't sure what to do about her. She wasn't one of the ones that had been cursed—but she was marked as the woman's protector. The rules had been abruptly changed, and it didn't yet know how to react.

While she worked, she talked. She had very little expectation that the revenant was going to listen to her, but hey, it was worth a shot. No matter that she could hardly hear herself over the thunder, the revenant would hear her no matter what was going on. It didn't have a choice in the matter.

"I understand why you're angry," she said, punctuating each word with a shovelful of dirt. She was already knee-deep in the grave, and very glad that she was used to a certain amount of physical labor. *Never thought I would be*

grateful to Memaw for making me chop all that firewood. . . .
"Silas Macreedy was a horrible, horrible man. I am sure
that he is in some version of hell, and he deserves to be
there." She dug into the sides, lengthening the hole and
making it wider. "He preyed on you and your family in
every way possible. There was no excuse for what he did.
In a fair and just world, he would have been caught and
punished. I cannot even begin to imagine how hard it was
for you, to see what he did to them, and as for what he did
to you—well, I'll be honest with you, I'd have shot him
too." *Of course, it wasn't just that you shot him. It was that
you served as his guide out into the woods, then shot his
ankles, then spent three days torturing him before you killed
him. On the other hand, I can't really blame you too much. He
was a beast.* She put her intent behind the words. Maybe,
just maybe, that would get through to the revenant. "His
son was just as bad. Even after all that came out, you got no
justice at all. The Macreedy family used their money and
influence to get you hung, to discredit everything you said.
They managed to sweep everything Silas had done under
the rug and a death curse is exactly what they deserved."

The miasma didn't seem mollified.

"But only the first generation. That was punishment
enough. Your curse ruined them, they all died in painful,
awful ways, and no one who was responsible for what happened to your family escaped. But it should have ended
there. The second generation was more honest, and before
he died, Everett Macreedy told his wife and children

what had happened and charged them with making it up to your family. That's where it should have ended." *Why punish the innocent? That's like the Mirror Curse, left on someone when you know you won't be there to take it off if things go too badly. Only much worse.*

"You shouldn't have continued the vendetta past them. Not like this. Brenda didn't even know she was a Macreedy until she found an honest psychic. She never did anything to you or yours. She is a good woman. How can you blame her for simply having the misfortune to be born to an idiot who vanished on her mother? I've looked into every nook and cranny of her life, and she has never been anything but a good person. There's no one left of your family to make further atonements to. You have to stop now."

The digging really was going faster than it should have. Then again, the hard part was yet to come. She'd been afraid as she got deeper that the walls of the hole she was digging would collapse in on her, or that she'd be digging in a rapidly deepening pool of mud and water, but the earth stayed firm and the water drained away, leaving her with wet dirt under her feet. The hole was waist-deep now.

"Six feet" was the prescribed depth of a grave, but not in this soil. Bedrock was only four feet down, which was good, since her kit bag was on the side of the grave and she would be able to reach inside easily. She'd hit the coffin soon—

Her shovel scraped along something that sounded hollow.

And that was when the miasma came together into a shape and loomed over her from where the headstone had stood. Vaguely human, with burning-hot green eyes. She looked up at it.

"You know nothing!"

The words didn't so much resonate in her ears as in her head. She was expecting that. The very few immaterial things she'd spoken with had "talked" like that. Memaw said that *some* things could make real sounds, but not many, and most of those had a way to become fully material, like the banshee. This one's words were laden with a terrible anger, as if it was trying to frighten her out of the grave. Each word hit her like a blast of ice.

"Then tell me I'm wrong about Brenda, and I'll leave you alone," she replied calmly, although every hair on her body was standing straight up.

"Unto the seventh generation!" it spat at her. *"Unto the seventh generation! That is the curse!"*

The revenant was not listening. There probably wasn't much there *to* listen. What was left of the spirit had devoted so much of itself to revenge that revenge was all that was left. But she still had to try. "Prove to me that I'm wrong about Brenda and I'll leave you alone," she repeated.

Instead of replying, it attacked.

It moved with unbelievable speed. One moment, she

was staring at the vaguely human shape; the next, she only had time to register that it was moving before everything went black. It flung itself on her, enveloping her, trying to suffocate her as it had so many of Brenda's relatives, after it had destroyed their lives, driven away everything they loved, and filled their sleeping moments with night-mares and made their waking moments a misery. It managed to cover her completely; and although it couldn't actually force its way down her throat past her shields, it *did* cut off her air, along with her senses.

But she'd been ready for that. And now that she knew the lightning was on her side, so to speak—

She fought down the immediate rush of *I can't breathe!* and concentrated. There was a spell, if she could keep from panicking long enough to remember it. . . .

Then the words formed in her mind, and the signs and sigils, and she dropped the shovel and got the hilt of her sacred knife, her *atheme*, in her hand. She pulled it from the sheath at her side, thrust it toward the heavens, and shouted—as best she could, with fading breath and against the muffling of the thing that had wrapped itself around her—the words to call the lightning to her.

White.

It wasn't a flash of light as much as a moment of sear-ing whiteness. A moment when everything stopped and she stood there, blinded, transfixed, like a bug on a pin of power, at the heart of the blaze of a light that was so much more than light.

And then—

Then she was standing in the rain with her right hand stretched up, knife pointing at the sky, her clothing steaming.

The miasma was nowhere to be seen, but that didn't mean it was gone. Just temporarily dispersed. She had maybe ten minutes before it was back.

Better dig faster.

So she did. She dug as fast as she could, uncovering the coffin, then prying up the lid. It should have rotted away by now, but it hadn't. It hadn't because the revenant needed the coffin and what was in it in order to survive and keep killing. And with every kill it made, it got stronger, so it could keep the coffin and its contents intact, and keep killing. It was a vicious cycle and one that needed to end now, or it would not end until the last person with Macreedy DNA in his or her body died. "Unto the seventh generation?" That was a joke. This thing wanted to live on in the only way it knew, and it wasn't going to abide by any term limit. Once it got done with Macreedy descendants, well, it might find some other targets. That was how these old curses went—if they didn't get weaker with age, and this one hadn't, the thing behind the curse had found the way to a mad immortality.

The miasma began to form again as Di levered up the coffin lid. She was not at all surprised to see the intact body of Taylor Marcham inside, the marks of the rope that had hung him still on his neck.

The rain stopped, cut off abruptly. The graveyard went deathly still.

The miasma poured into the grave in a flood of fury and hate.

Poured into the body.

Taylor Marcham sat up in his coffin, face contorting in a spasm of rage.

Di jumped on his chest, driving him back down.

The body struggled insanely for a moment, clawing at her boots, shredding her jeans with its fingernails. But she was a lot stronger than she looked, she had leverage, and although the century-old body was intact, it was fragile. It broke several fingers on her boots and tried unsuccessfully to buck her off while she beat at it with the shovel. Abruptly it went limp.

Di wasn't fooled. She drove the shovel down, decapitating the corpse. In the moment of relief that gave her, she fumbled along the side of the grave and groped in her bag for the jar of salt, the jar of blessed water, and the rope from the noose that had hung him—which, bizarrely enough, she had found in the little wreck of a county museum down the road. Shouting the words of banishment and blessing, she doused the body head to toe in salt, then holy water; she dropped the rope on the body's chest as the miasma surged out of the neck cavity and went for her again.

This time she didn't need the lightning. *"Fiat lux!"* she screamed, and another burst of white-hot light erupted from her, fueled by whatever that power was that inhabited her.

The miasma, again in vaguely human shape, was flung from her, breaking up a bit as it was repelled. She took that opportunity to get out of the grave, snatching up the jars of lighter fluid from the bag and flinging them into the grave so that they broke and splattered all over the body.

Then she called fire.

"Fiat ignis!" she screamed, pointing at that thing in the grave.

The body went up in a sheet of flame all out of proportion to the amount of lighter fluid she'd thrown in there.

There was the worst scream she had ever heard in her life, and a final bolt of lightning cracked out of the sky and slammed into the grave, flinging Di backward and onto her ass in the mud, blinding her again. Her nose filled with the smell of ozone and she blacked out for a moment.

When she came to, there was rain in her face, mud in her ears, the smell of burned bones and burned hair in her nose, and the graveyard was empty of menace, dark clouds, or anything else.

She had to somehow explain to the nurse at the emergency room why she had flash burns on her face.

Fortunately, she didn't have to explain to Memaw.

She came to herself with a start, staring at the dying flames in the fireplace.

Crap. Tomorrow is the first day of classes.

Well, if old memories are the worst the universe is going to throw at me tonight, I guess I'm going to be all right here.

Phooey. I am cream-crackered. She dropped her books on the top of the bookcase next to the desk and stared at the little kitchenette with a frown. *Lunch. Must make lunch. And my brain is full.* Finally, after a moment of indecision, she went to the stove to start hot water for tea. Tea and a PB&J was about all her brain was up to for the moment. She had known intellectually that college was going to be hard, but she hadn't really grasped that it was going to mean a racing start right out of the gate.

Speaking of racing starts . . . This building was full of other students, and there was no elevator. The staircase was at the far end of the hall, but she could still hear people running up or down it to get to or from their apartments for lunch. She could see now why the House for the off-campus types was a good idea. It had a library, a lounge, and a cafeteria . . . and when winter came in earnest, staying there between classes instead of going home was beginning to sound like a good idea.

As she made the sandwich, she cocked her head to the side and listened to the sounds from her upstairs neighbors. There was only one floor above hers—she'd really wanted a studio on the fourth floor, to prevent the inevitable herd-of-elephants above her head, late-night party noise, and bathroom leaks, but there weren't any available. So far, though, they hadn't been too bad. Or else the floors were thicker than she thought. They mostly didn't seem to use the floor as a trampoline, or a football field.

They were men, though, so their footfalls weren't exactly light.

Their names were Itzaak Meyer and Emory Sung, and she imagined that mealtime up there probably got pretty interesting. Probably American, maybe New York deli versus—well, she didn't know Emory's exact nationality, "Sung" could be Korean, Chinese . . . probably not Japanese. Kimchee versus sauerkraut?

Or maybe I'm wrong. Maybe they both like the same food. Hell, for all I know they both like Italian.

Wait, they were men. They wouldn't cook. Would they?

The kettle whistled and she made tea. She amused herself with those thoughts and ate her sandwich in neat little bites before working her way through the Moral Reasoning course homework. That was one of the Core courses that all Harvard students were required to take, and she had figured she would get it out of the way as quickly as possible. She hadn't quite known what to expect from the title Moral Reasoning, and then she'd seen that it wasn't just one course. She could choose one from among several options; she'd opted for Human Rights, a Philosophical Introduction. It seemed like a good solid choice, something she wasn't likely to flounder in.

That was her first course of the morning. Then came one of the Historical Study track courses, another Core Requirement; those assumed that you had a general foundation in history and elaborated on what they figured you knew. They were supposed to give you insight into how major issues had developed. She'd picked the course on Japan. She didn't know very much about Japan, and now would be a good time to work on that before she had to deal with Japanese folklore in class or nasty Japanese critters on the street.

I need to take a martial arts course.

Judo? Probably. Nasty critters were sometimes very physical in nature. It would be nice if she could ever find someone who actually believed they existed to teach her, but that was like hoping for a money tree to sprout.

The third course that rounded out her morning was a science class, also in the Core Curriculum. She'd picked a basic Archeology course, which had looked pretty interesting from the source description. Now that she'd gotten into it, it looked as if it was going to be more physical than mental, which was good, because she needed something that wasn't going to make her brain explode just before lunch. And who knew? She might be able to use some of what she had learned at some point. Guardians kicked around a lot of strange things.

After lunch was her first Folklore course, followed by nothing. Which would give her most of the afternoon for homework, and most of the evening for writing. Assuming that—

There was a knock on the door, which made her jump and spill her tea a little. She sighed at the interruption, swiped at the tea with her napkin, and got up. Well, maybe it would be one of the boys upstairs. Maybe one of them would be nice. Even handsome. Maybe he'd ask her out.

Maybe pigs will grow wings.

She opened the door, eyeballed the man standing there, half illuminated by the staircase window at the end of the hall, and immediately knew it was *not* one of the boys from upstairs.

It was a cop. She knew cops; how they stood, dressed, moved. She could spot a cop at five hundred yards. Even though this one was in his civvies, she knew cops, and this was one.

"Miss Tregarde?" the cop asked. "Diana Tregarde?" He had a nice voice, a calm tenor. He did not flash a badge. So whatever he was here for, either he was trying to find out something without being official or he really was off-duty. In either case, he knew her name, and obviously where she lived—and why did he know these things? She didn't have a car to be illegally parked, she was just another Harvard student. Her suspicion meter went up a couple of notches.

She nodded, but did not step aside nor invite him in.

47

Until she knew why he was here, she wouldn't either. Not just because she was paranoid—you couldn't live in Nixon's USA and not be paranoid—but also because she wanted no part of some fishing expedition. She didn't know anyone here in Cambridge except one other Guardian and she hadn't had any real friends to speak of back home, but that didn't mean that a cop wouldn't try to make something out of nothing.

And he knew her name.

For all she knew, that flashback last night had been a warning, telling her that something out of the past was going to come calling and make trouble for her.

The hallway was very, very quiet. So she wasn't the only one around here who had spotted him for what he was. Lovely.

The cop smiled, looking embarrassed. "I know you don't know me, but Lavinia Thurgood sent me. I asked her for a little help with something, and she told me you were in town and that you were better suited to what I need than she is. She says you're pretty good at exposing phony tea-leaf readers and Gypsies."

Well that was a bolt out of the blue. She blinked at him. "How do you know Lavinia?" she asked cautiously.

"She's a cousin," he said, and coughed. "I, ah, ask her for help sometimes when I get the kind of . . . you know . . . weird stuff. Stuff no one can explain . . ." His voice trailed off.

That made sense, since Lavinia was another Guardian.

One of the handful that Di had actually talked to; in fact, one of the first ones she had talked to, who had given her what she called "Arcanum 101," walking her through the basics of what it meant to be a Guardian.

She nodded. "I understand." For all that Lavinia knew her Ritual High Magic like no one else, she was not good with real-world stuff.

So, phonies. That had been Memaw's pet bugaboo.

That had nothing to do with Guardians, and everything to do with the fact that Memaw had debunked many a "trance medium" in her time. She took a very dim view of people exploiting other people and giving magic a bad name. Real magic, that is. Her pet peeve was the kind of charlatan who would use stage magic to convince people in some of the new witchcraft circles—people who didn't know any better—that he was the real deal, then take everything he could get from them.

There was one guy Memaw really, really hated. He'd been all over the country—he'd pull his song and dance number on some "New Pagan" group, milk them blind, seduce anything with boobs, then do a vanishing act. Then he'd turn up in some old lady's tea and séances Spiritualist group, and do the same there, minus sleeping with the women. And *then* he'd vanish and turn up at some Bible-thumping church, begging to be saved from satanism and use the same stage magic to convince them that he was really being besieged by demons and get into *their* pockets (and sometimes their beds). She still hadn't managed to nail him when she died, though not for lack of trying.

Memaw had taught Di everything she knew about debunking.

"First, you probably should tell me the problem." Di still didn't let him in, even though he was kind of cute. Actually, really cute. Black hair, faintly tan, like a young Ricardo Montalban. Black Irish, obviously—the many-times-removed descendant of some of the Spanish sailors from the Armada wrecked off the shores of Ireland back in the fifteenth century. Very, very cute. Still.

He stood in the hallway, looking uncomfortable, but did not ask to come in. He shoved his hands deeply into the pockets of his blue Members Only jacket and shifted his weight to one foot. "I'm one of a bunch of guys on that kidnapping case," he said slowly.

He didn't have to say more than that, because you would have to have been living in a cave not to know about it. She drew in her breath in a hiss. The kidnapping had been everywhere in the news, and it was making even the Harvard students nervous, though they were way, way outside the age of the victim.

Melanie Fitzhugh was eight years old; she wasn't a particularly pretty little girl, she was actually fairly ordinary, but that just made it all the worse. Every parent with a child could imagine the same thing happening. Melanie and her mother had been shopping and the little girl had gotten permission to play in a designated play area in the mall. She knew not to leave, but when her mother came back, she was gone. Other children at the play area told Mrs. Fitzhugh that a "policeman" had come to take Melanie to her mother and that she had gone away with him. There had been no other adults in the play area at the time, but it was supposed to be a very safe place, surrounded by stores, the perfect place to leave a responsible child for a few minutes.

Unless, of course, there was a predator in the area who was very, very clever. One who knew exactly how to approach exactly the kind of middle-class child who would trust someone dressed like a policeman.

Still, what did that have to do with debunking psychics?

"I'd like to know who I'm talking with and why before this goes any further," Di began.

"I'm not asking you to help with the case," the cop said, and finally produced his badge and ID, flushing. "Well, not directly. This would be strictly off the books." He handed her the badge and ID to look over, and shifted his weight to the other foot. "If you can, I'd like you to give me a hand with Chris, Melanie's mother. Some creep of a so-called 'psychic' got to Chris Fitzhugh and now we can't get anything out of her but 'Tamara says' this and 'Tamara says' that and 'Did you look into Tamara's leads yet?'"

"Has she been asking for money?" Diana asked, cautiously examining the ID. *Joe O'Brian.* Well, it looked genuine, and his very being did shout "cop"; she handed it back and he shoved it in his pocket again. "The psychic, I mean. That's what they usually want."

"No, which is why we can't get Bunko on it." O'Brian looked incredibly frustrated. "You'd think she was one of God's own saints, to hear Chris rave about her. I just . . ." He shook his head. "It's making us crazy."

She refrained from commenting.

"Her husband too. This Tamara is the only person that Chris is listening to, she's not even talking to him any-more." Joe ran his hand through his hair, disturbing it from its "regulation" comb. "If you can just prove she's a phony, I mean prove it in a way that Chris can't help but believe—"

Di shook her head. "I don't know. You're talking about someone who is desperate, and this psychic is giving her answers of the sort she wants to hear. That's like arguing with someone's religion. I mean, using only empirical evidence I can prove that half the saints in the Catholic calendar either never existed or were nothing like the legends—"

Joe flushed again. *Ha. With a name like O'Brian, I figured he was Catholic.*

"But that means nothing to what people believe, and belief is impossible to budge until people are ready, on their own, to hear the facts. Sometimes that never happens." It certainly had never happened with Memaw's *bête noire.*

He grimaced. "Would you at least check this chick out? See what she's all about? Find out if she's working an angle so we can shove a stick in her spokes?"

Clearly he was not going to go away until she said yes. He had the look of a man on a mission.

Okay. What can it hurt? Maybe I can find out an angle that Bunko can get her on.

"I'll go have a look at her, but no promises," Di replied. "And she had better be on a bus line, because I have no car. And it won't be right away. I have classes."

It was quite clear that Joe wasn't paying any attention to anything after yes. The tightness in his face eased, as if he had gotten some terrible burden off his back. "Here's her card, Chris shoves these at us by the handful," he said, sounding immensely relieved. "And here's mine. And thank you—"

"Don't thank me until I come up with something," she replied a little sourly. She let him babble on for a little more, until he finally got the hint and said goodbye. She closed the door feeling . . . odd.

Very tingly, antsy, oh-crap-something-is-up sort of odd. Storm-about-to-break odd.

Oh, hell. Guardian odd.

She looked at the psychic's card, but this time whispered the mage-sight spell and waited as her vision of the world settled into a new configuration.

The card changed in mage-sight, and it was not a good

change. It was haloed in a very, very nasty black aura with greenish edges.

She looked at the other card O'Brian had given her.

Oh, double hell. To mage-sight, the cop's card was overlaid with a red crusader's cross. It was a legitimate Call.

"I do not need this," she said aloud with exasperation, and put her back against the door, staring up at the painted tin of the ceiling.

She had hoped that everything would change in college. She'd never had friends in high school. She'd never had a date, much less a boyfriend. How could she? Before she'd turned sixteen, she'd been a practicing witch, living on the outskirts of a small town with her grandmother, who was known to be strange. And she had the feeling that even if she'd still been with her parents, kids would have sensed something "off" about her.

Until she was thirteen, for instance, she'd never really cared for popular music, preferring folk, jazz, and classical. She'd more or less gotten into popular stuff because of Simon and Garfunkel, Donovan, the Turtles, and the Irish Rovers, and then she had discovered Cream and from there she had ventured into the realms familiar to her peers. But her tastes were still eclectic, and even though 1968 was the height of the hippie revolution, with Woodstock a mere year away, in that small town, most of the adults voted straight Republican ticket. And Di was still the weird girl with the weird grandmother, the one who had been called

"Wednesday Addams," the one who made people feel just a little uneasy when they looked at her.

Thirteen, fourteen, fifteen, not even a hint of a boyfriend. No best friend. No slumber parties, no invitations to "study," which really meant to get together in the bedroom, giggle about boys, listen to records, and try to learn to dance by watching what the cool kids were doing on the dance shows on TV. No one hated her, but no one liked her either.

And she was too smart. The smartest kid in the school, as it turned out, which was one reason why she was at Harvard. No guys dated a brainiac, even when she bloomed at sixteen, and developed a great figure and the kind of long hair you saw in shampoo commercials.

And all her clothing, except for the jeans and leotards she wore after school, was handmade. Never mind it looked a thousand times better, and hipper, than the stuff you got at Sears; everyone knew her grandmother had run it up on her ancient treadle sewing machine.

And . . . there was the fact that once in a while she slipped, and said things that scared people. Things she shouldn't have known, things that people didn't really want anyone knowing.

Nope. No dates for Di.

At least they didn't egg the house on Halloween. They just kept their distance, whispered sometimes when they saw her. They never treated her badly, but they never treated her as if they thought she was one of them. She might just as well have been a *Star Trek* alien, blue, with antennae.

Heck, some of them probably thought she was a Vulcan in disguise.

Then after her sixteenth birthday, well, there was never any time, even if a boy actually had approached her. Between school, learning everything she could about magic, and keeping herself and others alive, all her waking hours were pretty much accounted for.

Isn't a Guardian supposed to have a life? She'd wondered about that. More than once, because the other Guardians she got a chance to talk to all said that things were getting a lot more dangerous than they had been before. There were more incidents, more things waking up, more things breaking through.

She'd asked Memaw about that, and Memaw had a theory about why so much weirdness was cropping up. She was sure it was the hippies, and truth to tell, Di was inclined to agree with her. Where once you had to go into the bad parts of big cities to find an occult store, or get the mailing address of one that would ship books to you, or find libraries with really obscure collections, now occult stores were cropping up all over. The stores were in college towns mostly, but there were science-fiction stores in bigger cities that would get you occult books if you knew what you wanted, and you could mail order most of them directly from the companies that were printing them.

And the hippies were buying them by the bucketload. Even the book that phony Anton LaVey wrote was getting snatched up, despite the fact that the former carnie was not the wholesale advocate of free love that they thought he was.

That was the heart of Memaw's theory—that all the weirdness and problems cropping up were a result of all these people dabbling in what used to be the provenance of a few who were trained and knew what they were doing. They were supplying the raw energy that allowed things that had been dormant to wake up and start making trouble. According to Memaw, the same thing had happened after World War I, when the Spiritualists had been tilting tables, trying to get hold of loved ones on the other side. And again after the Civil War. To be honest, Di couldn't see anything wrong with this theory.

Especially now, when she was looking at the card of a supposed "psychic" that was radiating bad juju.

Bloody hell.

Was this just a case of some manipulative bitch who happened to be dabbling in real magic? Even though she hadn't asked for money yet, that didn't mean she wouldn't; she could just be working a longer game than O'Brian was going to spot.

Or was it something more than that?

Or was it just a coincidence that this psychic was also into Bad Things as well as going after a woman at her most vulnerable?

Well, Occam's Razor. The simplest explanation was probably the best one, and this Tamara was probably just taking advantage of a grieving and frightened mother, and the nasty magic she was using had nothing to do with the missing child. She'd probably been a phony psychic for a lot longer than she'd been a dabbler in the black arts.

Actually, come to think of it, she might be getting paid— in a way. Black magic worked best when you had a source of negative energy, the sort produced by anger, hate, fear, or grief. Chris Fitzhugh would have plenty of that, and Tamara could just be using her as a spiritual "battery."

If that was the case, well, it could be difficult to pry her off. Difficult, but not impossible; the trick would be doing so without spooking Chris Fitzhugh in the process.

Dammit. It didn't matter. The Call was genuine, the real thing. As a Guardian, she didn't have a choice, and too bad if her regular life had to suffer for it.

As a Guardian . . .

She closed her eyes for a moment and sagged against the door.

She'd never had a "normal" childhood. She'd been on the front lines of a nasty war for a fourth of her life. She knew exactly how Vietnam vets felt.

Tired.

She could give it up. Guardians had, and she wasn't a sixteen-year-old steeped in comic book superheroism anymore. She had a life now, and she needed to think about how she was going to keep herself fed. Guardians didn't get a salary; there was no "Guardian Company."

Face it, as long as you're a Guardian, your life is never going to be your own.

She opened her eyes again, and stood there for a long moment, cards in her hand, her eyes going from the cards to her books, back and forth. She could quit. She would never taste the headiness that was Guardian magic again, but she could quit. Right now.

Lavinia could take this on. Right?

Well . . . not really.

Well, someone could. Someone else. There had to be someone else with the skill set needed to pick this thing apart and see Tamara separated from her prey.

Maybe.

She took a long, deep breath. She could hear the line from *Spider-man* echoing in her head, only it was spoken by Memaw.

Dammit. No, she had the power, she had the skill set, and she had the responsibility, and she wasn't going to turn her back on people that needed her now.

Tamara Tarasava was, indeed, on the bus line. And for once, Di realized that it was not so bad to have an aura that made people uneasy around her. She had no problem getting a seat, and not even the crazy-eyed guy in worn-out fatigues wanted to sit next to her. She stared out the window and watched as the streets they passed became progressively rougher and grimmer. Di realized immediately that she should have assumed Tamara would be reachable by bus from the start. After all, most clients that a "psychic" sees are not really the upscale sort. Most of them, if they owned a car, couldn't afford to drive it much. And that was a big "if."

She got out and walked the three blocks to the address listed on the card. This wasn't skid row but it was clearly a lower blue-collar neighborhood than Di's own; there were children everywhere, playing on front stoops, having a stickball game in the street, clustered around a basketball hoop nailed to the side of a house. Sniffing the air told her a lot; soul food, corned beef, hot dogs and beans, all in the same block. And beer. Cans had piled up in the gutter. People here apparently liked to party, but their preferred brand was "whatever is cheap."

As soon as she got to her goal, she recognized something interesting.

It wasn't the fact that it was a typical two-story house in a run-down neighborhood; most "psychics" worked out of their homes. It wasn't that there were no signs advertising PSYCHIC READINGS in the window. Lots of fortune-tellers didn't advertise. Palm reading and the like were still against the law in some places, even if the law had better things to do than bust a five-dollar fortune-teller.

It was that the area *around* the house was preternatu-
rally quiet. No kids playing in the street or the yards. The
houses on either side were shabby, but very quiet, and
seemed to lean away from the one in the center.

Di loitered in an inconspicuous spot for a while,
watching the place, putting up a little "avoidance" aura to
keep people from noticing her. The upstairs windows
were all tightly curtained, but with sheers of the sort that
would hide anyone who was looking out while giving the
person inside a reasonably good view. The ones downstairs were tightly curtained in red velvet. So when Joe
O'Brian had said Gypsy, he was being literal, or at least, that
was what this woman was passing herself off as. Frankly, Di
doubted that she was actually Romany.

Then she watched the people on the street as they
neared the house, and what she saw was even more interesting. *Everyone* hurried past the house. Some even crossed
the street twice to avoid it, and most cast an uneasy glance
or two at it as they went by. A cat, however, merely saun-
tered past. Mind, that didn't mean much. For all their reputation as psychic animals, cats were completely indifferent
to anything that didn't directly threaten them.

*So, Tamara has all the neighbors spooked, and I don't
think it's because any of them are sensitive. There couldn't be
that many people here who are even marginally psychic. So if
it's not outré, it's mundane. Something she's done has got
them scared to confront her in any way at all.*

Given all of that . . . no way she was going to walk

through that door right now. Mage-sight showed her nothing except that some of the same black-green aura that surrounded Tamara's card also enveloped her house. Di picked up no clues about what the woman was doing, whether it was garden-variety black magic, or just the residue of someone using her powers to exploit people. Mage-sight generally didn't tell Di anything about the strength of magic if it wasn't being actively used. So she could walk in there and find someone who had picked up *The Satanic Bible* and discovered she really *did* have the Gift and was gleefully using it to get whatever she could, or she could find someone who was more than that. Potentially, much more than that.

If it was someone that was more than that, without better preparation and shielding, Di was going to stand out like a neon sign. Possibly she would even if she was shielded. Guardian magic could be damned inconvenient that way. It often decided to advertise, and the sign it put out often read GOOD EATS to things that liked to snack on magicians.

Dammit.

The best thing to do would be to get more information from that cop. And the best way to do *that* was to invite him into her apartment. Oh, hell no. That was not going to happen. She still didn't know if this was one of the cops who occasionally harassed Lavinia, who'd just used her name to get himself in Di's door.

Righto then. Make an appointment to meet him at the station.

For which she needed a phone, and she was not going to use a pay phone in this neighborhood. She had a healthy sense of where it was and was not safe for a woman to stand around on the street, preoccupied with talking. So, back home, phone the number on the card . . . or rather, hope that the line was free, because she had a party line, and then call the number on the card . . .

Oh, jeez. Another complication. Hope that no one is listening in, accidentally or on purpose, because the very last thing I need is for my neighbors to decide I am a narc, an informant, or both. . . .

All right, set up a spell to tell her if someone on the party line had picked up.

I hate party lines. But it was all you could get at short notice in that building. And it was much cheaper than a private line.

Do the magic, then phone Joe O'Brian. Complications. Always complications. *Bloody hell.*

Set up an appointment that wasn't going to conflict with her classes. Unless she could get him to give her more information over the phone, which wasn't likely. Maybe phone Lavinia and ask *her* about O'Brian, see if he really was her cousin, or if Di was being set up.

She shoved her hands in the pockets of her jacket and headed for the bus stop. An hour wasted that she could have used for studying. And it was getting colder.

The ride back mirrored the ride out; the only person who wanted to sit by her was a tired-looking woman who had some sort of uniform on under her shapeless coat. Probably a maid, she was so happy to have a seat on the bus that she would have sat next to a wino who drooled.

Maybe Di was a little more sensitive than usual, but as she approached her building, still brooding about Tamara, she began to get prickles on the back of her neck. Not bad prickles as such, but there was no doubt that some-one in the apartment building was fooling around with magic, and inexpertly. Fantastic. Just what she needed. Another do-it-yourself wizard trying to vibrate his way to Middle Earth. By the time she reached her own flat, the prickles had localized.

To the apartment directly above hers.

She groaned. *Great. Just great. I have a budding wannabe Gandalf living upstairs. Just shoot me now.*

She waited apprehensively for some sign that this was yet another mess she as a Guardian was supposed to take care of, and finally breathed a sigh of relief when no such sign came. Then she made sure all the wards were up on her space, and strengthened them until she couldn't feel the tingle anymore.

There. That should keep what he was doing from in-terfering with what she was going to do.

First things first. She set up a little ritual circle around the phone with chalk and candles. She generally used birthday-cake candles, since they were the right size and colors for such a small bit of magic. First, the chalk circle—inside her personal wards, this was more of a size-limiter than a protection. She used a simple piece of blessed chalk and a string and muttered the circle spell under her breath. Then she set up the candles and evoked each element in its proper space—yellow in the north for Earth, blue in the east for Air, red in the south for Fire, and green in the west for Water. With all that in place, she was ready to work the actual spell. This was all personal; there would be no Guardian help here. Which meant that she needed to be as economical as possible.

"As economical as possible" meant minimal use of energy, and minimal use of energy meant that she had to give careful consideration to exactly what she needed the spell to do. It was possible to give whoever touched a phone on this party line while Di was making her call the illusion that they were hearing static. But that would take more energy than she intended to use, and on top of that, it might have repercussions. If someone wanted to make a phone call and got static, he or she might go from door to door to find out who had left the phone off the hook. And while that might not be a big deal, it just might, if someone found out that she was a witch.

So the best, safest, "cheapest," and simplest thing was just to set up something that would tell her when someone was listening. It was a spell that witches had been using for hundreds of years, and it was pretty obvious why a witch would want a spell like that. When you were doing something that was going to get you hung, burned at the stake, or otherwise shuffled off the mortal coil, it was a good idea to have a way to tell when someone was snooping around.

After casting wards around the phone, Di touched it, infusing it with a bit of power, and with her finger, drew the sigil against eavesdropping on the middle of the rotary dial. She felt the energy leave her, making her feel a little more drained than she had the moment before.

Well, at least it worked.

She picked up the handset and dialed Lavinia's number first, watching the sigil, or rather, where she had drawn the sigil. Only if there was a third party on the line would it flare into life.

The other end of the line rang twice before someone picked up; the moment the person's hand touched that phone, Diana knew it was Lavinia. Just as Lavinia knew it was her.

"Good heavens, Diana, you are a suspicious little creature. The sigil against eavesdropping indeed." Lavinia chuckled. "And of course you are calling about young Joe, because you cannot believe I would have sent him to you. If you had bothered to call me when you first moved here I would have told you all about him." Oh, dear. A social faux pas. The Queen was Not Amused.

Di rolled her eyes. "And you are entirely too credulous for a Guardian," she said crossly. "For one thing, I'm on a party line. And for another, you should know better by now. For all I knew this Joe O'Brian found your name on a casebook and—"

"And how would he have gotten your address then, if I hadn't given it to him?" Lavinia replied archly. "Really. You hippies—"

Diana suppressed the urge to make a rude noise. "I am not a hippie. But I'm considering becoming one, if only to irritate you." She settled down into the chair next to the phone and prepared to take notes. "Tell me about O'Brian."

"He's not really a cousin, he's the son of a very dear friend who always called me her cousin. He's a good boy. And more to the point, dear, he has had his share of cases he couldn't explain, and he's quite ready to Believe." The way Lavinia said the last word, you could hear the capitalization. "I have worked with him a time or two when I got the Call. Mind you, I never, ever let him see just what we were getting into, but he certainly knew that there were things that I took care of that he would never want to put down on his reports."

Well, if he'd gotten even a glimpse of what most Guardians got into, his hair would be white. "All right so far. You absolutely vouch for him?" She didn't need to capitalize anything. "And did you get—"

"Yes. And yes. This is something that needs to be handled, and not by me." Unspoken was the "by you." Di felt a headache coming on. Lavinia was a hell of a Guardian and the fact that she was still going strong at fifty and not dead was a mark of that. But her royal attitude sometimes left something to be desired.

Lavinia's tone softened. "Diana, dear, I don't have the

right skills. Your grandmother taught you how to debunk, yes, but this may be a situation where more than mere defensive *magic* may be needed, or even magic of the combative sort. Or as you have put it in the past, it is going to require mundane defenses—and perhaps, offenses as well. I know very well you have, and know how to use, firearms. I suggest that you get whatever you brought with you out and make certain it is cleaned and ready for use."

Di got cold chills then, not just at Lavinia's words, but at her tone. "I will," she said slowly. "Is this just a premonition, or have you gotten some sort of warning?"

Lavinia paused for a moment. She was probably trying to get a feel for the situation, which was what Di would have done in her shoes. Di let her take her time; this wasn't something you wanted to rush. "For now, just a premonition. Now call Joe, and tell him whatever it is you've seen or need to know. The two of you should take it from there."

Di knew a dismissal when she heard one. The audience with Her Majesty was over. "Thank you, Lavinia," she said. "Goodbye for now then."

"Goodbye, dear." Di waited for Lavinia to hang up before doing so herself. One retreated from the Royal Presence properly, after all.

Then she dialed the number on the card Joe O'Brian had left with her. With a much more businesslike manner, she arranged to meet him in the library of Dudley House between classes. That should be an appropriately neutral spot. She still wasn't going to let him in her apartment. Not yet, anyway.

Then she sat back with a sigh and erased the sigil on the phone, extinguished the candles in the right order, and wiped out the chalk circle.

Which left her with—

The tingle from upstairs, currently blocked by her general wards, but she knew it was still there.

Which wasn't going to give her any peace for studying unless she looked into it. It was just going to nag at her until she found out which of the boys it was, how deeply into magic he was, and got as much detail as she could without either of them thinking she was a busybody or a nutcase.

Curses.

But if she was going to go charging up there, she had better do it with a peace offering in hand. People were more likely to think well of you if you came bearing gifts.

One came immediately to mind, because if one of those guys had ambitions to be the next Merlin, her candles would be especially welcome.

She delved into the cupboard and came up with two of the plain white "smells good" unconsecrated ones, a couple of fat pillars that would fit very nicely in a bowl. She stuck her keys in her pocket, made sure the door locked behind her, then made her way down the hall, up the stairs, and back down the hall. The halls in this place were virtually identical, floor to floor. She wasn't sure what they had looked like in their heyday, but at some point in the fifties they'd gotten a renovation and hadn't been changed since. Linoleum floor, old tin ceiling with tiny, inadequate single bulb lights, white-painted walls, green-painted doors.

She could see now why there were studio apartments on the third floor and none to be had on the fourth. There simply weren't any studio apartments at all on this floor. These were the luxury apartments, a full story above the roofs of the surrounding buildings. Well, there was no accounting for what people in the early 1900s had wanted in their apartment buildings. Maybe the unblocked view, the unrestricted sunlight, and the breezes four stories up made up for the inconvenience of four flights of stairs.

Or—she tried not to grind her teeth a little, as she spotted an elevator door. One which did *not* have a corresponding door on the third floor. So that was how it was. If you paid the higher rent, you got to ride in style instead of schlepping up four flights of stairs.

On the other hand, do you really want to trust your safety to an elevator old enough to be your great-grandpa?

Maybe not.

So, Emory and Itzaak were in 4C. And there it was. 4C in old brass on the door. She knocked on it.

It opened immediately, and the face that topped the tie-dyed T-shirt could only belong to Emory, who was an exceedingly good-looking Asian man, taller than Di, with slightly shaggy hair. The first words out of his mouth were "Em! You're ear—" Then he blinked. "Oh. Sorry. I was expecting someone else."

It was pretty obvious that the "someone else" was not male. Not from the sheepish grin on his face.

Dammit. He has a girlfriend. He also was not the would-be magician. There were absolutely no "vibes" of any sort coming from him.

"Sorry, I'm your downstairs neighbor, Diana—"

"Oh, geez—" He ran a hand through his hair, looking distressed. "Are we making too much noise? Is it the stereo? Is it us? I keep telling Zaak—"

She had to laugh, and interrupted him. "No, no, not at all! I just thought I should introduce myself so if I *do* come pounding on your door, you'll at least know who I am. And I brought—"

By now the door was standing wide open and she could see right into the apartment. And she was jealous, because it was huge. A living room twice the size of her entire place, a big kitchen, and it looked like at least two bedrooms and the bath between. It looked as though she wasn't the only one living under these guys; there must be another studio and a one bedroom down there with them overhead. A shaggy, curly head popped out of one of the doors, pretty much confirming her guess as she held out her peace offering. "Candles," Di concluded.

The round little face beneath the curls lit up with a smile. "Candles! That's exactly what I need for my ritual!"

71

It was Di's turn to blink, her mouth almost falling open in astonishment that someone would just come out and *say* something like that in front of a stranger.

Her vibe-o-meter started to edge over into the red. It wasn't exactly going wild, but there was no doubt. Itzaak was the one trying to be a wizard.

Hoo-boy . . .

Emory rolled his eyes. "Zaak, how many times have I told you that you need to censor that mouth of yours before it gets you into trouble? What if this was a Jehovah's Witness?"

"Then I'd say I was glad our virgin sacrifice got here." Itzaak's grin was infectious, though Emory still looked a bit annoyed. The rest of him came out of the bedroom; he looked a bit like Art Garfunkel, only with black hair instead of red. He approached with his hand held straight out. "Hi! I'm Zaak, Comparative Religion. This is Emory, Applied Mathematics. He thinks I'm crazy."

She transferred the candles to Emory and shook Zaak's hand. *Oh, yes. Up to his neck in magic, and gods help me, he has the gift for it too.* "Di Tregarde. Folklore and Mythology. Why does he think you're crazy?"

"Because I don't believe in all that woowoo crap," Emory said with a touch of irritation, dumping the candles into Zaak's hands the minute Di let go, and shaking her hand himself. "This is all just a phase. He does this every year; we're juniors. Last year it was Buddhism. God only knows what it will be senior year." He rolled his eyes again. "Probably the Flat Earth Society."

"Aw, come on, Emory, you *know* I'm onto something this time!" Zaak didn't seem at all put out by Emory's attitude. "Did I, or did I not, manage to magic my way into that closed class?"

"Well . . . you got in. There might have been a lot of reasons—"

"And I'm going out with Angela Harris!" The grin got larger and more triumphant.

"Now that, I must admit, is close to a miracle." Emory shook his head.

"It wasn't a miracle, it was magic! The stuff works!" Zaak crowed triumphantly. "You just watch, my man, it won't be long before you're begging me to help you!"

At that moment the elevator door opened and they all turned to see who it was. From the happy look on Emory's face, it was exactly who he was hoping to see. Zaak reached for Di's arm and pulled her inside the apartment.

"Come in, sit down," he urged. "Are these candles hand-made?"

"My grandmother and I made them," she said. "Beeswax and bayberry. We got the wax from a honey farm."

"Better and better! Do you believe in magic? Not stage magic, that's Marshal's thing, I mean the real stuff." He waved at one of the somewhat battered armchairs and perched eagerly on the corner of the equally battered sofa, putting the candles down on a coffee table made of a door on two stacks of cinder blocks. They might have a lot of room, but her furniture was better. She really didn't want to know what the Indian bedspreads that covered the chairs and couch hid.

At least there weren't any busted springs poking her.

"Who's Marshal?" she asked. Someone who knew stage magic? That could be incredibly useful . . .

"Friend of ours, he'll be over tonight probably. So, do you?"

She shrugged. *Okay. Don't lie. It's never a good idea for a mage to lie, especially not around another mage. . . .*

"There's a lot of things you just can't explain by scientific means," she temporized. "I'm studying folklore, and you have to wonder where some of that stuff came from, you know? Every culture has some form of ghost, every culture has some form of shape-shifter, or vampire. Every culture has good and bad magicians. So, I guess—"

She didn't need to go further. With a potential believer in front of him, Zaak was off and running. All she had to do was listen and make vague noises once in a while. It was too easy, and (not for the first time) she was just a little appalled at how naïve these self-taught occultists were. She wasn't going to have to pry, Zaak was practically pouring everything she wanted to know right into her lap. And if she'd been the sort of creature he was likely to run into, a magician who got power by draining it out of others, who got what he wanted by controlling them, she could have made him hers within an hour.

It was quite possible that the only thing that had saved him so far was the simple fact that there were relatively few of that sort of predator . . . and so very many willing victims.

As she had feared, Zaak had picked up a handful of fairly dubious books, and now he was convinced he had the Answer. It wasn't that the books in question were *bad*, it was that, like Zaak himself, they were incredibly naïve. These "new Druids" and "modern pagans" wanted to believe that everything "out there" was just waiting to welcome you into a joyful realm of harmony, peace, and love.

Well, they were right about one thing. There was a great deal "out there" that was waiting to welcome you. But the universe was *not* a friendly place, all sweetness and light, and greeting the would-be magician with open arms. It was more like a tough neighborhood, filled with things that would be only too happy to mug you and take your metaphysical wallet. If you were lucky. If you weren't so lucky, they would beat you up and leave you bleeding in the metaphysical gutter. If you were *really* unlucky . . .

As it happened, maybe she could do something about that. And there was no question of *should she*, because as sure as rain on your picnic, anything bad that Zaak got into was going to end up involving her. Morality aside, it was going to spill over on her due to physical proximity.

And as for morality? Well, you didn't let a five-year-old toddle out onto the highway, now did you? Not if you were the sort of witch that Diana and Memaw had been *before* Di became a Guardian.

The big question was how she was going to handle this. Her mind was going a million miles a second, trying to juggle it. The obvious was to take him aside and play the Great and Powerful Oz with him and make him her student. It wasn't as if she couldn't do things that right now he could only dream about. The drawback was that she had no idea how good or bad an apprentice he would be. He could turn out to be nothing but trouble.

I don't need an apprentice. I don't want an apprentice. I could use some help, but right now, this kid is just trouble.

Okay, then maybe the subtle approach. He hadn't gotten into Harvard by being stupid. So perhaps the proper approach was to remind him that, like mundane physics, there was a physics of the metaphysical as well, and that every action had a reaction, every deed a consequence.

"I'm not saying I totally buy into this," she replied, when she could get a word in. "But aren't you mostly talking about influencing the way that people think? I mean I assume that magic has to mostly work in small ways, and that would be the most logical, right? So what you're doing now, that would be changing how people react to what you want. You're changing their minds for them."

That brought him to a screeching halt. "Uh," he said after a moment.

"Well, doesn't it make sense? The class you got into, and the girl that you got to go out with you . . . if magic did that, wasn't it by changing what they were thinking?" she persisted.

"I . . . guess . . ." By this point, Emory and his girl-friend had stopped sucking each other's faces, closed the front door, and were actually listening.

"And is that ethical? I mean, this is Harvard and they make us take courses about that sort of thing. So shouldn't you apply that Moral Reasoning class you took? They make us take it for a reason, you know, it's not just to bore us to death. Is it ethical to go into someone's head without their permission and monkey around in there?" Zaak looked as if she had just smacked him in the face with a fish, as if none of this had even occurred to him. Probably it hadn't. After all, when the toddler gorges on candy, he's not think-ing about the possible stomachache to follow. Over his shoulder, Emory was grinning.

"She's got you there, Zaak," said Emory's girlfriend, who hadn't yet been introduced. She took care of that herself. "Hi, I'm Em."

"Di." She smiled, then turned back to Zaak. "And did you really think it through? I mean, there are conse-quences to changing things. What if someone who needed the course more than you got bumped? What if what you did caused someone to fail or get sick so the course slot opened? And what if you're preventing the guy this girl is really *meant* to be with from ever meeting her because you've got her going out with you instead?" Not that she believed that anyone was *meant* to be with anyone else— but she would bet that he did.

Zaak was really looking ill now. "I—uh—"

"Isn't the law of magic supposed to be 'do what you will *as long as you harm no one*'? I don't think that means 'trampling all over someone else's life is okay.' " She raised her eyebrow in a Spocklike gesture she had perfected over years of practicing in the mirror. It was usually pretty effective.

It worked this time too.

"You seem to know a lot about this," Zaak said weakly.

"My Field of Concentration is Folklore and Myth," she pointed out. "I mean, come on."

She might have said something more, except that there was a knock at the door, and when Emory answered it, the newcomer turned out to be none other than Marshal, the guy whose "thing" was stage magic.

Zaak was only too pleased to change the subject and quickly introduced Di to Marshal, and vice versa.

Marshal was not as good-looking as Emory, but he was attractive in a mismatched features, cute-like-a-hound-dog way. He also had a sense of self-confidence about him, not cocky, just that he wasn't naïve and generally knew what he was doing. Emory had that sense too, but not to the extent that Marshal did.

"I should probably go," she began, shoving herself out

of the couch, which was no easy feat since it had tried to swallow her the moment she moved in from the edge of it.

"Hey, stick around, you're the first person to talk sense at Zaak since he started in on this magic kick," Emory replied cheerfully. "If you haven't got anything you have to do tonight, that is."

"Or someone you need to meet," Marshal added, looking at her with thinly disguised hope.

Marshal was someone else she was beginning to think she needed to talk to. "Well, the rest of my reading eventually, but . . ."

"Great! Let me get the beers." She managed to conceal a wince. Of course. These were college guys. College guys and beer went together like peanut butter and jelly. Where there was one, there would be the other.

She didn't much like beer, but on the other hand, a little lubrication might help her interrogation. And since she didn't care if her beer was warm, she could make one last quite a long time.

And at least they aren't breaking out the roach clips and the rolling papers. If there was one thing that a practicing magician shouldn't mess with, or at least, not without a *lot* of preparation and safeguards, it was drugs. Of any kind. Magic was all about control, and when you smoked, or dropped . . . your control went right out the window.

And that was bad, because when your control went, sometimes your protections did too.

Which was a little like being a drunk white guy, staggering into Bed-Stuy, wearing a Dixie flag T-shirt with twenty-dollar bills hanging out of his pockets. You were bound to attract attention, and most of it wouldn't be friendly.

Not a good idea. Oh, no.

Emory came back with both hands full of open bottles; she took one and settled in for the next few hours as the couch slowly pulled her into its saggy depths.

It didn't take much to get Marshal going either. He *loved* stage magic. And like his idol Houdini, he *loved* debunking, or at least the idea of it. He didn't bad-mouth Zaak's magic, though; he confined his ire to the "mediums" and "psychic readers."

After two beers she was able to steer him right in the direction she wanted, which was to tell her the stage magician's perspective on how they did what they did. "The best and least harmful of 'em are no more than good psychologists," he said with a shrug. "They tell you what you'd get from a good shrink, but they wrap it up in a much more palatable package, palatable for people that don't believe in psychiatrists, that is. Like, if the good advice is coming from the Great Beyond, they're more likely to follow than if it came from the guy on the chair next to the couch."

"Especially if you believe in the Great Beyond and not in shrinks," Di replied dryly. She shifted, holding on tight to the bottle. There was nowhere safe to put it down, so she was keeping it clamped between her knees.

"Exactly. Not to put down religion! But—" He shrugged. "I go along with Ben Franklin. 'The Lord helps those that help themselves.' You know? And even when it's done with good intentions, how ethical is it to toy with peoples' feelings about the ones they've lost? How ethical is it to give them false contact? I think it's immoral, personally. Even Houdini said that he had to stop proving to people that mediums were phony by working the same tricks, then revealing he wasn't a medium and *showing* them the trick. He saw that they'd have such hope, such happiness to think they were in contact with a loved one before he pulled the reveal. And even though they learned not to get tricked by mediums again, fooling with their feelings like that was a crime."

"So what about the bad mediums?" Em asked the question that Di wanted to, and Di silently blessed her for it. "I mean, what is it that they do that has you so riled up? If someone wants to waste money getting their palm read, is that so bad?"

Marshal's homely face darkened. "I'd like to string them up by their thumbs," he growled. "They're parasites. They're worse than—than—Nixon! Worse than the Mafia. They give people hope, and rob them blind, and it's all a lie." He leaned forward earnestly. "Look, there's all kinds of scams. Some mediums, they research you, or get someone to do it for them, and then they use stage magic to make you think that they're actually bringing in ghosts. These days, they'll have microphone pickups in the waiting rooms, have a stooge in there pretending to be another client who's there to dig for information. Sometimes they'll make you leave everything in the waiting room and the stooge will go through purses and coat pockets. Then, wow, you get in the dark room, and there's stuff floating around, there's noises, you might even see the dead person! But what you're seeing is a projection of a photocopy of the photo they got out of your wallet. And the rest, that's all sleight of hand, escape tricks, even some of the kinds of special effects you see in stage shows."

He spent a lot of time explaining how some of that stage magic worked—levitation, misdirection, table tapping and tilting, the "medium" managing to get free of the restraints put on him. In theory, Di knew how these things worked, but not the mechanics, and it was fascinating. To be honest, it made her admire stage magicians even more. So far as she was concerned, knowing how something was done didn't bother her—in fact, knowing how a trick was worked was only going to increase her appreciation of the skill involved in making it "invisible."

"Houdini spent a big chunk of his time showing these crooks up for what they were and you'd think by now no one would believe in them, but they're worse than ever. Like cockroaches. You stomp on one, but there's a zillion under the cabinets."

He finished his beer with a frown. Di prompted him into describing some of the ways that Houdini and others had caught the phonies, and took a lot of mental notes.

"Those are the old-style mediums. A lot of times these days the mediums and psychics do away with the stage magic—hell, most of 'em don't have the skills to pull it off anyway—and just concentrate on hot readings."

"What's a hot reading?" Zaak asked.

"What I told you about earlier. They get their information way in advance. Most of these people talk to each other, okay? They swap files. It's to their advantage to cooperate with each other. So you get tired of going to Madame Zuzu, and decide you want to visit Psychic Clarabell instead, well, Clarabell is going to call up Zuzu, offer to split the take, and get Zuzu's file on you, and when you walk in thinking she knows nothing about you, bingo! What amazing revelations! How could she know these things?" He snorted. "Then Clarabell ponies over part of what she got from you to your old psychic, and you think she's got a better connection than Zuzu."

"I don't get why you're so *mad* at these people though," Em put in. "I mean, aren't they offering a kind of comfort? Like a priest would?"

"Well, even at their best they're still offering comfort for money," Marshal pointed out, frowning. "And it's dishonest comfort. *They* don't want to comfort you, they just want your money. If you believe in all that psychic energy stuff, you know, and karma? They're giving you something that's counterfeit when it all comes down to it. It's not real, and when people find out it's not real, they are just shattered. At their worst, well . . . there are the outright crooks. Besides having pickpockets and thieves going through your pockets for information, they have pickpockets and thieves getting a couple checks out of your checkbook to forge, stealing your credit card numbers, and lifting your cash. And then, they get into the 'curse' scams."

This was the sort of thing Di knew about, and she watched the others' jaws drop as Marshal told them about the "cursed money" fraud, the "psychic surgeons," and all of the ways people were convinced that they needed to be rid of nonexistent "demonic influences." These were what she and Memaw had debunked, but it was all new to Marshal's friends.

"Hey, look, let me just show you something. Gimme a couple of seconds in your fridge, okay? Then you'll see what I'm talking about." With Emory's wave of a go-ahead, Marshal rummaged around a bit and came back. "Zaak, you're going to be my patient. Pull up your shirt, okay?"

Embarrassed, Zaak did so, revealing a bit of a belly. Marshal kneaded at it for a minute with his fingers, then suddenly seemed to plunge his hand halfway into Zaak's stomach! Even more astonishing, a few seconds later, Marshal pulled out—

A meatball . . .

"I'm telling you, Zaak, you really have to start chewing your food before you swallow it," he deadpanned. All of them laughed, even Zaak.

"That was all sleight of hand. If I had time to prepare, I'd have some blood in the tip of a surgical glove, or even just some cotton soaked in blood that I palmed along with what I was going to remove. Usually that's a piece of liver. Liver looks generic and really icky, and it's not hard to believe it's a tumor. And this is how I did it." He took the meatball and hid it in the palm of his hand. He kneaded the surface of the couch, creating a crease. This time though, he did the "plunge" in slow motion, and *without* concealing what he was doing with his other hand, so they could see all he did was fold his fingers up into his palm, then "withdraw them" with the meatball in them.

He did a slam dunk with the poor abused meatball into the trash. "Those guys are the worst. They make you think you're possessed by demons. They take all your money, a little at a time. They keep you scared to death. And you just might actually be sick, with cancer or something, and by the time you find it out, you've got no money and you're probably so far gone you die."

Evidently this was the first time Marshal had ever expanded on his particular hobbyhorse, and even Zaak was leaning forward to listen, his embarrassment mostly forgotten—except for a flush, once or twice, that suggested to Di that he'd fallen for some of those tricks.

Eventually, though, Di's reading assignments overrode her intense interest in Marshal's stories. She finished the last of her beer, put the bottle down on the table—the good thing about using a door for a table was that no one cared about bottle rings—and stood up.

"I really need to get," she said regretfully. "College is a

lot more intense than I thought it would be. And this is *my* dime I'm dropping here, so I'm not into pouring it down the drain. . . ."

"The voice of conscience," Marshal said with a laugh. "Tell you what, I'll walk you to the stairs. I'm 4A, right by the stairwell."

She clasped her hands under her chin. "Oh, *thank* you, gallant sir!" she said in a breathless voice. "However will I repay you?"

"Don't answer that, Marshal." Em laughed. "I'll kick your ass."

Marshal put his hand over his heart. "I swear, I had no intention of—"

"Yeah, right." Emory snorted. "Get outta here. See you tomorrow."

As soon as the apartment door closed behind them, Marshal lost every semblance of even mild intoxication, and turned to her with an intense look on his face. "All right, you wanted to know waaaaaay too much about psychic debunking. What's going on?"

Di hesitated for a very long time. Should she trust this guy she'd just met?

On the other hand, nothing about any of these four had set internal alarm bells going off. And he knew more than she did by a good mile. *Intuition sez—*

Before she could answer, Marshal persisted, a worried look on his face. "Someone you know getting scammed?

Friend? Relative? Seriously, if I can help—you know, use the powers only for good?"

That decided her. "Come on down to my place," she said. "This is going to take a while."

The next day, she wasn't alone when she was waiting for Joe O'Brian; Marshal was with her.

The library seemed to be frozen somewhere in the fifties, with hard upholstered chairs and sofas with spindly little Swedish-modern wooden legs, covered in beige fabric and what might have been leather. They clashed with the Victorian architecture, but then, Dudley House was, well . . . not the typical Harvard House. As the painting of Karl Marx downstairs, and the fact that for years in the sixties the SDS had kept a mimeograph machine in one of the bathrooms, might have told you.

Joe eyed Marshal, but didn't say anything as Di introduced them. When they all sat down, however, he leaned forward over his knees. "I thought I was just meeting you, Miss Tregarde—"

"Marshal's a stage magician," Di interrupted him. "I don't know enough about the situation yet to know what questions to ask, but he knows about the sorts of stage magic deceptions that this Tamara might be using, so I thought I'd bring him along to help us both out."

She gestured to Marshal, then sat back and listened as the two men slowly pooled their knowledge. Finally Marshal shook his head. "All right. This one just might beat me. Partly. I can't see immediately either her angle, or where she's getting her information; she isn't extorting money from the mom, and she's not getting publicity out of this."

"If she's really smart," Di said slowly, "she's got a confederate. Someone posing as a cop or a reporter, who can get at least some of the detail about Melanie from schoolmates or playmates or their parents. I'd bet on posing as a reporter, everyone wants to get his name in the paper, not everyone is comfortable talking to a cop."

Marshal nodded. "But what's her angle? That's the question." He drummed his fingers on the table beside him. "Thinking aloud here . . . I'd think she was just throwing random stuff out as these 'leads,' figuring to get some publicity if one of them actually pans out, except that from what you're telling me, the leads are anything but random. Most of them are typically vague, but they don't seem random, and they do seem to mean something to the mom. Nothing to the cops, but either mom is convinced that there's a hidden message there, or your phony is just doing a combination of hot and cold reading and coming up with things that mom zeros in on."

"Yeah, I don't get it either." Joe tried to get comfortable in the hard chair, failed, and tried another position. "That's what's so frustrating."

"So go at it another way," Di said. "Follow up on these so-called 'leads.' Prove they're dead ends."

Joe shook his head vehemently. "We'd look like a bunch of idiots, the papers would have a field day if they found out we were spending man-hours on a psychic's tips. And we can't waste the time—"

"Not you," Di interrupted. "Me. And Marshal, if he wants to."

"I'm in," Marshal said instantly. "I've done some searching for lost kids, so I kind of know what to look for and if we find anything that looks right or wrong, we'll stop and phone you. And no one is going to know we're associated with the cops. Come on! A couple of Harvard kids? Helping the *cops*? Never happen. Right? If we actually find a lead, which I very much doubt, and the press asks, you can call us 'private investigators for the family.' "

Joe sucked on his lower lip for a moment, then gave in. He got out his notepad and case file, and made a copy of the list of "leads" that Tamara had so far pressed on Chris Fitzhugh; Di made a second copy and gave it to Marshal. The lanky junior glanced at his watch and shrugged. "I've got a lab," he said. "I'll catch you back at the apartment, Di. We'll figure out what we can do with this, if anything."

Only when he was well gone did Joe turn back to Diana. "How much does he know?" the cop asked. "About—" he wiggled his fingers in a way probably intended to convey "the supernatural."

"Nothing," Di said. "But Lavinia said *you—*"

The silence hung between them for a moment, interrupted only by the sizzle of a fluorescent bulb somewhere in the library stacks. Then Joe sighed.

"Cops don't like things they can't explain," he said sourly. "So when they find things they can't explain, they make a little division of people who don't quite fit, people they can't actually *fire*, and they shove the things they don't want to think about at those people. And they hope that if the people in question can't make those things go away, they will at least be—or become—people that no one will listen to. In my case, I had the misfortune to be the guy who solved a murder because a ghost told him who did it."

"A ghost." Di nodded. "I can see where that would be a problem."

"It was worse because the ghost told me where to find the murder weapon, which was *not* what the lab said it would be, and which was right in plain sight in the home of someone who wasn't a suspect." Joe grimaced. "So I got put in *that* department, where we're all considered borderline loonies. And if we actually aren't borderline loonies to begin with, we sure are after we see a few cases. So we're the ones who deal with psychics. Such a treat."

"I'll do my best for you," Di promised. "It's entirely possible that if we treat these things as serious, and investigate them completely, then this Tamara will dry up and blow away. I . . ." She hesitated, then plunged on. "However, there's one angle to this that I didn't want to go into in front of Marshal. I went by the address you gave me for her, and I have to tell you, without even seeing this woman, she gave me the creeps. And I can think of something she *might* be getting from Chris Fitzhugh that would be as good as money."

Joe's brow furrowed. "Which is?"

"Despair. Some people . . . they can feed off that. It's a powerful emotion—and feeding off it is more common than you might think. You ever know anyone who would start an argument for no good reason, get people so angry they're about ready to kill something, then cut the argument off with some sort of apology, and walk away looking like they just had a turkey dinner?" She waited. She was pretty certain that Joe *had* had an experience like that. Maybe more than one. When she saw the light of reluctant agreement in his eyes, she continued. "And I'll bet that at least once, everyone except that person winds up feeling exhausted."

Joe nodded slowly.

"Despair's not as common an emotion as anger, but it's just as strong. If that's the case, Tamara won't care that her leads turn out to be nothing. From her point of view, it's even better to raise Chris Fitzhugh's hopes, then dash them again. That might be why she keeps bringing Chris these so-called leads, to keep her on that emotional roller coaster." Di pulled a strand of her ponytail over her shoulder and wrapped it around her finger. "If that's the case, she'll stay glued to Chris Fitzhugh for as long as she can milk what she wants."

Joe made a face of disgust. "Great. Just great. So—"

"So if that's the case, the solution is to get the poor woman so tranked up she isn't a tasty meal anymore," Di said bluntly. "If I were you, I'd call in the family physician. Talk her husband into it. Hell, get her checked into the hospital for a while. It shouldn't be hard, and it's not as if she's any use to the case at this point."

Joe groaned a little, but nodded. "All right. Thanks. I'll be in touch."

It seemed that Di's hunch was right. There was not one damned useful thing in any of those so-called "leads," and between them, she and what she was beginning to think of as her "gang" managed to run down every possible interpretation of each one. The whole group was in on it now, even Zaak, and despite Zaak's sometimes credulous nature, he had a good mind. He came up with possible interpretations even *she* hadn't thought of.

A lot of them were just ridiculous. This was Cambridge, and "look by flowing water" not only could mean the river, it could mean sewers, gutters, even water pipes. There was absolutely nothing to be done with anything that vague, but the gang sat down and made a *list* of every possible interpretation, and every possible location in the city that it fit, in exacting detail, just to prove how ridiculous it was. As Marshal pointed out, it wasn't always going to be necessary to do an actual search. It was only necessary to prove how impossible a search would be.

But what Di hadn't counted on was how personally involved all four of them were getting, including Zaak. Particularly Zaak. There were times when an outsider would have thought that Zaak was Melanie's older brother, not a complete stranger. Unlike Marshal, who was still focused on debunking the leech, Zaak was getting more and more impatient with them for not doing something about Melanie. He kept trying to talk them all into doing a "ritual of finding," though how he expected to get any real results when he had nothing personal from the missing girl, Di had no idea. Zach didn't always think rationally.

In retrospect, Di should have expected him to try something on his own. But hindsight is always perfect, and it wasn't as if she had—yet—appointed herself as his mentor.

When the time came for all of them to get together one evening, Zaak was nowhere to be seen, even though Di had come bearing the gift of pasta.

"He said he's tired." Emory shrugged. "I think he's more frustrated than tired. He wants to actually work on the kidnapping case, and that's not what we're supposed to be doing, right?"

Di nodded, and dumped cheese on her spaghetti.

"Joe's made that pretty clear. The department doesn't even want *him* doing anything serious about this case, much less a *bunch of meddling kids.*"

"Ro-roh, Raggy," said Marshal in a Scooby-Doo voice.

Honestly, Di didn't much blame Zaak. She was frustrated too. Was there more to Tamara than the fact that she was a psychic vampire? Di had gone out to her house three times now—though she had never yet dared to go in—and still had not come up with anything more conclusive than *this woman is bad news.*

She thought she knew what Zaak thought. He had said several times that he thought Tamara was behind the kidnapping. And yes, that was certainly possible, but why? Tamara didn't have a motive, not even as a psychic vampire; there were plenty of other desperate people in this city without taking the risk of kidnapping a little girl. And how had she done it? Had she used a confederate? The little girl had been taken by a cop; the other children were unshakable on that point. If she had a confederate, by now the cops should have gotten some clues to that, because surely they were as suspicious of Tamara as Zaak was. And you would think, with all of the publicity about the case, a confederate might be getting nervous.

It just seemed unnecessarily complicated. *Occam's Razor.*

Zaak wasn't sulking, he was in his room attempting something magical; Di could feel the energies building up in there. She figured he was trying a ritual to find the little girl, probably using her photo from the newspapers and a dowsing rod or a pendulum. He wasn't nearly trained and focused enough to pull that off, so it was going to be about as effective as walking the streets and calling her name. In fact, that was a pretty good analogy. She debated interrupting him, but it didn't seem all that important and doing the ritual would make him feel effective.

Joe had another so-called "lead" for them to check out; this one was a bit more specific, and it was going to require some good maps and possibly some legwork. Supposedly Tamara had "seen" Melanie in a room, crying and screaming; the room had a tall, narrow window that faced south, and she had heard a train in her "vision." She was sure it was in Cambridge proper. So they had to check neighborhoods near enough to train tracks to hear trains, looking for late-Victorian buildings with tall, narrow windows. This was, of course, a lot.

However, buildings where someone would ignore a strange child crying were a lot fewer, especially now. One of the other teams that the cops had was literally investigating every single report of someone hearing a child crying. Nothing had turned up, of course, except for a lot of exasperated parents and children delighted that they'd gotten so much attention for a tantrum, but this did narrow down things considerably, not the least because they could cross off *their* list every building that team had visited.

Tamara might have overstepped herself this time. She was adamant that the location was in Cambridge—not

Boston, not outside the Cambridge city limits—and there actually were not as many places that qualified as the "psychic" might have thought.

And as they worked their way across the map, cross-checking with the police reports, they discovered that up to 90 percent of that ground had already been covered. What hadn't been covered was beginning to look like a wash. The buildings were the wrong sort, industrial, windowless, too modern, or the windows were the wrong shape.

Di gathered up the plates and took them to the sink, and was just turning back to say as much when—

Every internal alarm she had shrilled at her. A fraction of a second later, an icy wind literally tore through the apartment.

Bloody hell!

The lights flickered and dimmed. It wasn't an illusion, either, the wind picked up papers and sent them all over the living room. Di's breath streamed away from her in a mist of ice crystals, it was suddenly that cold in the room.

Em shrieked, Emory reacted as any good boyfriend would by trying to shelter her; Marshal looked frantically around, trying to find a source for the wind and failing.

Reflexively, Di called up mage-sight and immediately put up her shields, because the place was literally full of malevolent energies, razor-edged dark things—

They're hunting—but for what?

She didn't have a chance to think further, as in the next instant, they all arrowed straight through the door of

Zaak's room. The wind died. The temperature dropped further.

And the door burst open.

Any other time, she might have laughed, for Zaak was wearing what he probably hoped were ritual robes, though in fact they looked like nothing so much as an old-fashioned granny nightgown. His hair was standing straight out too, giving him the look of someone trying to ape an Afro and not doing too well.

But she was not going to laugh. Because there was something *in* Zaak—and it was not nice, and definitely not happy.

It glanced wildly around the room, and its eyes lit first on Di.

It couldn't have liked what it saw, because it immediately switched its gaze to Em. With a horrible laugh, Zaak leaped at the girl before Emory could react, and tore her out of the other man's arms. Em opened her mouth to scream, and so did Zaak, though his scream was silent—

And a thick column of oily black smoke laced with that same malevolent energy poured out of Zaak's mouth and into Em's.

Zaak staggered back as Em straightened, looked around, and laughed harshly, angrily.

It was a male laugh, a horrible baritone.

And with that, Di's thoughts solidified from *what the hell is this?* to *oh, hell no*—

Di knew what it was. Or what it likely was. She'd been

studying these things long before she ever came to Harvard, and an interest in old horror movies had led her to *this* particular menace years before she was ever a Guardian. It hadn't been easy, doing that research in a small town, but Memaw had access to the libraries of a lot of friends, and many of them had books going back a long, long way.

This was a dybbuk, a kind of angry ghost, laden with hate and guilt, that walked the earth until it could find someone to posses. Whatever Zaak had been doing in his room had called it and given it an opening, but dybbuks never permanently possessed anyone of the same sex, and this one was male. With only two females in the room to choose from, one of them protected, it had leapt to Em. And it was a good thing that Di had obsessively researched them back when she first discovered they were real and not the figment of some movie writer.

Sulfur! I need sulfur!

She also needed to keep it *here*, and there was one good way to do that quickly; the means were even close at hand.

Di snatched up the familiar blue-and-white cardboard container of table salt from its place next to the stove. With a fast gabble of the words of consecration, she blessed the stuff, and before the dybbuk could run out the door—gods only knew where it was going to go if it got out of the apartment—she jumped over the couch and poured a line of blessed salt across the threshold. And then, in quick succession, she poured more lines across the windowsills, the fireplace, and the doors into the bedrooms. Only then did she turn, heart pounding, to see that there was no danger that it was going to escape at that moment.

The dybbuk was chasing Zaak—and in Em's hand, the spirit clutched the knife Em had been using to cut up the garlic bread. Whatever Zaak or Zaak's family had done to tick off this particular spirit, it clearly wanted Zaak's head on a platter.

"Grab her!" Di shouted. Zaak was shrieking. And Em was screaming furiously in that low baritone and waving the knife. But the dybbuk was not used to Em's body yet, so it wasn't so much chasing Zaak as stumbling after him like a movie zombie. So far Zaak was able to keep well out of reach.

She dashed into Zaak's room, hoping that she was going to find what she needed in there. Behind her, she heard Emory and Marshal shouting Em's name, and the thing that was in Em roaring furiously. She blinked in the dim light, trying to get her eyes to adjust to only candles.

Zaak dashed into the room and slammed the door, panting and leaning on it. "Light!" she snapped, and he flipped on the light switch reflexively. The overhead bulb, like all the overhead lights in this old building, was dim and very yellow, but at least now she could see. More to the point, this was Zaak's room and he was in it.

"I need sulfur, a shofar, a Bible, and candles. *Now!*" she snapped. He blinked at her for a moment, then began scrambling in a cupboard by the door. His bedroom was as big as her whole studio. The bed was up against the wall, and the cleared floor held his "ritual space." Di looked at his ritual circle and gritted her teeth. Idiot. Candles, little brazier with charcoal and wormwood, circle drawn in paint on a piece of oilcloth, candles at the cardinal corners. She recognized the glyphs chalked in around the periphery. A kabbalistic summoning circle and he didn't even specify *what for!*

Now, a Jewish exorcist would confine the spirit, interrogate the dybbuk, then persuade it to leave by sheer force of argument.

She wouldn't. Which was just as well, she wasn't going to have three or four days to talk the thing out.

She'd have to fight it. And probably its friends.

Zaak turned back to her with his hands full of the stuff she'd asked for. She said, "Find the Ten Commandments and make up a *cherem*, I want this thing to know we are *not* going to play nice! When I say, read the Commandments and tell the thing we are not going to accept it and help it find a home." Then she grabbed the shofar, took the sulfur and dumped it on the little circle of instant-start charcoal in the brazier, and picked the brazier up by its wooden handle. She wished she had her own *atheme* with her, but there was a sword on the wall that would do. She pulled it down, put the brazier right by the door so the sulfur smoke would billow out into the main room, and grabbed the chalk off his dresser. Then as Zaak shrieked, *"What are you doing?"* she yanked open the door and jumped out into the living room.

As she had hoped, although the dybbuk was strong, Emory and Marshal together had Em pinned to the floor and had gotten the knife away from her. Just as she managed to fling them both off, Di shouldered them aside and blew the shofar, the sulfur smoke blowing out into the living room behind her. Damn good thing that she had a great embrasure; there were a lot of ceremonies that involved blowing hornlike objects. Doing this cold, what she produced was kind of a *blat* rather than a trumpet sound, but it was no worse than trying to blow a Hawaiian conch shell or a Celtic *lur*.

The dybbuk froze for a moment, giving her enough time to enclose it in a chalk circle. "Light two candles and start reading!" she shouted at Zaak, and jumped over the chalk line to face it with the sword.

She couldn't understand a word, of course. She didn't know Hebrew. But the dybbuk did, and Em's face contorted in a hideous snarl, going so flushed and inflamed she looked like a demon.

"I know you can understand me," Di said sternly, holding the sword up in the proper guard position for a broadsword. "Out! Because I can, and I will, force you out."

"You are no rabbi," the spirit growled.

"I don't have to be." They stared at each other across the blade of the sword, and Di hoped, hoped, hoped that one of the three would realize that she knew exactly what she was doing, and ask . . .

And bless him, it was Zaak who stopped reading for a moment and sobbed, "This is all my fault! Di, you gotta help her!"

Ah, bingo.

There it was, the magic words, or an acceptable variation on them. *"Please help me."* She felt the hidden door inside her fly wide open and Guardian power flood into her. That was how she got the mojo when she wasn't actually Called. When someone had gotten in over his head and begged for help.

Immediately she felt warmer, as if she was encased in a second protective skin of invisible armor. Which, in fact, she was.

"Zaak! Start invoking holy names!" Didn't matter that she wasn't Jewish. Zaak was, and so was the dybbuk. She was just the Champion, and that was all she needed to be. He supplied the religious fuel, she supplied the muscle.

Zaak started gabbling out more Hebrew, and when he got to "Michae-el" the sword went up in a blaze of fire.

Nice.

"Out!" she repeated.

"You will not use that blade on your friend." It laughed at her.

"I don't have to. Oh ye who are condemned to wander, because of countless sins against your fellow man, oh unclean spirit, oh evil one, behold! Ye may not withstand the sound of the horn!"

Again, she blew the shofar, and this time the creature paled and shrank back, because it wasn't just the feeble *blat* of an amateur, this was the clarion call to arms that had taken down the walls of Jericho.

She took the horn from her lips and faced the creature again. "Zaak, more reading. *El Melekh* and *va-ya'avor.*" She had no idea what she had just asked for, but there were things moving through her now that knew a lot more than she did, and the words popped into her head. Zaak began to read in a steadier voice. The thing straightened.

"I will not be cast out!" it snarled. *"Behold, my name is Legion!"*

With that, it opened Em's mouth, and a torrent of malevolent *things*—shapes of black smoke—poured out of her. Em dropped to the floor, out cold, leaving Di trapped in the circle with not only the dybbuk, but as she had suspected, all his friends.

But the dybbuks, even if they had encountered exorcists before, had never met up with a Guardian. And they had only dealt with old scholars who seldom saw anything more lethal than a carving knife wielded against a chicken.

She actually knew how to use the sword she held.

She danced with it, in a pattern that owed as much to kata practice as to classical Western swordplay. The horde of black shapes, confined by the circle, whirled around her, trying to reach through her armor and past the lethal edge of the blade. But every time one tried, she sliced— and there was a sizzle and a line of fire, and the shape was gone. She wasn't quite sure how many there had been in the first place, but soon enough there were only a dozen.

Then six.

Then three.

And at last, only one, which hung in the air, as if stunned.

Now if this had been a movie, Di would have paused and said something significant, and the thing would have pulled some unexpected ability out of its ectoplasmic ass.

But it wasn't a movie and she didn't give it a micro-second to recover.

The sword flashed across the intervening space and cut the last of the dybbuks in two. It vanished with a shriek that practically deafened her, and a stink worse than the sulfur that was still fuming.

All the power drained out of her at once, as the "door" slammed shut once again.

She dropped to one knee, exhausted, and Emory ran to Em, who was starting to sit up.

"Somebody open a window," Di said, panting. "And put out that damn fire before we all choke."

Nobody said a word for a good long time, while the sulfur fumes cleared out and Di stumbled to a chair, laying the sword down next to it as she slumped into it. Emory helped Em to the bathroom, and a moment later, Di heard the shower running. Yeah, after that, the poor girl probably needed a shower. And then a second one to get the sulfur stink out of her hair.

Marshal, his eyes as big as dinner plates, brought Di a beer, then sat down as far from her as he could get, staring at her. Zaak, on the other hand, sat down as close to her as he could get, though he looked at his hands, not her.

Emory, who had left Em on her own in the bathroom, brought more beers, set them down, and sat down himself. He was the one that finally broke the silence.

"What the hell just happened?" he asked quietly.

Di slumped a little further into the chair and gave Zaak the evil glare. "Gandalf there decided that normal detective work wasn't getting anywhere. Didn't you, Zaak? What did you try to call? Specifically?"

"I thought"—Zaak gulped—"I thought I'd get a wandering spirit. 'Cause, y'know, something like that could go hunting for Melanie. . . ."

"Give me strength," she groaned. "Haven't you paid any attention to your own peoples' folklore?"

His mouth opened. Closed. Opened again. "Uh, no?" he said weakly.

She sat up and pointed at him. "When you do an unspecified summoning, you moron, you get what your *heritage* calls. And in your case, the only 'wandering spirits' that the Jews have, specifically the European Jews, are the dybbuks. Dybbuks are not particularly cooperative. What did I *tell* you about thinking things through?"

"I'm sorry," he said in a small voice.

"Well, you had better be sorry. Because the unrestful, unconsecrated spirit of one of your people found himself in the body of a *tryf*-eating *goyim*, and he was not even remotely happy about that. Which is, I expect, why he attempted to cleave a pound out of your butt with that knife." She slumped down again. "Add to that fact that he and his friends are out and about for a reason—said reason being that they were such pieces of crap on earth that they can't rest—and I trust you get the picture. I'd smack you like your old granny, but I'm too tired."

"Wait—" said Emory. "Spirit? Dybbuk? I'm lost."

It was going to be a long night.

Thank gods it's Friday.

Be careful what you ask for. You might get it. Di had wanted a little help, now she had more than she had bargained for. Or she would, when the quartet got over being rattled and started to realize that they had just witnessed some *real* magic, that there was such a thing, and that—because face it, they were all under twenty-five and three of them were laboring under a burden of testosterone—it had been pretty damn exciting.

Which meant that she wasn't going to be able to pry them off of her now. Zaak was already a Believer, and the only thing more fanatic than a Believer who gets evidence that he's right, is a Skeptic who gets evidence that the Believers are right. Ah, the zeal of the newly converted.

Which of course was what Emory and Marshal were. Maybe Em too; for the moment she was being really quiet, and seeing as she was the one whose skin the dybbuk had tried to take over, Di didn't blame her.

When Di had finally made all the explanations she cared to, she stumbled down to her own apartment, intending to sleep like a stone. She left them to clean up the mess. Fortunately there wasn't much of it.

She hoped Zaak had to clean up the lion's share.

She really, really wanted to go straight to bed, but she knew that if she did, she'd wake up with the whole apartment smelling like sulfur, and the curtains would stink for weeks. So she stood under the shower until she started to go all pruney, and then fell into bed with her hair still wrapped in a towel.

She must have been so tired she didn't even move all night, because she woke up in the same position she'd fallen asleep in.

Alrighty, then. She lay there, just enjoying the fact that she didn't have to get up for class, and that although she hurt, it was that good sort of after-workout hurt. She'd done a good job last night.

Trouble was, it hadn't been what she'd been Called to do.

And in the cold light of morning, she knew what she had to do. She had to stop dancing around the situation and stop trying to pretend that there wasn't some sort of magical connection here.

She had to visit Tamara.

With a groan that was strictly internal, Di pried herself out of bed and went hunting for some clothes. When you had hair as long as she did, it took some time to brush it out after you'd washed it, and that gave her time to think.

Occam's Razor.

What if the simplest solution was the one that Zaak kept insisting on? What if Tamara *was* tangled up in the kidnapping? Forget that it had been a male "cop" who took the kid, forget that it didn't *look* like there was any connection between Tamara and the Fitzhughs . . . forget about hunting for motives. Motives were what you figured out after you caught the bad guy. Concentrate on finding the kid and catching the bad guy.

Di put her hair up in a bun, grabbed a bagel and tomato for breakfast, and went shopping at the Star Mart. She was pretty sure that Tamara wasn't an early riser; most of her kind weren't.

Back home, she put almost everything away, then used

some of her purchases to do a little "special" preparation. A picnic shaker of salt got consecrated, and so did the water that went into a tiny spray bottle meant for perfume. Then she made a little corsage out of the oak, ash, and thorn leaves she'd picked up off the street on the way home and pinned it to the shoulder of her poncho. An iron horseshoe nail went into one pocket, and a silver crucifix into the other.

She called the number on Tamara's card. She wanted to do this before the Scooby-Doo team woke up and decided to go with her.

The woman who answered Tamara's phone had a curiously deep, throaty voice and a Slavic accent that was as phony as a plastic flower. Yes, there might be a booking free. She would go and see if someone had canceled. Why, Susan was in luck, one of Tamara's clients had phoned in to say she was ill. If she hurried, she could just make the appointment. "And bring a fresh egg," she added.

Well, well. I know where this is going.

The first, the *very* first thing she did was to write several identical notes saying exactly where she was going. She distributed the copies around the apartment. There was one pinned prominently to the bulletin board, one on the kitchen table, and in case something happened to her and Tamara actually figured out her real address, one under the pillow on the bed, one in the stack of manuscript, and one rolled up and stuck into the laundry hamper. She'd never had much patience for the sort of book or movie where the hero wandered off into danger without telling anyone where he was going.

Then she called Lavinia and told *her*.

With that done, Di packed the shoulder bag she'd bought at Goodwill. First in were the perfume bottle and the salt shaker, plus the egg, wrapped in tissue to protect it. Besides that, for verisimilitude, she dropped in a pack of gum from which she removed two sticks; a new (cheap) lipstick and matching nail polish; a new, unused comb; a freshly opened pack of tissues; a used paperback romance; and a bandana with peace signs all over it. Plus the three things that she actually needed—enough money for bus fare, Tamara's fee, and maybe a cup of coffee and a donut; her keys; and a wallet with a phony ID. She had a stash of them from when she and Memaw had gone after the phonies. This one was from when she was seventeen— perfect for the purpose now.

According to that ID, her name was Susan Rutherford and she lived in Boston. In the wallet were more things from those days. When you expected that a crook might be going through your purse, pictures were very important in firming up your faux self. She chose a few from a whole box of photos she'd picked up at flea markets; a kid in a high school football uniform, a generic middle-aged couple, and someone's granny. She also had a boy's class ring she'd gotten at the same place, wrapped with angora to make it fit; she wore that on her right hand.

She shielded herself to a fare-thee-well. No way she was going to walk into that snake den without every protection she could muster. She even had her *atheme* tucked into the top of her boot. She hoped she wouldn't need it, because it would be bloody awkward to get at if she did, with the boots being under the bell-bottoms of her jeans. Still, it wouldn't show that way, at least.

Simple turtleneck sweater, black of course. Nondescript gabardine jacket. And gloves, the all-important gloves. If she managed to get any evidence, she didn't want her own fingerprints on it, and it was cold enough that thin gloves wouldn't raise any eyebrows and they stretched over the class ring, showing the shape underneath. One thing she totally refused to do, not even to complete the disguise of being a high school senior. No way in hell was she going to totter around on a pair of three-inch platform shoes.

So Susan got on the bus, and read her used romance book all the way to her stop while thinking very hard about being Susan.

If Tamara's house had been creepy before, she had to force herself up the steps now. And that made her wonder . . . what had changed? Was it just that the woman was sucking so much misery off Chris Fitzhugh that she was getting more powerful by the day? Or was there something else going on?

The door was answered by someone who could only be Tamara herself. She ushered Di into a nondescript entryway, maybe five by five, painted beige, with a little bench too narrow for anyone to sit on against one wall. If there was a Richter scale for "something weird," Tamara pegged it at ten.

Physically, she wasn't tall, but she gave the impression of being tall. She had shoulder-length black hair cut in a Mary Tyler Moore flip, square, Slavic features, and deep-set dark eyes. She wore a purple turtleneck tunic over a black, calf-length Gypsy-hippie skirt with a print of tiny purple flowers, and black moccasin boots. She had a fringed purple sash around her waist, a tangle of amulet necklaces and love beads around her neck, big gold hoop earrings, and a dozen Indian bangle bracelets on each wrist.

She was a fraud. The fact she had asked for the egg proved it.

It wasn't *just* that— There was no doubt about it, Di could already sense the emotional whirlpool there, the woman was a psychic vampire. And it wasn't just that she was no more a Gypsy than Di was. Nor that there was a whiff—just a hint—of real magic about her, and it was not nice.

There was something else that was completely off about her. And Di, normally able to put her finger on the cause of *any* weirdness, could not pinpoint this.

Tamara looked at her for several minutes in absolute silence. Then without a word, she crooked her finger at Di and led her into the "consultation room," which in any other house would be the living room.

As Di had expected, it was dim and lit by candles; the curtains were drawn across the windows and the air was smoky and thick with patchouli incense. The only way in which it really differed from the far too many rooms of the same sort that Di had been in over the course of her life, was that this room had been decorated in purple, rather than the usual red.

Di noticed the strategic placement of mirrors behind her, near the ceiling. In the dim light, and with all that dark purple, it was very difficult to spot them unless you were looking for them. The way that the few lights were placed, anything in the "client's" hands would reflect very nicely in them.

The table, covered with a purple cloth, was bare except for an eggcup and a white saucer set to one side. Those were for later.

"Please," Tamara said with a toothy smile. "Sit."

Di sat in the indicated chair and put her purse on the table next to her. Tamara looked at it with arch significance, so Di pulled out her wallet and put the requested fee on the table. It was quite modest, only ten dollars, but for Tamara, this was a starting fee—she undoubtedly expected to make a good deal more from this particular pigeon. Tamara nodded, took the two five-dollar bills (which Di had marked, though Tamara wouldn't know that), and tucked them somewhere under the tablecloth.

What, not down your cleavage? You missed one of the Gypsy clichés? You haven't been watching nearly enough bad horror movies. Of course the cleavage would be hard to reach wearing a turtleneck.

"Take out of your bag some object that means much to you, and that connects to the problem you have come to me about," Tamara continued. "But do not show it to me. Merely hold it in your hand. The spirits will tell me all that I need to know."

That, and the mirror behind me.

Di pretended to fumble through the bag, going through the photos until she came to the one of the boy. She pulled it out of the bag and held it in her hand, shielded from Tamara's direct gaze—but no doubt visible in the mirror mounted above and behind her seat. Tamara gazed over Di's head, as if looking off into the distance. But Di was well aware that she was looking at the mirror.

"You have a lovely grandmother and loving parents," said Tamara. "They care much for you. So much that they are concerned about your love for a boy. No?"

Di faked a gasp. "They want me to go to college," she whispered. "But if I do—he's not going, he has to go to work for his dad. If I go away, will he forget me?"

Her response had told the Gypsy that there was money enough to send her to college. That would probably be bait the woman could not resist. Tamara closed her eyes and began to sway. "There is another, a rival to you," she intoned.

Di allowed a tiny whimper to escape.

"She has designs on this boy. She is not good for him, this girl. She does not love him. She only wants the things he will have, when he takes his father's business. But he does not see this." There was a sly little smile on Tamara's lips.

Di really, really did not like her. If there was ever a story designed to make a young girl paranoid and fearful, it was one like that. It didn't even matter if there *was* no other girl in the picture. Given a story like this, the victim would find *someone* she knew who matched the description of a man stealer.

"Oh, and she is, is not good for this boy. She will get him to do things that are wrong. To steal from his father so he can buy her presents. To go to places with her that he should not. You are a good girl; she will make him to think that good girls are dull. You know her, she is taller than you, not so pretty, sly, and—" Tamara made a cupping gesture at her own breasts that seemed faintly obscene. "Big bosoms."

"Juliet Whately!" Di exclaimed, making up the name on the spot.

"Yes . . . yes . . . but there is more . . ." Tamara frowned. "The spirits tell me there is more about this girl than you know. She has bad blood. Bad Gypsy blood. There is good Gypsy blood, and bad Gypsy blood, and hers is bad, bad, bad. . . ."

Okay, here it comes.

"This girl—bad things follow her. Bad things come when she calls. That is how she will get this boy, not just with her bosoms and letting him do what he wants with them. No, no. She has more." Tamara leaned over the table now, and stared into Di's eyes. "She is evil! Quick, take out the egg I told you to bring, and the spirits will show you!"

Di fumbled out the egg and handed it to Tamara. Tamara was as good or better than Marshal; Di knew what she was doing and was watching closely, but she didn't see the Gypsy swap it for her own egg, one she had prepared earlier, probably after Di's initial call.

But Di had no doubt that it was Tamara's egg, and not her own, that was placed in the incongruous little eggcup on the table between them, with the white saucer to one side.

"Think about the boy!" Tamara urged. "Think about the girl! The spirits will show us if he is in danger!"

Di clutched the picture hard enough to crease it, and stared at the egg as Tamara chanted. It was all she could do to keep from breaking up laughing when she recognized the words.

"Ue o muite arukō, namida ga koborenai yō ni, omoidasu haru no hi, hitoribotchi no yoru."

Ten years ago she'd learned that song. The only song sung in Japanese to ever hit the bestseller charts in the United States. It was called "Sukiyaki," a nonsensical title that was probably one of the few Japanese words that Americans would have recognized in 1963. Di supposed that, droned as the words were and without a tune, there weren't too many people who would realize where they came from.

All they would know was that it sounded exotic, nothing like any language they'd ever heard. Tamara was supposed to be a Gypsy, they would assume it was a Gypsy spell, and not that she'd learned the words from some sheet music she'd probably picked up at a used bookstore.

Tamara repeated the words three times more, each time getting louder. As she finished the chant the last time, she picked up the egg, and on the final *yoru*, she cracked it into the saucer.

Di faked a shriek, as any teenager would have, seeing the blood, the black sludgy stuff, and the hairy fibers, along with the half-formed chicken embryo, splayed out over the white china. Most teenagers from the heart of Cambridge wouldn't even know that it *was* a chicken embryo; all they would see would be something fetuslike.

"You see! You see!" Tamara said in triumph. "Already she has him! Already she places her curse on you and your love for him, and on him to draw him to her! Oh, you are in danger, and he is in danger, terrible, terrible danger!"

"Oh, God! Oh, God!" Di cried hysterically. "Tell me what I have to do! You must know what I have to do!"

"Fear not, I can save him, and you," Tamara crooned soothingly. "Listen to me—I will tell you what to do."

But Di feigned more hysteria, her hands shaking, repeating only that Tamara had to tell her what to do, had to write it down for her, finally convincing Tamara to write down her instructions when she shook and wailed too hard to "listen." With her lip curling a little in a veiled sneer, Tamara printed everything out on a sheet of paper on a yellow pad before tearing it off, folding the paper in half, and sliding it across the table.

117

Di made *very* sure that not only did their hands not touch, they didn't even have their fingers on that piece of paper at the same time.

"Do not tell your parents," cautioned Tamara. "They will not believe, and they will not understand. But you must find someone who can help you get enough money to take the curse away. We will give the money back, of course, but this girl, she puts the curse on money, for money is all she cares for. Your grandmother, maybe—?"

"Oh, yes! My gramma is the one who told me to find a Gypsy!" Di babbled, scrubbing at her face with the tissues from her purse—which she put right back in the purse when she was done. "Gramma will help me!"

There was a sly smile. "Trust in your grandmother," Tamara crooned. "The old ones, they know. They have seen. They believe in curses, in the power of evil ones. Your grandmother will help you."

Di babbled some more thanks, still sobbing, then grabbed her purse and rushed out before Tamara could tell her the time of her next appointment. She literally ran out the door, down the steps, and down the street, and only stopped running when she knew she was out of sight.

Not that Tamara would be concerned about her victim returning. She knew that the sort of child that Di appeared to be would phone as soon as she had her hands on the money.

But Di was only too happy to get out of that place. Luckily, Tamara had been concentrating so hard on the money that something had escaped her. Di had not been hysterical, and had not given her the sort of feeding that she usually got from her clients. She only hoped that Tamara was so sated on what she got from Chris Fitzhugh that she wouldn't notice the lack of response from Susan until it was too late, until Di had turned over this paper— written in Tamara's own hand, with her fingerprints all over it—to Joe O'Brian and the Bunko Squad.

Di went straight to Joe's station, hoping he was on duty. Like most precinct houses, it was a little shabby and very busy. The desk sergeant had one of those tall desks of the sort you saw in movies from the 1940s. He looked a little surprised to see someone like her walking in, and even more surprised when she asked for Joe. As it turned out, Joe was on duty, although he was not in the station at the moment. Di was sent to Joe's captain.

He raised his eyebrows when she came into his office; she stuck out her hand and introduced herself as he rose from his seat behind his desk. The office was scarcely big enough for the desk and a visitor's chair; the desk was one of those dreary gray metal things, and the visitor's chair, when she sat down on it, was enough to give someone back problems. She felt sorry for the captain if that was the sort of chair that *he* was stuck in.

The captain himself, Irish like Joe but big and ruddy, was named O'Grady. So the eastern seaboard tradition of Irish policemen was still alive and well here in Cambridge. Well, so close to Boston, she shouldn't be surprised. "There was something you wanted to see Detective O'Brian about, Miss Tregarde?" he asked carefully.

"Yes, but you will do just as well, sir." She smiled. "I've been doing a little poking around on Joe's behalf. I recently moved to Cambridge to attend Harvard and a mutual friend of ours introduced us; Detective O'Brian was looking for someone who could expose a phony psychic, and she suggested me. I did a fair bit of that sort of thing with my grandmother, mostly around Waterford." She watched his eyebrows climb a little further. "If you check with Detective Gabrielli in the Waterford Bunko Squad, he'll vouch for both of us."

O'Grady made a note of that, but she was pretty certain that when he got done talking to her he wouldn't bother calling the Waterford PD. "The woman in question is Tamara Tarasava. Detective O'Brian didn't go into details, he just told me that he'd like to have her discredited at least, and arrested on fraud if possible." All right, that was a bit of a fib, but Joe hadn't gone into a *lot* of details, so it was technically true. "He gave me her address, I did some preliminary work, and this morning I set up an appointment with her under an alias and posing as a teenager."

"Oh?" O'Grady looked a little more relaxed now, though his tone was still guarded.

"A teenager is naïve and vulnerable." Di smiled. "About an hour ago, I kept my appointment with this Tamara woman, and she pulled the 'egg trick' on me. I got you this—"

She carefully took the paper out of her purse, holding it by the very corner, and put it down on his desk. She explained in detail exactly what she had done, from the pictures in her purse to the phony ID. She finished, "I got her to write out the instructions for me. She wants me to get five thousand dollars, which I believe is in the felony range. I wore gloves, so the only prints on that paper are hers, it's in her handwriting, and it was taken from a legal pad that should be in her consultation room, so you should be able to get the impressions of these instructions from the top sheet. Will that be enough for Bunko to act on?"

The eyebrows stayed well up on the captain's forehead, but the smile he gave her was genuine. "I was skeptical when you first started to talk, Miss Tregarde, but I can see you know your business. We don't often get that kind of cooperation out of Harvard students."

"Just call me a public-minded citizen," she replied. "Now, if it were me, and I needed to actually catch Tamara in the act, for the second round it would be the grandmother, not the girl, that showed up with the cash. First of all, a teenager wouldn't *have* that kind of money to give her, and secondly, with that kind of money at stake, Tamara might bring in a confederate to make sure the pigeon doesn't get away if she has second thoughts about the deal. A young girl could probably outrun her and would certainly attract unwanted attention by screaming. Gramma would probably be easier to control."

The captain nodded. "Then if you can leave your name

and address if we need you to testify—" He handed her paper and a pen, and she wrote both out for him.

"Good luck with this," she said when she was done, and stood up to go. "Tamara is a piece of work I would like to see locked up."

They shook hands. Then the captain hesitated a moment. "If . . . we needed to do something like this again, on one of Joe's cases, would you be available?"

"Possibly," she temporized, and smiled ruefully. "It kind of depends on classes and exams. School comes first, and they aren't going to give me that degree for being public-spirited."

"Of course." This time his smile was quite warm. "I wish my daughter had your attitude about classes and exams. Thank you, Miss Tregarde. You've been very helpful."

With the captain's approval, she stopped at Joe's desk and left him a note. On impulse, she picked up one of his cards from the holder on his desk.

And inwardly cursed.

Superimposed on Joe's name was the equal-armed red cross.

She wasn't off the hook yet.

The upstairs gang wasn't in; not Emory and Zaak, and not Marshal. After knocking on Marshal's door, Di began to wonder if they were having second thoughts about being involved. They were probably avoiding her.

Not that she blamed them. What had happened last night had been pretty damned scary. Emily was probably frightened out of her mind, as well she should be, and the guys, once they got over the kind of numbed, shocky state that always followed an experience like that, might have decided that they wanted no part of her. She trudged down the stairs and back to her own place, carefully locking her door behind her, and sat down on the couch in a dispirited state of mind.

Not that *she* was to blame for any of this—she'd tried to keep their involvement strictly mundane—but they probably wouldn't remember it that way. Until she showed up, the worst thing that had ever happened to Zaak would have been acute embarrassment if someone walked in on him while he was wearing that ridiculous "ritual robe." It was unlikely that he would ever have tried anything as ambitious as conjuring a "wandering spirit," another new thing would have caught his interest soon enough. There had never been any manifestations of anything outré in their lives, and if they had not gotten involved with her, there never would have been.

Then Di had moved in downstairs and all hell had broken loose. Literally. She wasn't personally to blame, but on the other hand, it wasn't difficult to make the connection.

I wouldn't want to be around me either.

And if she was going to be honest with herself . . .

avoiding her from now on would be the best possible thing they could do. She could not honestly say that her presence was not in some part the catalyst for what had happened last night. She was dangerous to be around. Trouble followed Guardians, and even if they didn't know that there were such things, their instincts might be warning them. And if she, with all her potential Guardian power bottled up inside her, had somehow served as a kind of magnet for the dybbuks, then she actually was obliquely part of the reason why things had gone so pear-shaped for Zaak last night. She couldn't say for sure. She didn't *think* so; she was pretty sure that with Zaak's own high potential, eventually he would have attracted something bad anyway—

But she could not honestly swear that the fact that she *was* something of a beacon wasn't a contributing factor.

If that was the case then, the best thing, in fact, the only thing she could do in good conscience was to stay away. If they all shunned one another, if she put heavy shields on them, they might get normal lives back.

She rubbed her eyes with one hand, then got up to get water boiling for tea, fighting down an unexpected lump in her throat.

It wasn't as if she couldn't do this without them. She *could.* She'd been flying solo, more or less, since she'd become a Guardian. It was more that . . . she'd liked hanging out with them, and it had been kind of fun working things out with them, even though it was a serious situation. They all—even Zaak—had sharp minds, and different angles on the problems than she did. It was good being able to bounce things off them. Marshal's knowledge of stage magic was priceless.

But beyond all that, she *liked* them. She had assumed that they were friends, *her* friends. She liked having friends; she actually hadn't had any since—well—grade school. In a way, Zaak blowing things up had been good; while it added to her burden of worry that they would insist on helping her, and she would have to keep *them* safe as well as herself, it meant she would not have to hide her secrets from them. Well, other than being a Guardian; no one really needed to know that but another Guardian. But for the first time since Memaw died, she'd have someone she didn't have to hide her magic from. And for the first time *ever*, someone her own age would know she was a witch. But instead, it seemed that once again she was going to be the weird one, the one people avoided.

She wasn't particularly worried that any of them would spill the beans—who would believe them? Despite the popularity of horror movies, no one really wanted to know that there were such things as dybbuks and demons and vampires. Usually people who got a glimpse of such things quickly made up some rational explanation for what they had seen. And the few people who *might* believe them were . . . well . . . a few tacos short of a combo plate.

"Bloody hell," she said aloud, near to tears. She was just so damn tired of being alone. . . .

At least, before, she'd had Memaw. Memaw knew her, really *knew* her. Now she had no one. She was going to end up like Lavinia, behind a façade that she never dared crack. And one day she was going to have to face off against something she couldn't handle, and then she'd die the same way she had lived.

Alone.

She turned away from the stove, leaned her forehead against the glass of the windowpane, and cried quietly. She knew she was feeling sorry for herself, and right then she didn't care.

The cold glass was soothing, and the sound of the water coming to a boil at least forced her to turn away and pay attention to it. She had no appetite, so she poured part of the boiling water into her tea mug, got a hard-boiled egg and a banana out of the fridge, and ate both and drank her tea without tasting any of it. It was completely dark when she finished, and she stripped to her underwear and crawled into bed without bothering to go back upstairs to see if one of the others had come back. What was the point? Even if they were there, they'd probably pretend not to be.

She cried herself to sleep, which was stupid, and again, she didn't care. Tomorrow she could cowboy up and be the big bad brave Guardian who was bothered by nothing. Tonight she was going to feel sorry for herself until she got it out of her system.

She didn't stay asleep—not truly asleep—for very long.

A Guardian's dreams were seldom "just" dreams, and especially when a Guardian had been Called, her dreams were as much a part of the job as anything done during the waking hours.

She woke to the sound of a small child crying; the child sounded exhausted and hopeless. She sat up, and as she did, she realized that she was still asleep; she wasn't in her own bed. She wasn't in a bed at all but on a nasty smelling couch, a broken-down piece of furniture that stank of cat pee. There was no light and she couldn't make out a lot in the room, but she could tell that it was cold and mostly empty. The crying came from the left-hand corner of the room where there was something piled up on the floor; Di got up and cautiously felt her way to the source.

There was a small mattress there, or at least something shaped like a mattress. As she concentrated on it, she was able to see a little better. Definitely a mattress, maybe from a kid's bed or a crib; it was smaller than a twin and looked as dirty and stained as the couch. There was a heap of ratty blankets there, a child huddled in them, sobbing.

As her foot moved *into* the mattress, Di knew something else; nothing she could do here would affect anything. She wasn't actually *present* in any way; this was a vision. What she would be able to learn would be limited by a lot of things—for instance, she might not be able to move past the walls of this room to find out exactly where she was.

Knowing that, she invoked mage-sight, and saw the

walls, floor, and ceiling of the place glowing with the same black-green energy that Tamara's card had. The child turned her head to wipe her streaming nose and Di recognized her as the missing Melanie.

Hanging over her was a sense of deadly peril—a sense that something truly worse than death was in store for her. For a moment, a sign formed over the child, superimposed on her tiny form. Di didn't immediately recognize the sigil but she instinctively knew it meant doom.

Mentally, she cursed. So Tamara *was* the kidnapper, and she had warded this place strongly against detection. She was smart and probably paranoid; *she* was a magician, so she assumed there might be other magicians who would look for the child. It was a logical assumption; since there was currently a huge reward for Melanie's return, funded by one of the TV stations, there were going to be people looking for the child, and some of them might well be magicians. There was no other reason to have warded this room so heavily.

And if Tamara had warded the place magically, it was also warded psychically. The two abilities were often linked, and it was easy to add wards against mental intrusions. If Tamara was that smart, and that paranoid, this room was probably hidden in a place where no one would look.

Not surprisingly, the room itself looked nothing like the room that Tamara had described to Chris Fitzhugh. It might be a storage room in a basement, or a really big storage closet, or even some sort of storage shed; it had no windows at all. The floor was wood; the floorboards were worn, with spaces between them. The walls were painted but the paint was cracked and peeling. There didn't seem to be a source of heat or light.

The door opened.

There was light outside; the person who had opened the door was silhouetted against it. It seemed bright, but only in comparison to the darkened room. If it was electrical, it couldn't have been brighter than a 40-watt bulb, and it might have been from a kerosene lamp. Di tried to move past the door to see, but couldn't get near it, because of the personal wards on the person standing there.

The person in the doorway was Tamara. Because of the mage-sight, she was haloed in that awful energy. She didn't see Di, which meant this really was a vision—if any part of Di had actually been in this room, there was no way that Tamara would have missed her.

Tamara strode into the room, skirts swishing angrily, heels pounding on the wooden floor. She bent down, pulled the little girl out of her nest of blankets by one shoulder, and shook her until her teeth rattled.

"Shut up, you little bitch," Tamara snarled, and dropped Melanie back on the mattress. Terrified into silence, the little girl curled up into a ball and pulled the covers over her head.

Without another word, Tamara turned back around and stalked out the door, slamming it behind her.

Di really woke up this time, head aching and her heart

pounding. She sat up slowly, trying to extract every bit of information she could from that dream.

Tamara definitely had something to do with the kidnapping of Melanie; at this point, there was no telling exactly what her role was. Di was betting the Gypsy was the original, even the sole, kidnapper, but it was possible that Tamara was acting in collusion with someone. And at the moment, Di had no idea why she had snatched the child . . . but based on the little she had seen, it wasn't *just* to leech her misery along with that of her mother, nor was it to "discover" her and claim the reward. Melanie had seen her and could identify her; there was no way that Tamara was going to turn her over alive. So Tamara had other plans for the child, probably awful ones, plans that required her to keep the child alive for some unknown time.

If the vision was right.

Sometimes the visions weren't. Even though Di had "seen" Tamara, it didn't follow that Tamara had actually been there. Someone else could be responsible, someone who was using Tamara's powers to keep the child hidden. Or, it could be someone connected with Tamara, but because Tamara's was the only face Di knew, that was the face the vision showed her.

Twice in the past, she'd gotten it wrong. Once, when she thought she'd pinpointed a murderer, and once when she thought she had witnessed a particularly brutal rape. Fortunately Memaw had stopped her before she had gone rushing to report what she had "seen" to the police. In the first case, the murder was long solved; the vision had been meant to warn her not to stir up old, terrible memories for someone. In the second, she had been right about the rape, but wrong about the rapist; what she had seen was what the victim "remembered"—and the victim herself had been wrong.

But Melanie *was* in danger. That much she was completely convinced of.

The problem was, she didn't have a shred of evidence. There was no point in taking this to Joe; without evidence, he couldn't do anything either. For that matter, she didn't even have a location, so all she could do was to tell him that what everyone hoped was right—Melanie was alive— and what everyone feared was right—she was in great danger. What could she do with this information other than make Chris Fitzhugh more miserable?

For that matter, although Di herself was strongly convinced that this vision had taken place in present and concurrent time, it might be in the past.

"Dammit," she said aloud into the dark. She tried to think. What *could* she do? There had to be something . . .

Maybe protection? Could she do something that would make it difficult, or even impossible, for anyone to harm the child for a while?

Not through those shields . . . at least, not without something that belonged to Melanie. That was the problem, she had no personal connection to the girl. She'd need something *very* personal—hair, saliva, or blood—to get through the wards in place around her.

Di ground her teeth until her jaws ached, then went to the locked cupboard that held her magic books and grimoires. She took them all back to bed and spent the rest of a sleepless night leafing through them, looking for something, anything, that would help, and coming up with nothing at all.

She didn't realize that she had fallen asleep over her books until she woke with a start. There was a crick in her neck and the phone was shrilling away. Heart pounding, Di shoved everything aside and scrambled out of the bed, hoping to get to the phone before whoever was on the other end gave up.

"This is Joe O'Brian," said the tinny voice on the other end of the line in response to her hello. "Do you want the good news or the bad news first?"

"Good news?" she faltered.

"The bitch won't be bothering Chris Fitzhugh anymore."

The way he said it made her heart sink.

"Because?" she asked.

"She's bolted. We got a warrant for her based on your work—good job, by the way, the captain's impressed—and went looking for her last night. We knocked on the front door, and near as we can figure, she went out the back."

Di closed her eyes as her heart plummeted. She wanted to ask, "Why didn't you have someone watching the back?" but in the first place, that wouldn't do any good, in the second place, it wouldn't win her any points with Joe, and in the third—only she knew that Tamara was something more than a fraud and an extortionist. It all came back to evidence, of which she had exactly none.

"Any idea where she might have gone?" she asked instead.

"She's a Gypsy, she's probably halfway to Chicago by now." She could almost see him shrug. "At least that's one complication in this case that we won't have to worry about anymore. Thanks, Tregarde. I owe you."

"That's all right, Joe. I wish I could have done more—" she said, but he had already hung up the phone.

She carefully put the receiver back on the cradle, because if she wasn't careful she was afraid she just might smash it.

So Tamara was gone—and maybe that vision last night had indeed been reality, maybe even in sync with reality. She could well imagine why Tamara was angry, if she'd had to flee a half step ahead of the law.

Now she cursed herself for not taking something of the woman's with her when she had had the chance. With a physical object, she *might* have a chance of finding her.

Without one? Not with those shields in place. She stood there next to the phone in her underwear, feeling utterly helpless. And utterly alone.

Why am I doing this? she thought in despair. *Why? What's the point? I'm not actually succeeding at anything. Tamara isn't in custody, I have no idea where Melanie is, something horrible is going to happen to her, and I can't stop it. What good is all this power, all this sacrifice, if I can't save one little girl?*

She wanted to howl, scream, tear out handfuls of her hair, break something. She wanted to *hurt* something.

How much of her life had she given up? The chance for a normal life, for friends, for guys, for—well, everything that everyone else took for granted. She'd done it all in the name of helping people.

And now she couldn't even manage that.

What *good* was all this if whatever had given her this power couldn't even give her the tiniest little sign, the smallest bit of help, so she could—

Her thoughts shattered at the tentative knock at the door.

"Um. Di?"

It was Emory's voice.

Flustered, Di looked around frantically for a bathrobe. "You there?"

"Just a second, I'm not exactly decent—" She wrenched open the closet door and grabbed the first thing that came to hand, one of her old granny dresses. She pulled it on over her head. It was a light yellow cotton with short sleeves, wildly inappropriate for the season, but at least now she wasn't three-fourths naked. She ran back to the door, flipped the locks, then opened it.

She didn't think it was possible for her heart to sink further, but it did. All four of them were there, looking somber, and very much as if they too had had a sleepless night.

"Can we come in?" Emory asked somberly. "We'd like to talk to you."

Numbly, she nodded. *So they've come to tell me to bugger off in person. . . .*

At least they were going to give her that much courtesy and not treat her like she had suddenly contracted leprosy.

They filed in, and she closed the door, then turned to face them.

The foursome exchanged a look, then Emory took a deep breath.

Here it comes. "Sorry, we just can't handle—what happened. So . . . let's say we don't know each other, okay?"

"We talked things over last night," Emory said, brows creased. "All four of us. We went off to the Dudley and stayed there most of the night, talking. That stuff that happened— it was kind of hard to—" He took another deep breath. "I mean, it's not something that's easy to accept, even when it happened to you and you've got the evidence right in front of you—and—we wanted to talk it over somewhere normal, where we could look at things objectively and—"

"We want to help," blurted Marshal.

That was so unexpected that for a moment she didn't believe what she'd heard. "Um—say again?" she said stupidly.

"We want to help you," Emory repeated. "That's what we were talking about all last night. I mean, you didn't just pull all that stuff out of your ass. You weren't surprised, you weren't running around screaming, you recognized what you saw and you knew what to do about it. You're like Dr. Strange or something. You do magic to help people, and we think you've been doing it for a while. So we want to help. Not sure how, but you shouldn't have to do this alone."

All she could do was stand there and blink at them.

"Look," Emory said, "I know the only one of us that can actually do anything like what you do is Zaak and he's like the bumbling apprentice—"

"Hey!" Zaak said indignantly.

"Shut up, Zaak," the other three said simultaneously.

"Anyway—" Marshal made a helpless little gesture with his hands. "The thing is, we *know* this stuff is real now, and we can't unknow that. And we all work pretty good together. I mean, when you're running the show. So—um— can we, like, sign on?"

She felt as if her jaw should be hitting the floor and shattering at this point, she was so shocked. This wasn't happening. This *couldn't* be happening—

She watched their faces start to fall in reaction to her stunned silence, and realized that she had better say something before they walked out the door, thinking that *she* had rejected *them*.

"Yes!" she blurted. "Oh, hell *yes!*"

For a moment, they stood in stunned silence. Then Zaak let out a whoop, and the others began punching fists in the air and generally carrying on as if she had just offered them all brand-new Ferraris.

For the life of her, she could not imagine *why* they would feel that way—but she joined the celebration.

The celebrating didn't last forever of course. In fact, it didn't last very long at all. Di took a minute to change into something more practical, then brought them quickly up to speed, including her horrific vision from last night. They all sat on the floor, using pillows from the bed, while they ate deli bagels and cream cheese and lox that Marshal brought down from his place. Marshal took notes—it turned out he knew shorthand—while the other three listened with frowns of concentration.

"So why can't you just find Tamara or the kid?" Em asked finally, before Di had had a chance to explain what she could and could not do. "Zaak found my keys this morning."

"Because she needs something personal either from Tamara or Melanie," Zaak supplied before Di could say anything. "The more personal the better. Right?"

"Sort of," Di replied. "The problem is that if my vision is right, Tamara has her place shielded, and even if I had something from either one of them, I still wouldn't be able to *find* them, though I might be able to affect them. It's like . . . okay, like they're lights, and the shields are like boxes. I can't see anything past the boxes. Better yet, camouflaged boxes. They blend in with the background."

Marshal was drumming his fingers on the floor. "Okay, but can you tell one box from another? Could you tell by looking at the outside if Tamara was the one that made the box?"

She grimaced. "Technically . . . yes. Practically speaking . . . I'd still have to have something personal of hers. I could look for her signature energy, it's pretty unique, if I had that."

Marshal got up. "Then let's go." He offered her his hand; she stared at it.

"Go where? Tamara's place? The police have probably got it locked up tight—"

Marshal snorted. "I doubt there's any lock in this town short of a bank vault that I can't pick. Come on. We'll take the car."

She took his hand and scrambled to her feet. "Car? You have a car?"

Emory made a face. "Why do you think we let an egg-head like him hang out with freaks like us?"

Marshal swatted him. "Di, have you got some kind of traveling kit? You know, magic emergency supplies? From what you were saying it sounds like we'll have to move fast."

Wow. Marshal was *sharp*. "Yeah, it's under the bed—but I'm out of consecrated salt and water—"

"Zaak, you can do that, right?" At his nod, Marshal made shooing motions. "Make with the magic."

"Can any of you use a gun?" Di asked, deciding that if they wanted to be in, they were going to be *in*.

Emory and Em both raised their hands. "Bottom drawer of my dresser. Should be two handguns in there, a .38 and a .45. Make sure they're clean; I can't remember if I cleaned them when I put them away last, and make sure they're loaded. Then make sure the reloaders are full, you'll find the ammo in there with the guns. Every other bullet should be the silver ones."

Emory stared at her for just a fraction of a second, then nodded. "We'll take care of it. You guys go."

Marshal headed out the door at a trot, Di hard on his heels; Zaak closed the door behind them and Di and Marshal pounded down the staircase to the first-floor entry-way. "Ya can't pahrk yer cahr in Hahrvahrd Yahrd," he deadpanned as they sprinted past the wall of mailboxes and shoved open the door, getting a slightly hysterical giggle out of her. "But I have a secret parking place. Tell no one."

Considering that parking places were more valuable than diamond-encrusted platinum tiaras, she wasn't at all surprised at this admonition. What was absolutely astonishing was that his hidden parking place—for a tiny Austin Mini Cooper—was within a quick sprint of the apartment building.

It was a little nook that would never have fit a car that was any bigger, in an alley half a block away. Marshal rolled a Dumpster out of the way, pulled the car out, and she helped him push the Dumpster back into place. They both squeezed in and he shot the tiny car out of the alley and into Sunday morning traffic, what little there was of it.

"I give magic lessons to the kids of that building's super," he said, maneuvering the little beast around a dinosaur of a station wagon.

"What?" she said absently, trying to think how she could use Tamara's object to find something that didn't want to be found.

"The parking space, that's how I got it. I use my powers only for good." He glanced over at her. "Sorry, bad time for a worse joke."

"No, it's okay. I'm just thinking—"

"That's fine." He grinned. "You do the heavy lifting, I'll do the driving."

They got to Tamara's neighborhood quickly, taking

much less time than the bus trips had. When they reached
Tamara's street, though, he didn't stop, going straight past
the house with yellow crime scene tape crossing the door.

"But—" she protested.

"We don't want to be seen, do we?" he countered, and
she subsided.

He circled the block and ended up tucking the car into
another alley, parking between two garages. All the houses
here had walled-in backyards; they counted houses until
they came to Tamara's, and tried the gate.

It was locked, but Marshal solved that in next to no
time. They slipped inside and closed it behind them.

There was police tape over the back door too, but they
simply took it off, carefully, so that they could replace it,
and Marshal went to work on the locks of the back door.
There were glass panes in the door, and she supposed that
they *could* have broken one to get in, but then the cops
would know someone had broken in and . . .

Not a good idea.

There were three locks on the door, including two
dead bolts. But Marshal took a roll of felt out of his jacket
and unrolled it, and inside was a complete set—so far as
Di could tell—of professional lock-picking tools.

"Funny thing, not even the police question you about
these if you have business cards showing you're a professional magician," he said under his breath, as he worked
on the locks. "I've even gotten gigs doing parties for cops'
kids. And that's one."

She heard the lock click open.

"Back home, all the neighbors knew to come get me when they locked themselves out of their cars or their houses," he continued. There was another click. "And that's two. We're lucky, these are really old-fashioned. She never changed them."

"Maybe she didn't think she needed them," Di said dryly. "She might have had other protections."

He froze. "You don't think she—"

Di shook her head. "I'm not getting a sense of anything dangerous waiting, not on the door and not for a good way beyond it. For one thing, anything that was there, the cops probably already sprung, tossing the place. For another, I think she left in too big a hurry to actually set something up. I honestly think she thought she was immune from getting arrested, and it never occurred to her that her house could be invaded. Gods know she's got the entire neighborhood spooked. I bet there isn't anyone around here who would dare break in even if she left her doors wide open."

"That's comforting." He finished with the third lock, and the door swung open. "Nevertheless, after you."

She gave him a little mock bow, readied her defenses just in case, pushed the door completely open with her foot, and stepped inside.

She knew as soon as she crossed the threshold that whatever had been here was gone. There wasn't even that faint sense of menace she'd felt when she'd come here as Susan.

Marshal joined her in a kitchen that looked like an explosion had gone off. Tamara hadn't been all that good of a housekeeper, but drawers and cupboards were all yanked open and had been left that way, pots, pans, and dishes had been pulled out, canisters dumped out, leaving flour and sugar and coffee all over the floor. The cops had done a real number on the place.

"Wow. Remind me never to do anything to get searched," Marshal said, blinking.

"That's a good basic rule to live by," Di replied, and picked her way across the floor. "Remember we need to clean our shoes off when we leave."

"So we don't have evidence that we've been here—"

"So we don't track sugar into your car," Di corrected. "You park behind a Dumpster in an alley. You want roaches in your car?"

Marshal shuddered. "Right. So we're looking for personal stuff. You go left, I'll go right."

Di found herself in a small hallway; the first room she came to was the bathroom. It, too, had been pretty thoroughly trashed. There was no sign of a toothbrush, but she found a hairbrush on the floor and stuffed it into her pocket.

Then she got the oddest feeling. As if . . . the hairbrush wasn't what she needed. She took it out of her pocket and looked at it closely, then pulled one of the long, black hairs out of the brush.

It didn't look right.

"Uh, Di? I think you need to see this."

She followed Marshal's voice to a bedroom that for a moment looked to her as if it were the site of an Indian massacre. There were scalps everywhere.

Not scalps. Wigs.

That was why the hair in the brush didn't look right. . . .

Scattered among the clothing and other things on the floor were what must have been a good dozen wigs; all black, but as near as Di could tell, each one had been cut and styled a different way.

"Pretty useful if you're being followed or watched," Marshal observed, poking one with his toe. "Especially if you carry a spare one with you."

Di nodded.

Marshal picked his way across the bedroom floor; there was an old-fashioned vanity in one corner, a real beauty of an antique. It seemed that Tamara had made daily use of it, for there was a litter of makeup of all sorts on and around it. Most of it was spilled. Clearly the cops had been on a fishing expedition, hoping to find something, probably drugs, that they could use to charge her with.

One entire end of the bedroom was blocked off by sets of louvered doors. Marshal opened one door, revealing a closet full of clothing—not just the Gypsy-hippie things

Tamara had been wearing when Di met with her, but everything from sequined evening gowns to sharp business suits, to a couple of antique-style Victorian dresses. And above the clothing, ranged neatly, were more wigs in every possible color.

"What the—" Di stared.

"Chameleon," Marshal guessed. "I bet she did more than just tell fortunes."

"I'm beginning to think that the psychic scam was only the tip of the proverbial iceberg." Beneath the clothing were shoe racks, which were just as full as the shelves. "I'd love to know where someone with feet that size found shoes like that." She shook herself out of the contemplation of all that clothing. "Never mind, we don't have time to sort through all the hair around here to figure out what's hers. Look for a wastebasket; maybe you'll find some used Kleenex. I'll find the laundry hamper. And we should both keep our eyes open for things that look like they might be keepsakes."

Di found the laundry hamper, and discovered that Tamara sent her clothes out to be cleaned. A commercial laundry bag sat next to the hamper, stuffed full. Di extracted a pair of lacy undies that were a little frayed. That would have to do, since Marshal came up empty-handed.

Di was hoping, but not really expecting, to find Tamara's ritual space or tools. She had the feeling that Tamara kept such things far separated from her living space. Since she was working the left-hand path, that was probably wise. The residue of nasty magic was apt to attract equally nasty things, and you didn't want those things sniffing around the place where you lived and slept.

She checked her watch with an increased sense of urgency. "I think we've spent as much time here as we can. We have something, anyway. Let's get out of here."

Marshal locked up behind them, though there wasn't anything he could do about the dead bolts. They cleaned off their shoes, then sprinted down the alley to his car.

They found the others waiting somewhat impatiently for them. By then, Di had a pretty good idea of what she was going to do next, at least so far as finding Tamara.

"Help me move the furniture," she said, and when they had gotten it all cleared to the sides of the room, she flipped the rug.

The bottom side was a single piece of white canvas, with her own ritual circle beautifully embroidered on it. She and Memaw had spent all of one year making it. It was, of course, a "broken" circle; the circle was outlined in a nine-part braid of silk with some of her own hair braided into it, and it was completed only when she tied the loose ends of the braid together.

She unlocked her cupboard and got out her supplies while Zaak examined the rug with interest and envy. She took everything to the middle of the rug and raised an eyebrow at Zaak. "Watch and learn," she said, tied off the braid, and cast her circle.

The moment she did so, she sensed that little door

opening up in her again. The movement of power was slower and more deliberate, but it was obvious that she was finally on the right track, or it wouldn't have come at all.

Once her circle and wards were in place, she sat down cross-legged in the middle of the circle and cut the crotch out of the panties with a silver knife. Not her *atheme*; that was reserved for other things, and she didn't want to contaminate its potential power with anything of Tamara's.

She pulled several threads from the scrap of cloth, then disassembled her compass.

It looked like an ordinary compass; a glass cover, the needle resting delicately on a spindle, and the base. But there was no compass rose painted on the base; it was just a blank piece of white stuff. Ivory, though the elephant that had left that tusk had died of natural causes long before there was any ban on importation.

Everything but the lid was ivory, in fact, including the needle. The lid was a glass disk set in bronze. It was very, very old. Di wasn't sure how old, but the ivory had mellowed to a creamy shade.

She opened the bottle of rubber cement and lifted the needle from its place. She delicately dabbed a line of the adhesive on the needle, carefully laid three of the threads from Tamara's panties along it, then set the needle back on the spindle. She finished reassembling the compass, then changed position from cross-legged to kneeling, facing south, the direction of the Protector and Avenger, who could take many names, but answered as often to Archangel Michael as any.

She closed her eyes and clasped her hands over her *atheme*, holding it point down above the compass. She took in a long breath, threw everything out of her mind except the need to find Tamara's power, and released her own power through her knife into the compass.

When she opened her eyes and looked, the needle was pointing between west and south.

"Right," she said, realizing from the looks on their faces that there had probably been a physical manifestation of that discharge of power. "Now we have a guide. Saddle up and move out."

Zaak, Em, and Emory somehow squeezed into the back of the Mini Cooper, though Em was mostly on Emory's lap. Di and Marshal were in the front, following, as best they could, given the roads, the guidance of the compass. The streets around Cambridge were not exactly laid out in a logical fashion.

Still, that was the least of their worries. Once they actually got close to Tamara's power, the shields would begin to interfere with the compass. Eventually the needle would start to spin. Diana could only hope that the area they ended up in was something like warehouses—places without a lot of people in them. They certainly couldn't

call the cops and start a house-to-house search in a
crowded residential neighborhood on the basis of three
underwear threads glued to a compass needle.

But the needle continued to point steadfastly in one
direction, and they moved out of the city into the suburbs,
and then out of the suburbs of Cambridge into the suburbs of Boston, past Boston College—

"We are way out of Cambridge jurisdiction," Emory
said from the backseat, sounding muffled.

It was getting darker now, the sun going down, dusk
closing in. That was both good and bad. Good, because it
meant if they actually found the right place, they could
sneak up on it without Tamara seeing them. Bad, because
Tamara was clearly working some bad juju, and evil things
were stronger when the sun went down.

By the time there was nothing left of the sun but some
red streaks in the sky, they were out in rural Massachu-
setts. Farm country, lots of woodland and orchards. The
lights, slowly coming on as darkness fell, were few and far
between. Diana's hopes rose a little.

They turned down a barely paved two-lane road and
traveled about two miles along it without seeing any lights
at all other than their own headlights. Orchards? The trees
were spaced too regularly to be woods, but if these were
orchards they were long abandoned. Di felt in her kit for
her flashlight and trained the yellow beam on the compass. Her timing was good, because moments later, the
needle began to spin wildly.

"Ha!" she said, and Marshal glanced over at her, taking his foot off the gas—not that the car was going all that fast.

"Keep going," she told him. "It's around here somewhere, but I want to mark where the—"

"Where the effect ends." He stopped the car anyway and zeroed the odometer. "Now we know where it begins."

She shook her head ruefully. "I think you're smarter than I am."

"Naw. I was an Eagle Scout." He made a face. "Don't look at me in that tone of voice."

"I was just imagining you in short pants." That broke the tension a little as Em giggled and Emory guffawed. "Carry on, Scoutmaster."

Marshal growled something unintelligible and sent the car creeping forward again. It seemed forever before the needle stopped spinning and pointed back the way they had come.

"Stop," she said, and Marshal peered at the odometer.

"One point two five miles to the midpoint," he said, "roughly." He maneuvered the car carefully in an effort not to get off the pavement, taking so long to get going in the opposite direction that Emory made the impatient suggestion that they just get out, pick up the car, and turn it around.

Finally they were underway again.

"Stop us a little short and look for some place we

can pull the car off the road where no one is going to notice it."

"You're asking me to pull this poor little thing off the road?" The car bumped and lurched around a pothole. "Lady, the springs in ballpoint pens are stronger than the ones in my car!"

"Just—*there!*" She pointed ahead, at what looked like an overgrown gravel road intersecting with the rough lane they were on. Obediently, Marshal eased onto the track, which was a lot better than it looked; hardpacked dirt nearly as good as pavement—the weeds growing over it gave no resistance. They passed the nearly invisible remains of an old, crumbled fence. Once they were under the trees and away from the reach of the headlights of any car on the road, it would be hard to tell they were there.

They all got out. Diana distributed flashlights to the others, who played them on the ground, revealing a litter of cigarette butts and crumpled packages, beer cans, food wrappers, and a couple of empty bottles of harder stuff mixed in with the weeds.

"Well, that explains a lot," said Emory.

"Good thing it's Sunday night, otherwise we'd have company." Marshal got the rest of their gear out of the car's tiny boot, and looked at Di. "All right, Fearless Leader, what are we looking for?"

"Bonehead," she said affectionately. "Since there's no Haunted Amusement Park around here, it has to be the

Abandoned Farmhouse. Don't you ever watch any Saturday morning cartoons?" Marshal shook his head sadly. "No wonder the only culture you have is the stuff growing in your fridge."

"You know, Abandoned Farmhouse is also something that turns up in Cthulhu Mythos stories," Emory said soberly. "Ah . . . we aren't going to need any Elder Signs, are we?"

"Was that supposed to be a joke?" Zaak asked.

"No," Emory replied. "This is New England, and I bet not everything Lovecraft wrote about was something he made up."

That was just a hair too close to the truth. Di shivered, and not from the cold, though it was icy out here, and the darkness wasn't helping. "Let's get going," she said, wincing at the sound of her own voice. It sounded too loud. Instinctively, she wanted to whisper.

She led the way back to the road, then turned off her flashlight; the others did the same, though she could sense their uncertainty. "Wait for the moon," she told them. "It's almost full, and it should be coming up in a second. Em, Emory, you guys got your weapons?"

"Yep. We want to know where the rest of *you* are before we start going all Dirty Harry, though." Emory's voice sounded subdued. "How do we do that?"

"You all stick together; you've seen enough horror movies to know not to lose each other in the dark. If you do, those of you who are still together stop and let the stray find you. If I have to split off, I'll yell before I come anywhere near you."

"Got it." The moon was rising above the trees now, and as she expected, it flooded the road with light. With their eyes adjusted they could see reasonably well, enough to keep from spraining an ankle in a pothole or falling over a rock. They made their way cautiously down the road. It was . . . spooky. Far off in the distance it was possible to hear the sounds of cars and trucks on the highway, but nearby? Only the occasional noise of an animal scuttling through the dead vegetation, or farther off, the noise of something larger moving away from them.

"This really is going to be a haunted farmhouse, isn't it?" Emory said quietly.

"Well, it's pretty likely Tamara has holed up in the farmhouse that this orchard belongs to," Di replied. "Or at least something like that. I'd have suspected an old trailer home, but what I saw in my dream looked older and more permanent than that. I can't see her camping."

"Me either, not after that bedroom. I don't see anyone with that many wigs knowing how to rough it." Marshal peered up the road. "I think that might be what we're looking for, on the left. See where there's no drop-off at the edge of the pavement, like there is everywhere else? Like there used to be an access road there, or maybe a driveway."

They picked up their pace a little—as much as anyone wanted to, given the dim light. Sure enough, there was something like an overgrown track there. There was no sign of a gate, but Marshal and Di evidently had the same idea at the same time, for they both went straight up to what looked like an impenetrable barrier of bushes and weeds and discovered that the barrier was just a screen of dead stuff piled up to hide the road.

"Bingo." Di shivered again. "Either we have a mean old man out of a Scooby-Doo cartoon, someone farming weed, or Tamara. So wait—"

She closed her eyes and tried to see if she could sense anything.

Nothing but a vague but powerful feeling of menace.

"Anything on the radar?" Zaak asked. She shook her head.

"Sometimes these access roads go for half a mile," Marshal observed. "We might be too far away. Can we use the flashlights?"

"I think we're going to have to," she replied. "But . . . be careful, because that's just going to advertise we're coming. . . ."

"Like falling and breaking an ankle wouldn't?" Em put in. "Still, it might be worth it for someone to scout ahead of the group."

"That'd be me," Marshal replied. "Eagle Scout, remember? I won't go farther ahead than twenty yards. When I know that stretch is clear, I'll whistle a little, and you can catch up to me and then I'll go ahead again."

The sense of urgency that had driven Di out here argued against such caution, but the rest of her was in complete agreement. So that was what they did; the group huddled together, listening to the faint crackle of weeds being trampled underfoot as Marshal forged ahead. Then, at his excellent imitation of a whip-poor-will, they moved forward to his position, then waited for him again as he went ahead.

That continued for a while—it seemed like a very long time, but was actually a lot less than an hour—right up to the point where, instead of hearing his whistle, they heard him furtively making his way back to them.

"There's a farmhouse there, all right. Some lights at the rear, not many and not bright, and it looks like most of the windows are boarded up, so it's not as if someone is living there who has a right to be there. I think." He was whispering, and they all kept their voices just as low. "Di, you getting anything now?"

"This doesn't exactly work like radar," she whispered back, but she couldn't deny the heavy feeling of menace all around. "All right. We need a plan. Does that place look like it has a basement? Maybe a root cellar or something? And do you feel comfortable prowling around it a little? If not—"

"I'm comfortable, providing no werewolves jump me." He tried to make a joke out of it.

"I can try to do something to keep that from happening," she said quite seriously. "I can make you invisible to supernatural things, but so far as you making perfectly ordinary noises and alerting killer German Shepherds or anything like that—"

He sobered. "If you can do that, I'll take my chances. I was pretty good at teenage sneaking around."

She nodded, thought about exactly what they needed to know, and said, "All right. We just need to know the general layout of the place and where the doors and accessible windows are. And if there is a basement with outside access." Right now a basement room was the likeliest match for the room she had seen in her dream.

"Hiding" Marshal was magic she could do quickly; she'd done it a thousand times, although usually on herself. The process simply made the person in question blend in with the background, chameleonlike, at least to the senses of anything magical. Not so much invisibility, as making the eyes slide away, a forceful "not noticing." It wouldn't last long, but it didn't have to.

She was done with the casting by the time Marshal said, "Well, when are you going to make me the Invisible Man?"

"I already have," she replied. "Be careful."

"I will," he replied fervently, and slipped away, leaving them all in a huddle in the dark.

She tried to sense what was in the house, but other than the general aura of inimical magic, she couldn't get much without pushing. And right now, she didn't want to push. Tamara, though powerful, was not very skilled—or had picked up her knowledge piecemeal and had never been formally trained. Still, there was a lot of emotion fueling her power, and it wasn't just Chris Fitzhugh's anguish. Di realized that she had better tread very cautiously. Tamara might be the proverbial blunt instrument, but an untutored lout with a sledgehammer could kill you just as dead as an assassin with a stiletto.

Di didn't sense anything outside the house, but that didn't mean anything. There could be physical traps. There could be things that were hidden from her, the same way she had hidden Marshal. Maybe Tamara was conserving her magical resources.

Or maybe, just maybe, Tamara was arrogant enough to think that she wouldn't be found.

Di was used to waiting, though the others began fidgeting long before Marshal came back. The whip-poor-will whistle preceded him and he slipped in beside them in the shelter of their bushes with only a little rustling of dead leaves.

"The side facing us is the front. There's a wooden porch covered with Virginia Creeper which looks like a death trap; half the supports are busted and I wouldn't be any too sure of the floor. The windows are all boarded up, and I couldn't see any sign of anyone fighting through the weeds and the Virginia Creeper to get to the front door. Around left is that cellar door you were hoping for and someone *did* use that; the weeds are all busted down. There are a couple of windows on that side where the boards have been taken off, but the windows are dark. There's a car in the back, an old beater Buick. There's a back door with cement steps going up and the windows back there have light. It looks like a Coleman or a kerosene lamp, not electricity. The last side is all boarded up, and full of blackberry bushes, I didn't even try to get around it."

Di let out her breath in a sigh. "All right then. We're hitting this blind, and I'm sorry. My best guess is the kid is in that cellar. It's where I'd stash her if I was hiding her. So what we need to do is provide a distraction at the kitchen door while we snatch the kid from the cellar—"

"And we provide the distraction," Emory interrupted, and started to stand up.

"Oh, *hell* no!" Di whispered sharply, and pulled him down again. "If she's got the kind of juice I think she does, she'll be able to bring in stuff that will make that dybbuk look like Captain Kangaroo! No, I want you guys to put the grab on the kid, while *I* do the distraction! Chances are the kid's nowhere near the cellar door. She might even be locked in another room. The door's probably old enough and the frame's dry-rotted enough you can bust it off the hinges, but *I* can't. And I'm leaving you with the guns. If there's a confederate, he'll be down there."

"Oh," said Emory.

"All right. I'll go hit the back door and start a ruckus, while you wait at the cellar. As soon as you hear the noise start, break in and try to find Melanie. If she's not there, head up into the house but stay clear of where the noise is. Zaak?"

"Yep. Got the kit." Zaak sounded steadier than she thought he would. Excellent.

"Remember, blessed salt and holy water will probably chase off anything she's left on guard. If that doesn't work, try the horseshoe nails. If that doesn't work, try brute magical force and bullets. And if *those* don't work—try what worked on the dybbuk. It's worth a shot, and unholy things usually will at least react to the holy backed by faith."

"Gotcha. Give me a sec . . ." Zaak rummaged in the bag and came up with the salt container, which he proceeded to empty into one pocket of his jacket. She nodded with approval. "Got the squirt gun of holy water in the right pocket, and the horseshoe nails in a bag on my belt."

Horseshoe nails—better make sure they all had them. "Yeah, wait a sec, give everybody one of those. Stick them in your pockets. Cold iron is pretty effective as a repellant for the things I can think of she'd have as guards—they can still lob stuff at you, but they won't be able to get close enough to slash at you, and claws and teeth are generally their weapons of choice." She took a deep breath. "All right. Let's do this."

They did their best to slip through the brush and weeds in Marshal's wake, though only Di was as quiet as he was.

Their eyes had adapted to the darkness while they'd waited, flashlights off, for Marshal to return. The house had probably been white, and probably was now the silver-gray of bleached wood, so it stood out pretty well—and it helped that there was a vague haze of light at the back of it. Di left her friends all at the cellar door, an old-fashioned double door that she hoped had stairs behind it and not a coal chute. There was a padlock on it, but Marshal was already at work on it. Now, more than ever, she was grateful that lock-picking was included in his set of useful skills. She made a mental note to tell other Guardians it might be a good idea to start picking up stage magic tricks.

"Whistle when you get the lock off," she whispered; he nodded, and she moved quietly on to the back of the house.

Sure enough, there was a chunky old car back there, something from the fifties, not iconic enough to be cool, too lumpy to be good-looking. She couldn't tell the color.

She scooted around so that the car was between her and the house and studied the area around the back door. She could now detect wood smoke; the light wind had probably been carrying it away from them before. So there was some form of lantern in there, and a wood fire.

There weren't any moving shadows. Did that mean anything? She peered in the car windows; the backseat was loaded with dark bundles. Smart; the house was probably stuffed with rats and mice; anything Tamara wanted to keep safe—like food—she was better off keeping in the car. Carefully, Di tried the closest door; it opened easily, letting out a whiff of apples and salami.

The whistle she'd been hoping for sounded softly from the side of the house. All right. Time for the fireworks.

Tamara clearly was not expecting anyone to find her here. Chances were she hadn't locked the back door. After all, it would be a nuisance to have to unlock it just to get into the car for breakfast.

She brought up all of her defenses and walked quickly around the car and up the cement stairs. Bringing power into both hands, she kicked at the door.

As she had hoped, it flew open and smashed into the wall, sticking there. She jumped across the threshold before Tamara could do something to block her—

Most of the light in the room was coming from a Coleman lantern in one corner and a woodstove on the opposite wall; this was a kitchen, but there was no furniture in it—and the reason she had not been able to see any moving shadows was because Tamara was kneeling on the floor, naked, with her back to the door, in the center of a piece of canvas. Painted on the canvas was a ritual circle, though Di didn't recognize the signs painted around and inside the circle. Tamara leapt to her feet and whirled as Di crossed the threshold.

And that was when Di froze, because the very last thing she had ever expected Tamara to have was a penis.

It was a good thing her defenses were already up, because otherwise that moment of paralysis would have cost her dearly. As it was, when Tamara screeched an obscenity and blasted her, it pretty much all splashed off her shields. The attack steadied her, though, and she gave back as good as she got.

Tamara's shields were not as well made as Di's, but they were insanely strong, so the result was the same—nothing got through. They battered at each other for at least five minutes, when a volley of gunshots under their feet startled them both for a moment. The sound rattled Tamara more, though, and Di got in a hit that sent the kidnapper staggering back, narrowly avoiding the stove.

Tamara pushed off the wall and snatched something out of the old zinc sink under the window, then lunged for Di, an enormous butcher knife catching the light from the lantern as it passed *way* too close to her eyes. It was Di's turn to flinch back, her concentration broken. Then Tamara was on her again, and it was pretty clear that no matter what other skills the kidnapper had, Tamara was a solid knife fighter.

It was all Di could do to keep out of reach of that blade while she tried to refocus her power. But as she had pointed out, shields didn't do squat about material things, and that knife was as material as you could get. All she could do was fall back on the half-dozen jujitsu lessons she'd had. . . .

Which seemed pitifully few now. Her side hurt, she was panting and sweating, while Tamara was just as energized by rage and insanity as when this fight had started.

And then—a miracle.

Tamara made a stab at Di that was identical to something the jujitsu instructor had taught her to counter. Everything snapped into place, as if it were all preprogrammed. With focus and complete confidence, Di moved out of the line of Tamara's stab. She grabbed Tamara's wrist at exactly the right moment to catch the kidnapper off balance. She pulled, ducked under Tamara's arm, and flipped the "woman" over her shoulder and into the wall.

There was a shuddering *whump* as Tamara hit the wall, followed by a strange, gurgling noise.

Di straightened, as Tamara slid down the wall, flopped over—

And revealed that the knife had been driven into Tamara's chest. The kidnapper's hand was still clenched on the hilt even though "her" eyes were already glazing over with death.

There was a strangled little sick sound at the door. Di whirled to see Marshal and Emory moving to block the sight of the body from the child in Zaak's arms, and Em holstering her gun.

"Um—we came to see if you needed—guess you didn't," Marshal gulped.

"Thirty seconds ago I did," Di replied, feeling as sick as Marshal and Emory looked. "Move. Out. Over by the car. Quick."

She started for the door, which got *them* moving. Her mind raced; she needed to figure out a plausible scenario, and she needed to figure it out fast and make sure it was simple and that they were all letter-perfect in it.

By the time they were all in a huddle at the car, she had it.

"Okay, we need a story that is going to hold up enough to get us off. Marshal, go get your car and bring it to the front of the house; you and Emory and Em will take Melanie back to the last town we passed and get hold of the law. Wait!" She held up her hand at their shocked expressions. "Wait and hear me out. We can't turn up with a kidnapped child and a dead body unless we've got a good explanation, one the cops will buy.

"Here's ours. We came out here because we heard the place was abandoned and we were gonna scout it out for a party. Confess to the lesser crime they can turn us loose for, see?" She paused. "Okay, give me the guns. What were you shooting at, anyway?"

"There was something guarding the kid," Emory replied, his voice a little shaky. "Something bigger than me, and hairy. We emptied on it, it went down, Zaak hit it with water and salt and it just melted away."

She nodded. From that description, she had no idea what it was, only that it was a good thing they'd *had* all that weaponry. She took the guns, including Zaak's squirt gun, and shoved them all into the bag Zaak had been carrying.

"So the story is, you three got here and heard the kid screaming and crying. You busted into the basement and got her and ran. Zaak and I will go back to where we all got out of the car and wait for you. The cops will want you to take them to the house, and when you do, they'll assume

Tamara was too late to stop you, so she killed herself. Himself." She paused, thrown for a moment, then shook her head to clear it and continued. "While you're gone, Zaak and I will get rid of anything that looks occult and set up a bucket or a tub or something and put some water to heat on the stove in there, so it looks like you interrupted Tamara in the middle of bath time. Got it?"

They nodded, but Marshal asked hesitantly, "But why— I mean getting rid of—"

"Because this is freaky enough without starting a big old satanic witch scare," Di said bluntly. "*I* want to figure out what the hell she—he—was doing and why, and for that *I* need to grab the evidence. But the cops don't need to know any of that. Because if they did, sure as anything, they'd start looking for a cult, and there isn't one. Tamara was just one lone lunatic, but looking for a cult will start them sniffing around anything from Halloween supplies on up, and none of us need that kind of scrutiny."

She looked directly at Zaak when she said that, and he nodded.

"So, are we straight?"

They all nodded. Marshal took the best of the flashlights and went off at a run and Zack handed the little girl to Di. The poor thing was so exhausted by all she'd been through that she'd actually fallen asleep while they were standing around talking. She was heavy and more than a bit smelly, but Di didn't care—she was alive and safe. They'd completely beaten the odds on this one.

Marshal came back a lot sooner than any of them had expected, headlights blazing with welcome light. The tire tracks would give veracity to their story. Emory and Emily got in, wrapping the little girl in a blanket from the boot of the car. She didn't even wake up. And then they were gone, Marshal revving the engine as hard as it could go.

They didn't get back to their respective apartments until dawn. The telephone woke her up about noon. She fumbled her way to it—she'd fallen into bed still clothed and just rolled up into the blankets—and answered.

"Joe O'Brian," he said after her bleary hello. "Don't bother trying to tell me you had nothing to do with it. Lavinia says otherwise. Am I welcome in your apartment yet?"

"Uh . . . yeah?" she said.

"Good. Get your spook squad together in an hour. I'll bring the grinders and beer." Before she could respond, he hung up.

When Joe arrived, out of uniform, he was carrying two big sacks of grinders and a case—and had Lavinia in tow. Di had managed to wake everyone up and get them assembled, though there were dark circles under their eyes and all of them—including her—were still feeling kind of shocky.

Joe didn't say much after she let him in, just distributed the sandwiches and beer and let everyone settle down.

"Right," he said, taking charge of things. "First of all, is there any evidence I have to make disappear?"

Di shook her head. "Zaak and I were careful. We wore gloves, I never had any blood on me and I made sure Zaak didn't get any on him. I don't think the little girl has any idea how many people there were or who we all were, and I think I left a pretty plausible looking scene. I even polished my prints off the junker car where I touched it."

Joe let out his breath in a sigh of relief. "Good job," he said, breaking into a smile for the first time since Di had met him. "All right, here's what I know. Tomas—that was Tamara's real name—was turned down for sex change operations three times. No one would talk on the record, but the last shrink said—off the record—that no doc in his right mind was going to do that kind of operation on a raving loony like Tomas. We found all kinds of interesting things in that house, including a rent-a-cop uniform, so now we know there wasn't a confederate. But the big one was this—Tomas was operating as Tomas-the-bookie as well as Tamara-the-tea-leaf-reader, and one of the clients was named Fitzhugh."

As one, their jaws dropped.

"Well . . . that explains a lot," Zaak said, recovering first.

Di nodded. It did—how Tamara knew about Melanie and Chris, probably how Tamara knew about the shopping trip too—

"We're getting the details out of Fitzhugh now, but damn if Tomas wasn't slick. 'Tamara' was never around when the old man was, so he never laid eyes on his wife's pet psychic. We're gonna spin it as debt and extortion, and that's what the Fitzhughs think it is, but I want the real reason. That's why I brought Vinnie." Joe nodded at Lavinia, who was casually, but fastidiously, eating her meatball grinder with a knife and fork.

Di put down her sandwich and got the still unopened bag into which they had stuffed Tamara's canvas circle and every bit of occult paraphernalia they could find. She spread the canvas out on the floor and was reaching back into the bag, when Lavinia exclaimed, "Of *course!* Cybele!"

"Who?" said Joe, as Di snapped her fingers and echoed, "Of course!"

"Cybele is the Phrygian earth goddess, which is not important. What *is* important is that like most ancient goddesses she has both a light side and a dark side—and that historically her male followers castrated themselves to turn themselves into priestesses." Lavinia was off and running then, explaining that Tomas was probably invoking Cybele's dark side in hopes of getting the sex change he wanted by magic. Her explanations digressed into the realms of Anatolian mythology. Zaak followed her account with great interest, Emory and Marshal with frowns of concentration; Em and Joe were nodding but looking vaguely lost whenever Lavinia swerved off the modern path.

Now Di was very glad Joe had brought Lavinia, who was, aside from being a Guardian, a first-class scholar of Indo-European religions and mythology. She'd never have figured out Phrygian from those glyphs on the canvas, but once Lavinia did, it all made perfect sense. So to speak.

She wondered if Tomas was not a Gypsy at all, but some wandering Anatolian . . . even a descendant of those long-ago priests of Cybele.

Whatever the case, one thing was absolutely true. It was seldom wise to awaken one of those old, old gods and give them a foothold in the modern world. Their worship was often violent and bloody, and the sacrifices they demanded were generally extravagant. The Greeks and Romans had given Cybele room among their gods as the Magna Mater, or Great Mother, but there were dark things said about the worship of the Magna Mater, and human sacrifice was the least of them.

Who knows what that thing was that was in the basement. There wasn't a lot known about Phrygian myth, so it could have been a Satyr, some sort of Minotaur, or something Di had never heard of.

Lavinia finally wound down, and Di returned the stuff from Tamara's lair to the trash bag it had been stored in. At Joe's look of inquiry, she said, "Incinerator in the basement," and he nodded. He even helped her take it and the rest of the burnable trash down there, and they stood together to make sure it all went to ash.

"So. Can I count on you and your spook squad again?" he asked casually, as they watched the flames. "Can't exactly ask Lavinia to go hiking across country in the middle of the night or breaking into spooky old houses in the middle of nowhere. She'd probably break her hip."

Di snorted. "She's tougher than you think. She's more likely to bitch the whole time, but . . . yeah." She thought about it a moment. Even after being confronted with a very dead body last night, her friends had handled themselves well. Earlier, they hadn't been put off by the dybbuk, and this afternoon, no one had said anything about bailing or not wanting to be involved. Finally, she nodded. "You can count me in. I'll have to talk to the others, but—"

It was Joe's turn to snort. "After all these years in my department, kid, I can tell you there's two kinds of people out there. The ones that see the weird shit and just block it out and never want to think about it, and the ones that get addicted to it. Your bunch is addicted. You'll see."

By the time they went back to Di's apartment, Lavinia had her coat on and was saying goodbye. Zaak was promising to take the bus to visit her next weekend. "A pity I cannot convince Diana to do the same," Lavinia said dryly.

"Diana has only just moved here and hasn't figured out the bus schedule yet, old woman," Diana replied, just as dryly. "I'll let Zaak be the trailblazer. Thanks for coming over and giving us the lowdown, Joe."

"My pleasure. I just like to have all the pieces to put together, you know?" He shook hands with everyone, there was the usual jockeying at the door, and then he and Lavinia were gone.

This time it was Emory who put his back to the door. "Okay, we have to know. Are we still in?"

I guess Joe was right. "You're in as long as you want in," she affirmed. "Joe was just asking if he could count on us for next time."

"There's going to be a next time?" Emory exclaimed with glee.

"Idiot." Em punched him in the bicep. "He wouldn't have asked if there wasn't."

Zaak looked as if he had suddenly run out of steam, though not enthusiasm, and yawned hugely. "I think I need to sleep lunch off," he said ruefully, as he set off a chain reaction of more yawns from the rest of them. "Good thing I don't have Monday classes."

Di groaned, as did Marshal. Di added, "No class, but dammit, if I don't get that library book back today, I'm going to get fined."

"I've got a freshman to tutor," Marshal said, making a face. There was more congestion at the door, then they were all gone, and she went to grab her book bag. She had her hand on the knob when there was another knock.

It was Marshal.

"I figured we could go together," he said. "I'm going to introduce you to a friend of mine who's organized a karate club, so you can get hooked up for when you can't carry a gun. And maybe I could find out if you'd rather go to the Carlos Montoya concert or something else with me on Friday."

She stopped dead in her tracks. "Marshal, are you actually asking me on a date?"

He tugged her elbow to get her going again. "Is that so strange?"

"It is for me," she admitted. Then she grinned. "Carlos Montoya sounds great!"

And the possibility of having *something* like a real, normal life?

Priceless.

Drums

This novella takes place a few months after the end of Sacred Ground, *in 1995. Cell phones are not commonplace; they are the size and weight of a brick and all they do is make phone calls. Satellite television is available, but it requires one of those big honking dishes that sit in the front yard—dishes that are at least ten feet in diameter and move from satellite to satellite to get their feeds. They cost a small fortune, and generally you rent them. (And we had one in our yard.) The Internet as we know it is in its infancy; Microsoft released the Windows 95 operating system, which included built-in support for dial-up networking and TCP/IP (Transmission Control Protocol/Internet Protocol), key technologies for connecting to the Internet. When Windows 95 with Internet Explorer debuted, the Internet became much more accessible for many more people. Most people connected by dial-up, and 14k connection speeds were considered blinding. There is no Homeland Security, no Patriot*

Act. And eBay has just started. So has Craigslist. Newsweek printed an article by Clifford Stoll, in which he wrote, "The truth is no online database will replace your daily newspaper, no CD-ROM can take the place of a competent teacher and no computer network will change the way government works." If the world in this story seems vastly different from the world of 2010 . . . it is.

Outside the window, it was an absolutely amazing fall day, the sort of day that made you glad to be living in Oklahoma, where mild fall weather could stretch well into November. Jennifer Talldeer would have loved to have been outside, but she had bills to pay and the paperwork part of being a private investigator had to be done or no one would be paying her. The tapping from the other keyboard ceased, and Jennie looked up to see that her partner (in every possible sense of the word), David Spotted Horse, was frowning at the computer screen.

She resisted the urge to ask what was wrong. It was probably his law school coursework; after getting his PI license he had decided to go back to school and get his degree, then pass the bar. It had seemed like a great idea at the time, and he *was* only taking a couple of courses per semester. But there was often a conflict between what was legal and what was right, and David was often left fuming, knowing that the answers that would get him great grades were not necessarily the moral high ground. When he was angry, he got focused on the cause of his anger, and that wasn't a good thing in a PI; that meant the work suffered.

He was also a pain in the ass when he was angry, a state that made part of Jennie question whether the decision to share business, house, and bed with him had been the right one after all.

There were other lingering issues in their relationship. She knew he wanted to get married—"make it legal"—and when he got into one of his moods, Jennie had niggling little doubts that maybe getting married would make things worse. And then the coldly logical part of her brain would point out that *now* it was easy, if things really went sour, to just say, "Sorry, David, it's been real," cut him a check for his part of the business, and show him the door without legal tangles to sort out or any reason to feel guilty.

Think about it, that chilly voice in her head would continue, *he's gotten a great ride out of you—thanks to you, he has that license, and thanks to you and Grandfather, he's getting to be respected in Medicine circles. If you have to call it quits, he is way ahead of where he was when he walked back into your life.*

Sometimes it all felt positively schizophrenic. She *knew* he loved her. She'd seen how he was with her own eyes—well, her spirit eyes—when she almost died. And most of the time, she knew she loved him. She'd been infatuated before, and this *wasn't* infatuation. But if there was one thing that Jennifer Talldeer was good at, it was second-guessing herself and analyzing everything half to death. It was part of what made her a good PI, but it wasn't the sort of thing you could just shut off.

David looked up, saw her watching him, and shrugged sheepishly. "Is there any way to turn off this talking paper clip? It keeps trying to correct my English. And no, I don't want to send a letter to Broccoli, California."

She blinked. *"Broccoli?"*

"Berkeley." He sighed. "This thing could give your Grandfather lessons in contrary."

She laughed, all her misgivings forgotten, and walked him through turning off the "helper" and adding a word to the dictionary. They'd recently bought a second PC for David, since he was getting his own cases and had gone back to school, and of course the fresh-from-the-box software hadn't been properly beaten into shape yet. "You could still take it out and shoot it," she reminded him, when the thing balked momentarily at doing what he told it to do.

"Don't tempt me," he growled. "Damn thing, can't even scalp it."

The phone rang, interrupting what could have been one of David's funny pseudo-Luddite rants—pseudo, because David wasn't really anti-tech—and a glance at the caller ID made her wave frantically at him to hush.

She picked up. "Talldeer," she said.

"Explain to me how you got those artifacts away from

Jack Collins, and please, please tell me that you didn't do anything illegal," said the weary voice of the chief of police in tiny Luska, Oklahoma. "I have a big old box sitting on my desk, right this minute, that has everything in it you described to me."

She smiled. Jack Collins, scum that he was, had been selling Native American artifacts on a new online auction site called eBay and it had taken the devil's own time to track down the real person behind the anonymous ID. He claimed that he'd inherited the stuff he was selling from his grandfather. She knew, but could not prove, that the items were looted. When she'd gotten his real name and address, she'd gone to the chief and explained the situation, and then they both tried to talk to Collins separately. Most of the artifacts hadn't been all that important, and it wasn't as if he was selling bones, but a couple of pieces had been Medicine objects, and they needed to be in proper hands, not hanging over someone's mantelpiece.

Collins, predictably, had laughed in her face, told her to go to hell, and slammed the door. The chief hadn't had any luck either.

"Nothing illegal," she said demurely. "I only convinced him that a hundred dead Ghost Dancers were coming for him."

The heart and soul of that plan had been David's. David was into serious car audio competitions, which turned out to be the key to everything. He'd discovered, quite by accident, that subsonic tones played through certain speakers could rattle the walls of a house without anyone actually hearing anything.

Now, something like having your walls shake for no cause was guaranteed to make almost anyone convinced they were being haunted. When David suggested that this trick might convince their target that holding on to the artifacts was a bad idea, Jennie had agreed that the idea had a lot of merit.

They needed more than that to deal with a hard case like Collins, though, so David did a little more research. It turned out that Collins had ticked off the guy who did the maintenance on the co-op satellite dish he rented. Normally when someone didn't pay the satellite bill, the maintenance guy would arrange for every channel to—briefly but repeatedly—play a nastygram telling the renter to call the 800 number and settle up with the company.

Being able to "take over" the satellite feed was exactly what they needed. At Jennie's request, and because Collins had pissed him off, Cliff had arranged a very different feed—one that made it look as if the television was possessed. Cliff had friends with video cameras, Hollywood aspirations, and extremely creative minds.

Add to that a half a dozen little dirty tricks out in the yard, and Collins had spent a terrified night locked in his bathroom. And this was the reward. The box of artifacts had been on the chief's desk this morning and all anyone had seen of Collins was the dust from his truck.

"So long as nothing's going to come back across my

desk, Ms. Talldeer, we're good." There was a dirty little chuckle. "So officially, I don't know about anything, and you never left Tulsa County."

"I have witnesses," she replied. "Lots of witnesses. I was at an ICOT meeting." She was too. It had been Cliff and David and their friends who'd been trespassing on Collins's property.

"I'm glad to hear that. That's all I needed to know, Ms. Talldeer. You all have a good day."

She hung up the phone and shook her head at David's expression. "You enjoy that sort of thing way too much," she said.

"Don't pretend you don't," he countered, and sighed. "Now back to the real world—"

The phone rang again, and the caller ID showed an unfamiliar name and number. She picked up on the second ring. "Talldeer and Horse, Private Investigations," she said formally, hoping it was paying work. There was never enough paying work. "How may I help you?"

"You'd be Ms. Talldeer?" said a voice as unfamiliar as the name on the other end of the line. Begay?

"I would. How may I help you?" she replied.

"I—do you watch people? Do surveillance?" The man sounded hesitant.

"That's one of the things we do. Would you prefer to discuss this on the phone or in person?" She was getting a very odd feeling from this conversation. She wasn't sure why. David had stopped even pretending to type.

"In person, please. Can we meet at Goldie's on Thirty-first? In an hour?" All right. He wasn't asking to meet at a bar, or worse, Lady Godiva's Gentleman's Club. That much was in his favor. "I think we can manage that. Should I ask for you by name?"

"You'll know me when you see me, but the name's Nathan Begay. Thank you. I'll see you there."

He hung up. Jennie replaced the handset and looked at David's expectant face.

"Well, I *think* we have a client. . . ."

Nathan had been correct. She did know him the moment she saw him. There were just not that many people in Tulsa whose faces practically shouted, "Navaho." In fact, she would venture to say that there weren't any other Dineh within the city limits. The desert-weathered skin was part of it, but to the discerning eye, there was a Dineh *look*; she often thought that the Dineh were not unlike the land they lived in; their faces looked like wind-carved sandstone.

He was obviously looking for her as well, and waved as soon as she got through the door. If he was annoyed or disappointed that she'd brought David along, he didn't show it. They slid into the booth on the opposite side from him. There was nothing in front of him but coffee; she took the cue and ordered the same. Since it wasn't more than three, and the eatery was practically empty, and since the little teenage waitress clearly would *much* rather have been discussing her latest boyfriend with the girl in the other section, they didn't even get dirty looks for so minimal an order.

Begay looked woeful. "This is gonna sound bad," he said. "But . . . I want you to follow my gal. My ex-gal. That's why I didn't want to talk over the phone."

Jennie blinked slowly. "You're correct. It does sound bad. You do know this state has stalker laws, right?"

He nodded. "And I could tell you that this isn't what it looks like, and you wouldn't believe me."

"We wouldn't disbelieve you, either," David pointed out, his tone carefully neutral. "It's not our job to believe you. It's our job to do what you hire us to do—so long as we don't break the law doing it and so long as you don't use what we give you to break the law afterwards. Has she got a restraining order against you? We'll find out if she does, you know."

"No. No, nothing like that." Begay turned his cup around and around in his hands, staring down at the black surface of the coffee. "I guess I should start at the beginning," he said, his voice heavy with reluctance. "It started in Albuquerque. Caro—Caroline—is a jeweler, She wanted to learn traditional Dineh silversmithing and my brother gives classes. That's how we met—at my brother's. We hit it off right away, and then we did more than just hit it off. I'm a welder so I can work anywhere, and when she moved back home to Miami, I came along too. Things were good. I mean, at least I thought things were good. I'm a rez boy, pretty solid in the Good Red Road. She's Chickasaw, but she hadn't paid—I mean she'd never been into—" His heavily tanned skin flushed a dark red.

"Pretty assimilated," David said shrewdly, and Begay nodded.

"She kinda liked that I had a foot in both worlds," he continued. "She saw how I didn't have to be assimilated to do all right in the world. Went to a couple of gatherings with me, couple ceremonies while we were still in Albuquerque. After a while, she started looking things up and talking to people, and it wasn't just for her jewelry. One thing led to another and she decided she was gonna get back into her heritage. I thought that was a good idea at the time."

"At the time?" Jennie prompted, telling herself not to frown.

"Well, the first thing she got into was the dancing, and I thought that was a great idea, but then after a while she wouldn't—I mean, she didn't want me around when she was practicing, and then she was practicing more and more, and then"—he shook his head as if it weighed a hundred pounds—"then she told me not to come around any more at all. And I don't know why. And now she doesn't let anyone come visit, not even her old friends. I know, 'cause they asked me about her. I don't know what's going on—" He looked up at Jennie, and although his face was almost expressionless, there was pleading in his eyes. "I just want someone to go out and watch her. Make sure she's all right. That's all. If it's something I did, or didn't do . . . I'd like to know, but mostly I want to be sure she's not doing anything . . . dangerous." Then he stopped, and took a deep breath. "No. I'm lying. I think something's wrong. I think there's something wrong with her. Whatever it is, I want to fix it if I can, or help her if I can't fix it. I want to hire you to find out what it is, so I can do that. Does that make sense?"

David was nudging Jennie's foot under the table in a way that told her he wanted them to take this case. Of course, stalkers would use the same kind of excuses and rhetoric: "I only want what's best for her, I want her to let me fix her life." Her gut was telling her that this guy was on the level, but her gut could be wrong.

"I know that right now I sound like I'm a crazy person," Begay said heavily. "I know I sound like a control freak. But there's something wrong. I can feel it. Why would she be chasing everybody off if there wasn't?"

Jennie kept from drumming her fingers on the table with an effort of will. Talk about being torn—her instincts said one thing, her head said another, and if David didn't stop nudging her under the table, she was going to dump her coffee in his lap.

Her instincts won out over her logic. "Provisionally, we'll take this," she said, stepping hard on David's foot, which didn't do much since he was wearing boots. "If you've been on the level with us, we'll find out quickly enough." She gave Begay just enough of a glare to let him know she was serious, and that just because he was Dineh, they weren't going to let him coast. "For starters, you can give us a list of her friends, so we can ask them ourselves."

If he really was a stalker or a control freak, she'd find out really fast. He'd either refuse to give her the names or he'd give her phony ones.

He was so grateful he didn't even argue over their fee, just handed over the retainer in cash, then wrote down a list of names and numbers from a little well-worn address book he kept in his shirt pocket. At the bottom, he added Caroline's address. It was in Cherokee County near the Spring River, between Vinita and Miami, but back of beyond nowhere, on a little section line road that probably wasn't even paved. "She has about sixty acres out there, all to herself," Begay said, looking wistful. "I liked it. Peaceful. Green. Nice change from New Mexico."

He must have noticed something in her expression and shrugged. "Before you ask, it isn't worth much. Too much rock to farm or graze if you were planning on running any size of herd. The only timber that'll grow there is blackjack oak and scrub. She told me a neighbor once got a nibble from a wildcatter—until they actually came out and took a look. Got right back in the truck. Told him they'd spend more on broken drill bits than they'd ever get out of the ground."

Well, that solved *that* question—if he was telling the truth, and there was no reason to think he wasn't at this point. He wasn't after her land for the mineral rights.

Begay left in a battered old pickup truck with new Oklahoma plates. Jennie and David turned their attention to the lists. Most of Caroline Gray's friends—or at least the ones Begay had listed—were women.

They exchanged a look. "He wouldn't have given us women's names if he wasn't playing straight with us," David pointed out.

"If they're not friends or relatives of his that will take his side." She had to counter that but—David was right. Especially if *she* was the one who went to talk to them. "I have to be sure."

David shrugged, then grinned. She could never resist that grin. He looked altogether too much like the actor Lou Diamond Phillips when he grinned like that. "I'm better at sneaking around than you are," he pointed out.

"Under some circumstances, that wouldn't be a recommendation." She bared her teeth at him. "All right, take my BRAT, you'll be able to hide it off the road easier."

They had anticipated needing to split up, so they had brought both cars. David's five-year-old VW Fox wasn't exactly suited for off-roading, but though Jennie's Subaru BRAT was five years older than David's car, she'd kept it impeccably maintained and it would be perfect for David's mission. They swapped keys. "We really need to get cell phones," David said, as they walked out to the parking lot.

She snorted. "When they aren't the size and weight of a brick, maybe." They both had business-band radio, the kind that plumbers and other repairmen used. It made her sigh, sometimes. Things had been a lot simpler when she'd been solo. "I can just see you tramping through the woods with a brick on your belt."

"I could always use it for self-defense." He gave her a two-fingered salute and slid into the driver's seat of her BRAT. Before she'd gotten into and started his Fox, David had already peeled out of the parking lot.

She had to smile a little at that. He'd looked like a kid given parental permission to play hooky. He had probably been going stir-crazy, confined to the office like that.

Well, he was about to find out how boring a stakeout could be. Within a couple of hours he would be envying her as he tried to find a place to watch this gal that wasn't infested with chiggers.

It might have been a trailer, but it was a good-looking one, comfortable, and clean enough to serve as a sales brochure. The tiny living room had two nice plush beige love seats with a drum with a Plexiglas topper serving as a coffee table between them, and gorgeous Pendleton blankets thrown over their backs. "I'm baffled," said Terry Redwing, spreading her hands. "Honestly. Caroline's always been sort of a hermit, but not like this. I leave messages on her answering machine, I never get callbacks. I write, and I get no answers. And when I drive all the way the hell out there . . . she seems spaced-out. I don't know what to think. I mean, when she's working on a design you can tell her mind is on that and not on your conversation, but . . . it's like she's in a fog now."

Terry was the third of Caroline's friends to say virtually the same thing. Jennie decided to probe a little. "Not like . . . drugs?"

But Terry shook her head. "No, and not like booze either, and believe me, I'd know. Half my family is alcoholic." She grimaced. Jennie nodded sympathetically. Alcohol was a big problem for Native Americans, on or off the rez. "No," Terry continued, "it's an exhausted-type fog, like she's not getting any sleep. And . . . if I didn't know better, I'd say she was afraid of something. But what? It can't be poor Nathan; he hasn't been out there in a month."

"You're sure of that?" Jennie probed.

"As sure as I can be without tailing him," Terry replied decisively. "There's a lot of powwow people out that way and they all know his truck. If he'd been by there, I'd have heard drum talk. There's a lot of us worried about her. Something's not right."

Jennie nodded. Begay either had all these women buffaloed, or he'd been on the level. Just as her instincts had said.

So, all things considered, maybe it was a good idea to start looking at other possibilities. "How much do you know about Caroline's family?" she asked.

By the end of the day, she had learned a lot about Caroline and her family. There was no record of mental illness in the Gray family so far as the records at Vinita or the Indian hospital at Claremore were concerned. Of course, if Caroline had gotten hold of some bad peyote at a peyote rite, all bets were off—but no one, not even the people who had reason to know and would talk to her off the record, had seen Caroline at any of the rituals. A few folded bills handed over at the liquor stores near where she lived produced nothing useful. The rest of the Grays seemed to be down near Muskogee, which was a bit of a drive just to go harass a relative on a daily basis. But none of her friends had seen or heard anything to lead them to think that any member of Caroline's family was stalking or abusing her.

So. Begay was out. Peyote was probably out; in fact, most drugs were probably out. No history of mental illness— though that didn't mean she wasn't having a schizophrenic, psychotic, or manic-depressive break, just that it was less likely. Family abuse was out. What did that leave?

Not much. Or at least, not much that Begay could fix. Still . . . maybe Caroline had a secret, one she didn't want Begay to learn. Some teenage indiscretion? A pregnancy? Maybe a child?

That seemed the likeliest. As Jennie drove down to the QuikTrip where she and David would meet and swap cars, she debated whether or not she should just tell Begay they hadn't found anything. What gave them the right to invade Caroline Gray's privacy if she had a child or some other secret she needed to keep? Nothing, that's what.

But her instincts kept nagging at her. Surely, if Caroline was hiding something like that, one of the people she'd spoken to today would have given her a hint of it. But they were all as baffled as Nathan Begay.

She pulled up to the pump and refueled the Fox, then pulled aside. She got a cold drink from the station's convenience store and waited for David with the college public radio station on, but not really listening to it. She was so deep in thought that she jumped when David tapped her shoulder.

"The most exciting thing that happened all day was when the gal came out to fill the bird feeders," David said, looking overheated but oddly energized. "I'd say come home when her lights go out."

Jennie sighed. "I probably will. All I got was a big fat nothing." She detailed the results of her interviews, while David sucked down the drink she handed him as if he'd been sitting on the surface of the sun all afternoon.

When she finished, he tossed the cup into the nearest trash bucket and passed her the keys to the BRAT. "I'm debating something, 'cause I don't want to skew your impartiality," he said as she got out of his car.

She fastened him with a look. "Do not hold out on your partner," she said flatly.

He grimaced. "Okay. I'm not Grandfather, and I'm not you. But something down there feels like bad Medicine."

She blinked. "Surely not—"

He shook his head. "Whatever it is, it has to be new. There's no sign, and no 'feel' of burial sites, a village, or anything out there. And she's lived out there for years without any problems—"

"Until now." She sucked on her lower lip. "All right. I'll keep that in mind. You get some food. Make sure the Little Old Man doesn't talk you into making nachos and calling it dinner. I'll be back when I'm back."

He nodded. He knew to keep the base station tuned to their frequency, *especially* when she was on a nighttime stakeout. Of course, if she *did* run into trouble, he couldn't do much more than call the county sheriff, but at least that was something. . . .

She drove off in the ruddy light of the setting sun, and as she made her way down unpaved section line roads, with weeds growing up on either side of her, something else occurred to her.

Caroline was all alone out here. She'd be easy prey for someone who wanted an isolated place for a pot farm. Someone who would threaten to hurt people she loved if she narked on them. Organized crime, for instance. Around those in the know, that country song "Okie from Muskogee" was a laugh, especially the line "We don't smoke marijuana in Muskogee" because if pot wasn't the number one cash crop in this part of the country, it was only because nobody was trying all that hard to count the money coming from it.

Even more likely was someone putting a meth lab on her property.

If either of those were true, it would account for the fear, the sleeplessness, and the isolation. She wouldn't dare let anyone come around, for fear they would discover what was going on. Or worse, encounter the people who were responsible.

Well, she couldn't do too much to check that out tonight. And she wasn't going to do that alone at any event. That would be a two-man job, maybe three or more. She could call in some favors, do a very discreet search, and if she found something, talk to Caroline—there were ways to make contact without getting Caroline in trouble. . . .

Hell, if it's a meth lab, I can just blow the sucker up, she thought grimly. *One Molotov with a long-burning fuse and that would be it.* That would bring the fire department and the sheriff and there would be nothing they could lay at Caroline's door. *And if it's weed, well, I'll tamper with the water supply so it all dies.* Out on rock like this, the weed would all be in pots, each pot watered by a drip system, and all of it under the trees so it couldn't be spotted from the air. Easy enough to put something in the reservoir that would kill the roots. Lose the crop often enough and they'd give up, try somewhere else.

David had drawn her a little map that showed a good place to stash the BRAT under cover of some brush, and another spot that was good for surveillance. She arrived just at dusk, marking her way in carefully so she didn't make a hash of getting back out again. David might be better at this, but only marginally.

The lights came on in Caroline's trailer. Jennie watched her—or at least her silhouette—moving around inside for a while before even that ceased. Was Caroline reading? Watching TV? There was no sign of the flickering bluish glow of a television. Maybe she was working on her jewelry? But no, Begay had said her jewelry shop was in the middle of the trailer, in what would have been a second bedroom, and not at the end that held the living room and kitchen. Of course, from here Jennie couldn't see the kitchen door, or the path out into the woods, but why would Caroline go trampling around in the woods in the middle of the—

Then Jennie heard it. Coming from the woods.

Drums.

The sound put the hair up on the back of her neck and put a knot in her throat. It should have been innocuous, but it wasn't. David was right.

All thoughts of meth labs and weed plantations went right out of her head as she inched toward the trailer, moving as furtively as any of her Osage ancestors. A quick glance through the windows proved that there was no one in the trailer now, not in the kitchen or the living room, and the insistent pounding of the drums continued, very clearly coming from the woods behind the trailer.

Every drumbeat told her that something was wrong here, very wrong. Not the music itself . . . it was relatively simple, traditional drumming and singing. She didn't recognize the song, but there was plenty of Native American music she didn't recognize, even things in her own Osage tradition. No, it was what came *with* the music—the sense that something had been called, something that didn't belong.

It took an agonizingly long time to work her way through the woods; she didn't dare risk slipping and breaking something, and doubly did not dare risk being detected by whatever was out there.

But finally she saw light through the scraggly blackjack oaks—the light of a fire, a proper campfire from the conical shape of it. She inched forward, moving from bit of cover to bit of cover, until at last she could see the figures dancing there.

One was Caroline, in a "trade cloth" dress, splendid with ruffled hem, ruffled collar, rows of colored ribbons, and topped with a ruffled white apron of the sort that had been traditional since the 1800s. Outsiders might pardonably have mistaken it for an attempt to replicate a pioneering woman's dress. Caroline was dancing in the modest and stately style that went with that dress—nothing like the shawl-dancing that Jennie herself did. The half-terrified, half-entranced look on the woman's face was enough to make Jennie's heart plummet.

There was no wonder at the cause for that look. Dancing with her was a strange man, at least six feet tall, dressed in ancient Osage costume. Deerskin leggings, deerskin breechcloth, a trailer of otter fur behind stretching from his neck to the ground, two strings of shell beads crossing in front and in back, deerskin shirt, buckskin moccasins, finger-woven sash, leather belt with quill embroidery, knee rattles of deer hooves, horn armbands, and a blanket. On his head he wore a deer tail head roach and an elk horn roach spreader; there was a feather in his roach and another attached to his scalp—oh, but they were *not* eagle feathers. They were *owl* feathers! In his hands were his coup stick and his fan—again, decorated not with eagle but with owl feathers. . . .

And he had no paint.

He had no paint.

And that told Jennie that although he seemed as real and solid as Caroline . . . this was no living man. This was a *mi-ah-lushka*.

A ghost. And not just any ghost, but the ghost of an Osage who had died without honor and was put to rest without paint. One of the Little People. Jennie had had dealings with them before. . . .

He danced with Caroline and around her, keeping her as mesmerized as a cobra with a bird. And Jennie could feel, could *see*, the life force draining from her to him. She wanted to jump up and scream, to run in there and *do something*, and she knew she didn't dare. She might be signing her own death warrant if she did.

She would certainly be signing Caroline's.

The *mi-ah-lushka*'s expression was both greedy and possessive. How he had gotten this hold over his prey, Jennie had no idea, but he wasn't going to let go easily. The Little People never did.

And she couldn't go charging in there and claim Caroline was under her protection either, because that was not true. Any lie she told would be ammunition to be used against her. Bad idea.

But although this certainly answered one question— why Caroline had dumped Nathan Begay—it raised far more than it answered. What was a *mi-ah-lushka* doing here? There weren't any traditional Osage sites on Caroline's sixty acres, and certainly not any traditional Osage burial sites. And why Caroline? She was Chickasaw, not Osage. He should have no hold over her and no connection to her.

It was obvious what he was getting from her—life force—but why? The Little People generally had plenty of power of their own, so why would he need to siphon it from her?

So despite wanting to rush in there and do something fast and violent to free Caroline from bondage, instead Jennie backed away, slowly, taking care to mask herself both with stealth and with Medicine. If she had any hope of dealing with this situation, it was imperative that the *mi-ah-lushka* not know she was there, not be aware that she was a Medicine Woman . . . and above all, not be aware that she was the kind of Medicine Woman he had never known in his corporeal life.

For Jennie Talldeer was Kestrel-Hunts-Alone, schooled in both Woman's Medicine and Warrior's Medicine, in both the Tzi-Sho and the Hunka Medicines. In short, in every sort of Medicine, of every clan and *gente* that the Osage boasted. And in Medicine outside the Osage Ways. She was a pipe-bearer in the Way of the Lakota. She was entitled to wear the Eagle Tail Feather as well as the Eagle Under-tail Feather, yes, and carry the Eagle fan too.

But the *mi-ah-lushka* were cunning. If she confronted him prematurely and was defeated, he would learn all this, and swiftly contrive counters for her.

So she fought her wishes and followed wisdom, inched her way off of Caroline Gray's land, and down to her car, and headed home.

Grandfather pursed his lips. Jennie and David waited patiently for him to decide to speak. He would say what he was going to say in his own good time and there was no point in trying to hurry him. Finally, instead of speaking, he got up and went to the filing cabinet Jennie'd gotten from a law firm—one that had a handsome wooden case around it, so it didn't look out of place in the living room. It held nothing she considered important, just bits of this and that she and her family had picked up over the years and thought too interesting to throw away. She'd often joked there was fodder for a hundred books in that cabinet alone.

Grandfather went straight to the bottom drawer, where old tourist brochures were filed. "Little Old Man," Jennie began, "what on earth—"

"It is something I remember, from the fifties," he replied, his voice a little muffled as he peered into the drawer. "Route 66 days, when everyone along here was trying to make a tourist trap. Aha!" He pulled out a yellowing brochure and handed it to her.

The cover read, THE FAMOUS INDIAN LOVER'S LEAP AT PARK HILL, and showed a lovely, high rock bluff over the Spring River. The brochure described the "scenic view" and the facilities, which seemed to be confined to picnic tables and a souvenir stand, and listed motels and diners in the area. Only at the bottom of the brochure was there anything about the name of the place.

The son of an Osage chief fell in love with a Chickasaw maiden, and meant to run off with her. He captured her, but she would have nothing to do with him, for she loved a warrior of her own tribe. Knowing her kidnapper would never let her go, and in despair for her true love, she tore herself loose, leaving her buckskin gown in his hands, and flung herself to her death on the rocks below.

Jennie blinked. She turned the brochure over and checked the map. Sure enough, it wasn't that far from Caroline's property.

Some say you can hear him after sundown, drumming to bring her back. And on moonlit nights you can see her standing at the top of the bluff, poised to jump.

Wordlessly, Jennie passed the brochure to David. Grandfather shrugged as she met his eyes. "I always thought it was some damn fool thing they made up," he admitted. "I'd never heard any story like that in the lore, and you can bet they thought the idea that you might see a bare-naked gal standing on the top of a cliff would bring people to stay the night."

"Hey," said David, passing the brochure back, "I'd stick around to see it."

He and Grandfather exchanged knowing looks. Jennie made a face at both of them. "Did you ever go out there to find out?" she asked.

Grandfather shook his head. "No. You know how it is, the boys weren't interested in some sissy lover's leap, they wanted to see the snake farm. Never got around to it." He paused. "It's certainly beginning to look like for once the

Heavy Eyebrows got the legend right and it was *us* that forgot it."

"Or maybe someone was psychic and dreamed what happened." She watched him carefully file the brochure away and return to his seat. "Well, now we know where the *mi-ah-lushka* came from, and why Caroline. When she set up her little practice space down in the woods and started playing the drum CDs to dance to, it must have sounded like an invitation with his name on it."

"I think you ought to check this out further," Grandfather cautioned. "This story might not be recorded in Osage history, but it might be in Chickasaw. Try them. I'd like to know why he became a *mi-ah-lushka;* the reason could be important to getting rid of him."

Jennie nodded. "Sounds like tomorrow is a good day to visit the Five Civilized Tribes Museum."

The trip turned into a family outing, to David's chagrin and Jennie's amusement. Grandfather was probably going to drag David around the museum and take every opportunity to point out Osage superiority to the Cherokee. The Little Old Man got a bigger kick out of that than a cold war Russki proclaiming how Russia had invented everything.

She, meanwhile, was going to the research room. Her history of restoring important artifacts to the appropriate hands gave her *carte blanche* in practically every Native

museum and tribal archive in North America. She probably could have asked to take rare books or manuscripts
home and the people in charge would let her. And if she
wanted to camp out for the night in the rare book room,
they'd probably offer her a cot and a sleeping bag and hand
her the keys. Not that she ever abused the privilege, but at
times like these it was damned useful.

Hours later, she thought she had reviewed everything
pertinent that was available in this museum. And she had
an answer to why a chief's son would end up a *mi-ah-
lushka*.

According to the fragments she had put together, after
the girl had leapt to her death, the Chickasaw had pursued
the Osage man. Rather than standing and fighting, he
had fled, and been shot in the back and killed.

That was one strike against him. Cowardice.

Then, in revenge, the Chickasaw had stripped his body
and thrown him in the same river where the girl had died.
According to the records, his body had never been found.

That would be why there was nothing in the Osage lore.
Being stripped and thrown in the river meant that the
man had never been properly given burial rites or face
paint, and that, combined with being shot in the back and
cowardice, pretty much condemned him to *mi-ah-lushka*
status after death.

The Chickasaw version of the legend completely dis-
missed the man after the "shot in the back and thrown in
the river" part, and gave the much more important (to

them) "and the ghost of the maiden is seen on the top of the bluff to this day . . ." part in much greater detail.

Jennie took her notes and thanked the archivist who had helped her, then went in search of David and the Little Old Man.

They were waiting outside; David looked more amused than annoyed, and as usual, Grandfather looked inscrutable. "So," he said, as Jennie emerged into the late-afternoon sun, "it looks like you found what you needed."

"I'll tell you about it as we go. I left a message on Begay's answering machine to come by the house; we'll grab Chinese on the way home. Then we'll see if he fires us for playing Ghostbusters."

"Good!" Grandfather lit up. "I want pot stickers, and mei fun. And Mongolian beef."

"I think you were a Mongol in some previous life," she said, her mind already working on how to get Caroline out of the clutches of the ghost.

"I know he was," muttered David.

Begay listened quietly and without interruption while Jennie worked her way through everything she and David had done. When she got to the part about seeing the Osage dancer with Caroline, even though she hadn't yet revealed what the dancer was, he sucked in a startled breath, his eyes widening, but remained silent.

"Now . . . I don't know how much you know about us . . . besides that David and I are PIs," she began cautiously, and waited.

"You're Medicine People," Begay said, as if he were saying, "It's dark out." "All three of you. Your honored Grandfather is the strongest, as he would be, but all three of you have strong Medicine. Anyone with eyes can see that. And *you* saw the dancer with Caroline. So—that dancer. He's not—"

"He's a ghost. An old, bad one," Grandfather put in.

To Jennie's surprise, Begay put his face down in his hands for a moment. When he looked back up, there was a welter of emotion in his eyes. Relief was prominent. His next words told her why.

"I saw him," Begay said, his voice sounding strained. "I snuck out to her place once, and followed the drumming and saw him. I knew what he was—or I thought I did. And I thought I was going nuts. I've never seen a ghost before— I've never seen anything like that. I—"

He broke off, shaking his head. Jennie sympathized with the poor man. He had seen what had stolen his woman from him, he couldn't fight it, and he wasn't even sure it was real. And in a moment it would hit him that no, he wasn't going crazy and yes, it was a ghost—but he *still* couldn't fight it and it *still* had his woman.

"You wouldn't normally, unless you were skilled in Medicine," she said. "But he's sucking her life away from her, little by little. That makes him stronger. The stronger he is, the easier it is to see him."

Begay sat straight up. "We have to stop that, stop him," he said, his voice hard and flat.

All three of them nodded. "That's exactly what we're going to do," Jennie promised.

"As usual, you're scaring the hell out of me," David said as the two of them drove out to Caroline's place. The BRAT rattled over the uneven road; the last light of the sunset faded behind them as they headed east. The air smelled of dust and honeysuckle. "I mean, I know you can handle this. This is what you do. But the last time I looked one of the Little People in the face, I was hoping it actually *would* be the last time. And they were more or less on your side then. They won't be now."

She nodded, keeping her eyes on the road. She was behind the wheel, and out here, you had to watch for many things more exciting than the occasional bunny or possum darting in front of you. Deer, goats, wandering cattle, and the occasional escaped llama had interrupted her journeys before this, sometimes abruptly. "You have to remember, the Little People are never really on anyone's side but their own. You'd think Osage blood would get a pass from them, but they're so full of hate most of the time that your only chance to have them as allies is if they hate something else more."

She could see him nodding out of the corner of her eye as she switched on the headlights. He didn't ask what her plan was, which made her grateful, since she didn't actually have one, other than to try to catch the *mi-ah-lushka* by surprise and bluff him.

But it was too late for second thoughts. The sun was already down, they were within a minute of Caroline's place, and the only choice other than to let this thing *have* the woman was to try to face it down. Allowing the *mi-ah-lushka* to have his way was unacceptable for any number of reasons. Primarily that it would be flat-out wrong, but coming a close second was that increasing his personal power that way would make him more of a hazard in the real world than he already was. Like a serial killer, he wouldn't stop at just one victim.

Begay's truck was in the driveway when they got there, exactly as Jennie had planned. Caroline hadn't kicked him out, which was good. It meant that the spirit didn't have complete control over her yet. Jennie and David pulled the BRAT in beside it, bailed out, and sprinted up a set of nicely made wooden stairs on to a tiny deck at the front door. Through the door they could hear arguing—trailers weren't known for soundproofing—but it didn't sound too bad . . . Caroline was tearful and Begay was pleading. David knocked on the door and the voices within fell silent.

Begay opened the door and nodded, indicating with a sideways motion of his head that they should come in. They edged past him into the narrow living room.

"I only got here a minute ago," Begay said, closing the door. "I haven't had time to say much except I didn't want her to go out dancing, like you said."

"Like *they* said? Nathan Begay, who *are* these people? And what are they doing here?" Caroline stood in the middle of the living room, arms crossed defensively, looking bewildered. And exhausted, and thinner than she should be. Things were clearly getting way out of hand.

"You're Caroline Gray," Jennie stated. "I'm Jennifer Talldeer and this is David Spotted Horse. Mr. Begay asked for our help. We're private investigators, but we're also Medicine People, and Ms. Gray, you are neck-deep in a Medicine problem that is only going to get worse. You think you're hurting now—but believe me, this is nothing compared to what that spirit thing out on your back forty is planning for you."

Caroline blinked at them as if she couldn't quite believe what she was hearing. "I think I had better sit down," she said carefully.

"Caro, I think we had all better sit down," Begay replied. "You really need to listen to these people."

David and Jennie explained how Nathan Begay had contacted them and what they'd done since. When Jennie got to the part about watching Caroline dance and seeing the ghost, the young woman gasped.

Since she didn't interrupt, Jennie carried on, outlining what the spirit was and what her research had uncovered.

While she talked, one emotion after another raced across Caroline's face. Relief, fear, more relief, a flash of anger, and finally, acceptance.

"You saw him. You actually saw him." There was a touch of pleading in there, not unlike Begay's own reaction.

"More than that, Ms. Gray, it didn't take someone able to see the spirits to see him." David came in like the good tag-team player he was. "That means he's getting stronger, and the way he's getting stronger is by feeding on you. That's bad all the way around, and it's not going to stop unless we stop it right now."

"We'd like it if you would stay in the trailer tonight and let me handle this thing," Jennie said. "I don't entirely know what it ultimately wants from you, but the *mi-ah-lushka* are rarely friendly. In life, this man had no compunction about simply taking what he wanted. That won't have changed now that he's a spirit."

Again that flash of anger. Good. "What are you going to do?" Caroline asked. "I won't stand for it if it's going to put Nate in danger."

"Force it to leave you alone, I hope," said Jennie. "Right now, his thinking is still stuck in his own time, and so far, he's only come when the drumming calls him. I doubt he knows about Nate, and he may not understand that we are a lot more mobile in the twentieth century than he was in his; I'd like to keep it that way." She stood up. "So if you'll let me take your boom box out there, I'll see about putting an end to this in a way that if he's angry at anyone, it will be at me."

Caroline and Begay exchanged a look; Begay's was anxious, and so was Caroline's, but Caroline finally nodded. "It's right by the door," she said, pointing with her chin.

Now it was David's turn to exchange a look with Jennie. "You're sure you want to do this alone?" David asked.

She nodded. "I'd rather he didn't know about anyone but me and Caroline. If this doesn't work, then nobody but me is going to be in line for his malice. That means you'll be my ace in the hole for the second try. Let's just keep this simple, one-on-one for now."

Jennie could tell David didn't like it, but he didn't argue with her. She picked up the boom box on her way out the door, pulling a red flashlight out of her pocket to keep from ruining her night vision while still avoiding the worst stumbles on the path. It wasn't too bad actually, there was so much rock here that the path was almost a series of natural rock terraces, relatively flat and easy to walk on, the sort of thing that rich people paid small fortunes to re-create on their property. Off in the distance, she heard a barred owl whooping, but near at hand things were unnaturally silent. The wildlife knew, then; they were giving this spot a wide berth at night.

When she got to the clearing that was Caroline's "practice space," she saw that it was another big expanse of flat rock, perfect for dancing on if you were doing the

traditional women's dances. It would be hell on your feet
if you were going to do fancy dances, like the shawl-dance
Jennie favored; it would be like dancing on concrete. Caroline had laid a fire in the middle, ready to light. Jennie
put the boom box down on the edge of the clearing and got
out her lighter. She had the fire kindled and going quickly;
Caroline certainly knew how to build a good fire. When
the wood was burning briskly, Jennie went back to the
boom box, bent, and pushed the Play button.

The sound of drums filled the small clearing. She
shoved her hands in her pockets, waiting. There was a bad
feeling in the air, like a thunderstorm about to break, a
feeling she knew very well. It always felt like that to her
when she was about to go head-to-head with bad Medicine.
She flexed her fingers a little, keeping her eyes fixed on the
place where she had seen the *mi-ah-lushka* the last time.

There was a sudden spike in the "bad feeling" and
a sharp sense of fear and dread came over her—that was a
warning, the result of her protections. Her senses had been
honed by years of dealing with these things. Caroline likely
wouldn't have felt a thing, or if she had, she might have
mistaken it for a brief fit of nerves.

Just as if Jennie was being lured, that warning thrill
was quickly submerged in an incredibly seductive urge
to give in, let go—just relax—and let whatever was going to
happen, happen.

She fought it off without trouble but she could see how
easy it would have been to be ensnared by it. If Caroline had

been deeply immersed in her practice steps, she probably wouldn't have noticed anything. The power would have crept over her, ambushing her, making her more susceptible to the *mi-ah-lushka* when he finally did appear.

As he was doing now. Gradually, like the Cheshire Cat fading into view smile first, the spirit materialized at the edge of the clearing, in the half-light of the fire. At first, it was just a shape formed out of smoke gathering in a gap between two trees. Then the colors and shapes of his costume swam into focus, details emerging as she watched; shirt, leggings, regalia, then his backwards-incorrect feathers on either side of his deerskin roach, and last of all, his face. The same eagerness and greed she had seen the last time she had watched him were quickly replaced by surprise, then anger.

She held up a hand, frowning at him, before he could lash out at her. She needed to get him off balance and keep him surprised and off balance. He would feel her protections; that might be enough. At this point, he wouldn't have planned on a confrontation with a Medicine Person. "Come no further, paintless one. You are not welcome here any longer."

He snorted derisively; she could feel him pressing at her protections. His eyes narrowed with annoyance and speculation. "And who are you, woman, to tell me where I am and am not welcome?"

"I am Kestrel-Hunts-Alone, student of Mooncrow, student of Fox Laughing, student of Sees-Far-Mountains"—

she recited her Medicine lineage as she had memorized it long ago, ending with—"who studied under the hand of Watches-Over-The-Land."

That got his attention; as she had anticipated, he knew of Watches-Over-The-Land, so she had pegged his time period about right. He looked a little more wary, but he still had plenty of bluster. "So you are a Medicine Woman. Well done, but what has that to do with where I am and am not welcome? These are not the lands of the People of the Middle Waters, and what I want is not one of our blood." The implication was that any proper-thinking Osage would agree with him that Caroline was fair game.

"Did you not learn your folly with the first Chickasaw maiden?" Jennie asked severely. "The one who threw herself to her death rather than abide in your hands? Take wisdom from that lesson. You are not wanted here. I, a Medicine Woman of your people, tell you this. We are not at war with the Chickasaw any longer. There is no woman here for you. Go, and do not return."

He laughed scornfully. "Firstly, what if she gives herself to me freely? And secondly, you are but a woman and a living thing, though you have Medicine power. What can you do to me that is worse than what I am now? I will do what I will do, and you cannot stop me."

"I think that you are wrong," she replied. She pulled the first of her packets from her pocket, then broke open the soft paper napkin and, with a sweeping motion, cast a handful of corn pollen on the air between them.

He stepped forward boldly. Or rather, tried to, pushing against the invisible barrier she had created. She waited to see what he would do.

"This is small and weak," he mocked, but there was, for the first time, some hesitation in his tone. He made a trumpet of his hands and blew through it, following the curve of the pollen she had thrown. She felt a pressure inside her head and then a kind of *pop*, and he strode across where the barrier had been. Then he stopped and stood with his arms crossed over his chest, saying without words, "If that is all you can do . . ."

She debated going offensive this early in the confrontation. It might do more harm than good. Still, if she could hurt him now, it would give him second thoughts.

With a mocking little head nod, she took on the look of her spirit form. Once her spirit form had merely looked like a bird; now it was that of a woman who was half-warrior, half-bird—exactly the sort of shape that Kestrel himself might take, to show that he was something other than a human spirit. For Jennie to be able to assume this half-and-half shape meant that she had a great deal of power in the spirit world.

But she wasn't ready to step out of her body and into that world, not just yet. For her to take this shape meant she *could*, and that was all that the ghost needed to know for now. His eyes flashed with anger and arrogance.

Weapons appeared in his hands.

She gestured. The bowstring snapped, the arrows crumbled. "You will not harm me, spirit," she declared.

"So you say," he replied, but now there was uncertainty in his voice. "So you say."

"And I say, and say again, go from this place. Leave this woman alone. You are not wanted here." She made her tone as firm as she could.

He tried to push toward her. She held out her hand, palm facing him, this time putting up a barrier by will alone. She felt him shoving against it, but she was able to hold against his force; she betrayed by not so much as a frown how hard it was. If he kept it up much longer, she would start sweating from the exertion, and that wasn't something she could hide. He was a *very* powerful spirit even now. She didn't like to think what he would be like with more stolen power.

His frown grew with every passing moment. Finally, he stopped pushing against her barrier, cursed, and stamped his foot like a petulant child. "You think you have won," he growled, turning his eyes away in a refusal to look at her.

"I know I have," she countered, raising her chin and dropping her spirit form. "You are not welcome here. The Chickasaw woman is not for your taking. Nor is any other. Go. And do not return."

There was one moment when she wasn't sure what he was going to do. He appeared to gather himself and grew a little taller, his expression full of fury, his hands crackling with energy. He stood like that for a moment and she braced herself for an attack—

With a snarl, he turned about—and vanished.

The feeling of storm-about-to-break left the clearing. She waited a long moment to see if he would reappear and strike at her when she relaxed her guard.

Nothing.

Still she waited. The *mi-ah-lushka* were tricksters, and not in the amusing sense.

Still nothing.

Gradually, the normal sounds of the night crept into the clearing. Faint rustlings in the trees and grass, crickets. She jumped when a cicada went off nearly in her ear.

Jennie bent and turned off the boom box, then hefted it and headed back up to Caroline's trailer.

Caroline, Nathan, and David all looked up as she opened the door, but no one said anything. They just stared at her as if they weren't quite certain she was real. Setting down the boom box, Jennie broke the silence.

"He's gone," she said flatly. "I wouldn't practice down there again if I were you, but he's gone."

Caroline was sitting next to Begay on the couch and holding his hand. She rubbed her free hand across her eyes.

"I could use a cup of coffee," she said.

"So how did all this start?" Jennie asked, slumping down into an old recliner. She felt as drained as Caroline looked. *I think I'll have David drive home.* . . .

"I thought I was going crazy," Caroline said, unconsciously echoing Begay's words. "When I was practicing one night, I saw something out of the corner of my eye, looked up, and there he was. When I blinked, he was gone. But he kept reappearing. At first I thought, well, maybe I'm just somehow calling up an image out of my subconscious."

Jennie raised an eyebrow. "Did you think you were hypnotizing yourself somehow, dancing?"

Caroline shook her head. "I was just trying to find an explanation that wasn't—out there. I mean, I'm not one of those people that hangs around Peace of Mind bookstore telling anyone who'll listen about all the ghosts they're channeling. I *like* rational."

Jennie nodded; while she didn't exactly understand that attitude, she could sympathize with it. The spirit world seemed to scare as many people as it lured. Maybe more, actually. Despite wanting to *know*, for a fact, that there really was an "other side," a lot of people didn't really want that other side to intrude on *their* world. It scared them when it did. Because that meant that there were things they couldn't simply take for granted anymore.

"So . . . when he didn't go away, even when I stopped and stared at him, I thought maybe I was waking up an image out of the past, or somehow tuning into it, like a television getting a channel it wasn't supposed to." Caroline sighed. "After a few more times, it felt like I should just relax and let well enough alone. Soon I got used to seeing him there. Then one day—he spoke to me."

"What did he say?" That was David, cutting to the chase as usual; the question on the tip of Jennie's tongue was, "How did you understand him?" She was used to traveling in the spirit world and speaking to the creatures there. It was unusual for someone who didn't have strong Medicine of her own to be able to understand the spirits.

"He said, 'Dance with me,' and it wasn't a request." Caroline shivered. "It was like I didn't have a choice."

"Then?" Jennie prompted.

"Then, well . . . I couldn't resist him. Even when I tried, even when I wanted to stay up here, even when I locked the door, once the sun went down, it was like there was something dragging me down there. I'd light the fire, start the tape, and there he would be, and we'd dance. And it was horrible, like sleepwalking. He didn't flirt with me, no, he was just dancing around me like he owned me, and I couldn't help myself. I'd dance for two, three, four hours, and it felt like he was draining all my energy away. I'd feel half dead when he finally turned me loose, I'd sleep until noon and wake up still feeling half dead." There were tears in her eyes of frustration and anger. "I sent Nate away because I was afraid. I was afraid if it wasn't real, then it was a psychotic break, and I didn't want to hurt him. And if it was real—that scared me more, because I knew he'd want to do something, and he'd get hurt confronting the thing. Maybe worse than hurt."

"That would be about right," Jennie said dryly. "He was used to commanding people and getting what he wanted. Seemed to me that he was something of a spoiled bully when he was alive." She shivered a little. "Hard to tell what he's become as a *mi-ah-lushka.*"

"You've used that name before, what's it mean?" Caro asked, leaning forward anxiously. "Other than 'ghost.'"

The cup of coffee went unnoticed in her hands.

Jennie wasn't particularly in the mood to tell ghost stories, particularly not after facing one down, but she sensed she wasn't going to get away without some sort of explanation.

"Well, we Osage have the usual sort of expected after-life if you show courage and strength and the general litany of virtues in life," she said, trying to make it sound very matter-of-fact. "But our people figure if you aren't any of these things, instead of going onward, you stick around, kind of half in the living world and half in a shadow spirit world. It's a pretty unpleasant place, that shadow, which you'd figure, if the only things there are other rotten bastards."

Caro chuckled weakly.

"The *mi-ah-lushka*—we sometimes call them the 'Little People,' because some of them actually are quite small— are the general name for all the nasty things that live that kind of half-life. Most of them seem to be the spirits of particularly cowardly men, men who died without honor, without paint, and never got a proper burial. All of which your 'friend' there seems to be. Some of them are just vengeful—there is, or was, a set of them out at Claremore Mound that are the spirits of a bunch of villagers that were massacred, and let me tell you, *no one* is safe on that mound unless they're Osage, and sometimes not even then." She smiled wryly as David cringed. "The story goes that any man who goes up there at night, or at least at the dark of the moon, comes back singing soprano or pitching for the other team, if you know what I mean."

Begay rolled his eyes, but he didn't look as if he disbelieved her.

"There are others, things that aren't ghosts, but mostly, even Medicine People don't see them anymore. They don't much like modern stuff, so they stay hidden. So these days, when an Osage says *mi-ah-lushka*, he means 'nasty ghost.' " She took a long drink of lukewarm coffee. "They aren't just limited to going after Red blood either. They can go after anyone who pisses them off. Some of them have figured out the modern world well enough to really mess with you, even kill you. And as far as they are concerned, when you piss them off, you and everyone around you becomes a target. So, Caroline, your instinct to keep Nate out of this was dead-on."

The jewelry maker glanced at Begay, who squeezed her hand.

"But it's over now," Caro said, and sighed. "I think maybe I'll stick to practicing with that ICOT group."

Jennie nodded. "Safer. The drums called him, but I doubt he'll be able, or even inclined, to follow you into Tulsa. Just keep the drum music off your property. And don't hesitate to call us if you need us."

Jennie stood up and stretched, feeling aches all over. Despite her protections and precautions, she'd been "bruised" a good bit by the force of the spirit's will. She tossed David her keys. "Home, James, and don't spare the horsepower."

"Yes, madam," he said with a little bow.

There was something not quite right about the day.

It had started out badly; overcast, humid, threatening-but-not-quite-going-to-rain. She hated those kind of days, and so did David; they snapped at each other all morning, and Grandfather had taken the hint early and made himself entirely scarce, which was just as well. Some people called this "tornado weather," because conditions were good for big supercells to boil up. But it wasn't just the weather that was making them all nervous. Every time the phone rang, both she and David jumped, and whenever Jennie picked up the receiver she had a feeling of dread, for some reason expecting bad news.

Lunch was in keeping with the day, lousy barbeque sandwiches that had too much spice and garlic and not enough sauce, on buns that had gone soggy by the time David made it home with them. After they had both picked at the food and tossed most of it in the compost pile—the phone rang again, and finally it was bad news.

"It's Nate. Nathan Begay," said a weary voice on the other end of the line, a voice that sounded as if the speaker was in pain, and was having trouble with his mouth. "I'm in the Indian Hospital in Claremore. The thing's back and it kicked my ass." There was a long pause. "I can't face it again."

Jennie swore, and David went as alert as a hound that has caught a scent. He focused on her, but managed to keep quiet.

"We'll be right there," Jennie said, and hung up. "Begay," she told David, looking bleakly at him across her desk. "The *mi-ah-lushka* is back, and Nate got hurt. Bad enough to end up in the hospital."

It was David's turn to swear and look stunned. Well, he should. They had both heard of Little People messing with live folks, but they weren't usually able to physically beat a man badly enough to land him in the hospital. "We need to roll?"

"He's at the Indian Hospital in Claremore. Let me grab the kit; we need to get him smudged before he gets an un-wanted visitor." She fished her "traveling Medicine kit" from under the desk as David took off like a sprinter, then grabbed her purse, and headed out the door at a run. David had already gotten his car started; she yanked open the door and threw the kit inside, hurling herself in after it.

David had been in the area long enough to know where the speed traps were, and between them, he bent the law over backwards. Jennie was grateful that he was driving; even more grateful that Begay was in the Indian Hospital. Nobody was going to say a thing about smudging, chanting, or any other carrying-on, as long as the participants didn't start stripping to the skin and taking it into the hallway.

Another advantage: they knew her there, and she got the same access to patients that chaplains did, including after visiting hours, and no fussing about whether she was kin to the patient or not.

Begay was in a four-patient room, and he looked like hell.

David stopped in the doorway and stared.

"I know," Begay managed out of a swollen face that looked like it belonged to the loser in a bar fight. "Told 'em I was thrown by a bull and trampled."

That was an excuse that would definitely wash around here, especially now that it was rodeo season. Jennie nodded as she stepped past David and began setting up for her ceremony. This wasn't the first time she'd done this sort of thing, confusing the trail and the "scent" so a *mi-ah-lushka* couldn't hunt someone down. "Don't talk right now. Wait until I'm done."

She had the feeling they hadn't arrived a moment too soon; there was a malevolent taste to the air in the room that vanished once she was done with her cleansing and smudging. A passing nurse warned Jennie not to overwhelm the smoke detectors, but since no one in the room was on oxygen, she otherwise left them alone. Jennie was used to working in hospital rooms; she and Grandfather got a fair number of calls from people in here, or their relatives, wanting to be sure that there was nothing bad lingering around someone who'd gotten sick or hurt.

"All right," she said, once the sage and cedar bundle, the hawk-wing fan, and the abalone shell were put away. She sat down in the chair next to Nathan's bed. The other three patients pretended they were asleep, but she could almost feel them straining their ears to listen. What would they make of it? There were plenty of Native Americans who didn't believe, or were Christians. . . . Still, if the other patients thought all three of them were crazy, that wouldn't necessarily be a bad thing. If they disbelieved hard enough, that very disbelief was a kind of shield.

"Went over to Caro's place, later than usual," Begay said with difficulty, around his split and swollen lip. "She was gone. Boom box too. Started for the clearing. Heard the drums before I got there. Then . . ." He shook his head a tiny bit. "Dunno. Got hit in the back of the head then, not sure. Stuff hitting me, me hitting trees. Wound up by the trailer. Got the truck goin', got as far as QuikTrip. Clerk called cops, cops called ambulance."

Jennie's heart plummeted. The spirit was stronger. A *lot* stronger. It had ambushed Begay before he even got to the clearing, and now it was clearly able to work in the waking world; if the *mi-ah-lushka* was strong enough to bash the poor man in the back of the head with a heavy branch, there was no telling what was going on while it beat him further, maybe indeed throwing him against trees as he tried to stumble out.

What was clear was that Begay had given up. The despair in his voice told her that, and the sag of his shoulders, and the way he wouldn't look straight at her. She didn't need to hear him say it—it was all there in front of her, his capitulation as easy to read as a highway sign. *How does an ordinary man fight something that's already dead?*

Well, damn if *she* was going to give up that easily.

"Can you stay here and keep watch?" she asked David abruptly.

"You're not—" He stopped himself just in time, before putting his foot in it, which showed a lot of restraint on his part and better sense than he'd had before.

"I'm going to get Grandfather," she replied, and tried not to lose her temper at the relief on his face. "I've heard of Little People that were this strong before, but I've never seen one. Even the ones that were going after that contractor were only doing little things in the waking world, not beating people up. But there has to be something we can do besides let it take Caro."

"I—" David began, but she was already out the door and out of hearing range before he got any further.

She hoped he hadn't been about to say "I don't know what else we can do." Because she'd have smacked him with a chair if he had.

She'd left her Medicine bag with him, and the moment she got into the car, she realized that was a mistake—because everything went eerily quiet and very, very cold.

She felt a presence beside her and heard a mocking voice say, "The trail has disappeared. But you are just as good for my purposes. Come fight in *my* world, if you dare."

And then she felt a shove, and for the first time ever, found herself *physically* in the other world. As he said—his world. The one that was half of the waking world, half of the spirit world.

She was standing next to the car, but everything was grayed out and dim except for her and the *mi-ah-lushka*, and the car itself was empty.

"So," said the ghost, a sardonic smile on his lips. "Will you give this up and admit defeat? Or must I beat you too?"

With an effort of will, Jennie tried to change her form to something better suited to a knock-down, drag-out fight than a skinny, undersized woman—

And nothing happened.

She knew immediately why; it was because she was here physically. She could change her spirit form, but not a real, solid body.

"So you've descended to knocking a little woman

around?" she replied, trying to put up a brave front. This was probably how he beat up Begay—and Jennie hadn't even known this sort of thing was possible.

"Oh, but I am *mi-ah-lushka*, I have no honor to be concerned about," he retorted. His eyes flashed. "Only what is mine, and what I will have. That is all that concerns me." He stepped forward, hands already formed into fists.

Well, she might not be able to change form, but she wasn't exactly helpless. She'd had big brothers—and some martial arts training too. Dirty-fighting stuff. She hadn't been taken by surprise the way Begay had, and she hadn't been knocked half silly by a hit in the head.

Yet. And I need to figure out how to get back to the waking world, fast!

Meanwhile, when he swung his fist, she wasn't where he was aiming; and as his hand passed through empty air, she grabbed it to throw him—

Or tried; he was still a spirit—he could decide to be solid or not, and he reacted as quick as a rattlesnake. Her hands passed through where his arm had been, and he reappeared ten feet away.

"My world," he said, and vanished to appear at her side. This time he managed to backhand her before she could kick him. Her head rocked back on her shoulders and she staggered. The pain started a moment later, in a hot wash all down the left side of her face. He disappeared and materialized on her other side.

This time she caught his fist and managed to wrench it

enough that he gasped, then kicked his feet out from under him—and ran.

She had no other option, really. He could keep fighting forever. She couldn't. She needed to get back to the real world. But how?

She looked back over her shoulder, expecting to see him in pursuit, and only a hint of movement in front of her warned her to dodge as he appeared right in front of her. He didn't telegraph his blow, just punched; she ducked just enough that he hit her forehead instead of her eye, but he still knocked her to the ground and her head nearly split with the pain.

As he pounced on her, she rolled out of the way, got onto her knees and *finally* managed to concentrate. With a word of prayer and a lot of intent, while he was still sprawled on the ground, she hit the back of his neck with both hands clasped together.

There was a flash of something and she found herself on her knees in the parking lot. There was a huge knot forming on her forehead and she was bruised from head to toe.

David came running out of the door and headed straight for her. "I felt something bad," he said, landing on his knees beside her, already fumbling in the kit for the smudging stick. With a shaking hand, he got it alight, and did for her what she had done for Begay. She stayed bent over her knees, panting, feeling every ache.

"He pasted me," she said, getting her breath at last.

"He ambushed me, brought me into his world, and pasted me."

David was silent as he finished, extinguished the stick, and put everything back in the bag.

"I didn't know that was possible," he said finally.

"Neither did I," she said grimly. "But that's how he managed to beat up Begay. We can't fight him in his world. He's way stronger than us and he can fade in and out at will. Unless we can find a way to tap into that—"

"Brute force isn't going to cut it." David fell silent as he stood up and offered her his hand. "Let's get back to Grandfather. Maybe he has some ideas."

"I didn't know that was possible," said Mooncrow, deeply troubled. "I've never heard of such a thing."

Jennie held the ice pack against her forehead. "I—I'm at a loss. If you don't know what to do—"

"I didn't say that." For once her Grandfather was being entirely straightforward and not posing things in riddles. "I know what to do. Obviously we don't have the whole story. We need more information." He raised his chin, fire in his eyes. "I am not giving up. This *mi-ah-lushka* cannot be permitted to continue in this way. I do not like what he can do now, and if he takes this woman, I do not think he will stop with her."

The phone rang, and David went to answer it. When

he came back, his face was even grimmer than Moon-crow's. "That was Caro," he said, his voice tight. "She said that she doesn't want anyone else hurt. Not you, not me, and especially not Begay. She said to leave her alone with the ghost. She says she's pretty sure that he thinks she's the gal that killed herself rather than be taken by him, be-cause he's calling her by a name she doesn't recognize. Basically, she wants us to stop trying to stop him and she wouldn't take no for an answer."

Jennie felt tears of anger and frustration welling up in her eyes. "Dammit!" she swore angrily. "That means we can't do anything. She's not under my protection any-more, and—"

She couldn't help it; she broke down, crying silent, hot tears while her head felt ready to split. She didn't like losing at the best of times, but losing like this? It was—unacceptable. Caro was going to die, danced over a bluff, danced until her heart gave out, or even danced out in front of a car. The ghost was going to win, get what he wanted, and then, who knew what would happen next?

"No, we are not powerless," Mooncrow declared, steel in his voice. "This is one of *our* people. He was punished, and he does not accept that punishment. He is harming others, he harmed *you*. He raised his hand to you, an honored Medicine Person. We do not need this woman's permission to stop him any longer. Now, we are duty bound to stop him."

She looked up sharply, and pain stabbed through her

skull, pain she ignored at the sight of the expression on her grandfather's face. This was not the Little Old Man. This was not the Medicine Person. This was the Warrior.

"What can we do?" she asked humbly. "How can we stop him?"

"I told you, I do not know—yet," Mooncrow said, pushing himself up out of his chair. He stood tall and straight, towering over her, and she was suddenly aware that while he might be lean, he was all muscle, and he exercised more in one day than most teenagers did in a week. "But I know who does. The most patient of all, the one to whom all things come."

She blinked at him. This was not a spirit one approached lightly, and generally it was the other way around—you were led to her. "Grandmother Spider . . ."

He nodded. "Yes. Her web has caught all of the stories of our people—not the ones that we tell, but the ones as they happened. She is without pity and tells the dry husk of the truth, not the storyteller's tales. Now we—more precisely, you—will go to her."

It wasn't that easy or that direct, of course. First, they used the little cedar-lined room that they occasionally used for a sweat lodge as an ordinary sauna and baked Jennie's aches and bruises until they wouldn't interfere with her ability to move into the spirit world. And although Mooncrow normally was not one to let her have *anything* that might interfere with her visions, he himself gave her a couple of acetaminophen to further dull those aches.

Then there was the ritual bath, to cleanse her, mind and spirit as well as body, of everything except what they needed to know. Most of the time when she went into the spirit world, her questions were met with riddles, but she sensed that this time things would be different. The *mi-ah-lushka* had knocked everything out of balance. He had done what was not supposed to be done. The spirit world would be troubled, and there was no time to frame this in the sense of a "teaching experience." This was a rare time for action in both worlds.

Jennie and Mooncrow sat in the middle of the living room wearing simple, comfortable clothing, David sat between them, holding a small drum. They had all spun additional protections and deceptions around the house, layering new protections atop the very formidable ones Mooncrow already had in place. If the ghost could make his way through them, he was no longer just a ghost but something approaching a god.

And if that happened, well . . . Caro's fate would be the least of their worries.

Mooncrow looked up at Jennie. She nodded. David started the drumbeat as Mooncrow began to sing.

Jennie let the song guide her, as it had so many times, and without any effort at all, slipped free of her body to walk in the proper spirit world.

To her, the spirit world was as real and solid as the world she lived and worked in every day. For one of her ancestors, in fact, there would have been no sense of transition; the landscape of the spirit world would have been identical to the physical world he knew well. Now, the world Jennie lived in was very different from this one. Here, despite the passage of centuries, things were unchanged; not even the light hand of the tribes had made a mark on these lands.

As she got her bearings, Jennie realized she was not among the trees that spread on either side of the Arkansas River; she was somewhere farther north, in the kind of forest generally found around the Kansas border. The Osage had been the dominant force up and down the entire length of the Arkansas River, so she could have found herself anywhere along its banks or miles to either side.

The one thing that always indicated that you actually were in the spirit world was the weather; it was always summer. It was never very hot and seldom rained. Some tribes called it the Summer Country. She took a deep breath of air that was clean in a way it never was in the waking world, scented only with dust and old leaves.

Despite the apparent calm, Jennie could tell there was something wrong here. It was very quiet—an uneasy quiet. The spirit world sensed something out of balance, but it did not yet know what.

The ghost must be strong enough to hide his actions

and intentions even from the guardians of this place. To say this was a bad sign . . .

It meant it was possible that she would be the first one to tell them what was going on. She could only hope they were not inclined to shoot the messenger.

Well, there was no hope for it. She lifted her arms, and they became wings; she shrank, and with a thought, became the Kestrel of her spirit name, and sprang into the sky. With rapid wingbeats, she threw herself up through the branches, her falcon eyes spotting gaps that falcon reflexes aimed for. In a moment, she was out of the tree shadow and into the sun.

As soon as she cleared the tops of the trees, she saw Red-tailed Hawk, the spirit more important to her people even than Eagle. Her sharp falcon eyes picked out every detail though she was still far below him; how each feather in his tail and wings moved, catching the updraft and holding it, how the hackles of his neck blew a little as he shifted position. He was circling, circling, purpose in every motion of his feathers. He was watching for something. She darted upwards, and saw the moment when she came into his sharp gaze. His head swiveled and tilted, and she felt his attention focus on her. He knew who and what she was, of course.

"Little Sister!" he called, his voice piercing. "The world is uneasy; dreams are disturbing and portents are vague. Something is amiss. Have you brought us word from the waking world?" Now Jennie knew that he was not just *a* hawk, he was *the* Hawk.

"I have, Honored One," she said, feeling a little more hopeful, since this was speech more direct than she had ever gotten from a spirit creature before. "One of the Little People is acting as no *mi-ah-lushka* has ever acted before."

She explained as succinctly as she could, soaring with Hawk over the treetops. When she had finished, he voiced a note of dismay, a thin, plaintive scream that slicked her feathers down. "This is not good," he said. "This is not good at all. We must find Grandmother Spider. All things come to her web and break their necks therein. If anyone has the wisdom to see this ended, it is she."

"As you say, Honored One," she replied eagerly. "Lead, and I follow."

Hawk tilted his wings, and sideslipped west; she followed, beating her wings hard to keep up with him. Perhaps this would go better than she had hoped; she was being led to Grandmother by someone important. Grandmother would surely take her seriously.

A clearing line appeared in the trees ahead—it was the river, cutting through the forest, winding and curving like a fat, lazy snake. This Arkansas never flooded and never changed its course, so the trees of the spirit world grew right down to the banks, changing from the oak, beech, and chestnut that no longer grew in the waking world to thirsty cottonwood and willow. Again Hawk sideslipped, and they flew over the gray-green water, his eyes searching the shadows under the trees. Finally, he spotted what he was looking for and headed for the bank and a patch of mingled sun and shadow where a tree had toppled over long ago, leaving a gap.

She saw it too; the great orb of the web stretching from the lowest branches of the standing trees to the ground, strands shining silver where the sun touched them. And in the middle, the squat shape, weaving industriously.

Hawk landed ponderously beside the web. Jennie hovered for a moment before setting down beside him. They both bowed. "Grandmother," Hawk said politely. "Honored Woman. I bring news concerning the troubling of the world in the mouth of a seeker of wisdom."

Grandmother looked at both birds with her eight eyes, which glittered like jewels. "Tell me the news," she demanded, and Jennie complied. As Jennie spoke, Grandmother wrapped a bit of silk around and around, as if she were wrapping up Jennie's words to store them away. Maybe she was; it was hard to tell what she could and could not do.

"This explains much," Grandmother said, when Jennie was done. "It is one thing to adapt and change. It is quite another to take and hold and gobble up. I sense this spirit is one that would not be satisfied with a single mouthful; he would devour what he has taken and look for more. So, speak. What is it you want to know?"

"I know some of what he was, this *mi-ah-lushka*. I think the secret to besting him lies in what I do not know." Jennie bobbed her head nervously. If being in the eyes of Hawk was hard, being beneath the eyes of Grandmother Spider was positively unnerving. "You know more than the tales, Grandmother. You know the history, where the tales end, and what the tales do not say. I would know that about him—what lies in the places between the words I have heard." She waited while the huge spider hung above her, all eight legs splayed out along the strands of the web.

The web trembled, and for a moment Jennie was afraid that Grandmother was angry with her. But then a dry chuckle came from the great spider, and Jennie knew that Grandmother was not angry, only amused. "So, so, so. And that is wisdom indeed. Now you will hear, and may you find your answer in it."

Grandmother went to the edge of her web, one careful leg at a time, as delicately as a dancer on pointe, moving out of sight among the leaves. When she returned, she came back with a little bundle of silk held carefully in her two forelegs. "Now watch," she said. "And learn."

She began to unwind the silk, and as she did, a bright spot appeared in the shadows under the web. It grew swiftly, opening like a window into another time and place.

Jennie found herself looking into an Osage camp of the very oldest sort, at such a distance that she saw the camp laid out before her. A rough ring of rectangular longhouses—pole frameworks covered with dark brown bark sheets—stood in a clearing. Next to the longhouses were a large meetinghouse and several small, circular sweat houses covered with hides. Crop fields surrounded the village, planted with beans, corn, and squash. Beyond lay the forest, full of game, and the prairies where the buffalo were, buffalo that would be hunted by enormous parties sent out a few times a year for that specific purpose.

Between some of the longhouses were bowers made of branches driven into the dirt and topped with platforms of brush to give shade to the women and children of the camp as they worked or played. It was summer; the trees around the clearing were in full leaf and the camp was full of women working: scraping hides, smoking meat, cooking, sewing, grinding grain, or mending garments. There were a few older men among them, mostly making weapons and instructing the children. If the style of the lodges had not told her that all this was taking place long before the Heavy Eyebrows arrived, the Osages' clothing and the utensils they were making would have told her that. Decorations were quill embroidery, beads were bone, shell, antler, and stone. Tools were bone, antler, stone. There were mostly naked children everywhere. By modern standards they were very well-behaved children—but then, each had tasks to do. The village was almost certainly pre-Columbian.

By the position of the sun, halfway down to the horizon, it must have been late afternoon; shadows stretched out over the crop fields and the beaten-down grass around the camp. The men would still be out hunting for the most part; women farmed and gathered in the woods, though it was not unheard of for a woman to be a hunter or a man to tend the crops. Jennie's point of view shifted, until she saw a young warrior emerging from under the trees, a string of rabbits and squirrels in one hand. The moment she saw his face, she knew him. This was the one who had become the *mi-ah-lushka*.

He seemed very popular among the younger women. If she was reading the body language right, he flirted with almost all of them, and in most cases, got at least a saucy answer back. The older women, especially the grandmothers, seemed far less impressed. Certainly they were not nearly as impressed with him as he was with himself.

He was very handsome—well, she knew that, since he was very handsome even as a spirit—and he was dressed quite casually: breechcloth, leggings, and moccasins; the eagle feather that showed his *gente* was on the correct side of his roach. So, he was Hunkah, was he? Interesting. He seemed to be very proud of his muscles too; Jennie was familiar enough with the posing techniques of muscle-builders to tell that he was deliberately flexing them. It occurred to her that the stereotypical jock-jerk seemed to be eternal.

Her focus was drawn to one young woman in particular. The look in her eyes was impossible to mistake; she was like an infatuated groupie with a rock star parading in front of her. The others might have been attracted to the young man, but this one was obsessed.

Well, this certainly was not the Chickasaw girl he had tried to kidnap. And the legend said nothing about *this* young woman.

The young man distributed his game to some of the women, including his "biggest fan," and went to his own lodge. The look that particular woman gave him as he went inside should have set fire to the bark roof.

Grandmother Spider nodded in her web. "There is much that is commonplace and to watch all of it would take you the same time that it took to happen." She rapidly unwound the silk, and the scene became night. There was some quiet movement—the young woman. She slipped out of her lodge, made her way to a spot near the river, and—oh, surprise—met the young man. From the way they were all over each other this was hardly the first time they'd met by night. Grandmother Spider made a strange little creaking noise and unwound more silk before it turned into a voyeur session.

It was another day—the young man wore a buckskin shirt in addition to his leggings and breechcloth and stood inside a lodge that must belong to a Little Old Man, for Jennie could see many sacred objects in it, along with a small shrine for the sacred Hawk Bundle. The hunter stood beside an older man—one who was clearly a man of importance—who was probably his father. There were several other, even older men there—Little Old Men—and they were consulting the sacred Hawk Bundle. She wondered why they were using it, since it was reserved for decisions of war or peace. The Hawk fell with its head in the direction of peace. They all left the lodge; there was a group waiting outside for them. While the young man waited, his father and the Little Old Men spoke at length with several men in a different style of dress than they wore—though the Heavy Eyebrows probably would not have seen the distinction. Their buckskin shirts were cut differently, down to their knees or lower; their leggings were different too. Jennie didn't know much about the pre-Columbian regalia of other tribes, but she suspected that the visitors were Chickasaw—probably the very clan she had been researching.

So this was why the Little Old Men had been pondering peace or war. The Chickasaw must have approached the Osage for a parley. It was possible that they were attempting to join the Osage in a buffalo hunt; the larger the hunting party, the greater the success. That would account for why they were so close to Osage lands, when both the Osage and the Chickasaw had quite a warlike reputation.

She tried to remember her history; usually it was the Choctaw that warred with the Chickasaw, simply because their territories were closer. Maybe the Chickasaw felt it was better to ally for a hunt with someone they hadn't recently been fighting with. She knew there was *some* intersection of territory, but didn't think it was much. The

Chickasaw were Mississippian; the Osage were further west and north.

She would have suspected the young Osage warrior to be opposed to any overtures of peace, but instead, he appeared bored. She was beginning to get a sense of this fellow; vain, more than a bit lazy, and self-centered. Definitely the sort who would avoid anything that might interfere with his pleasure. He probably enjoyed hunting, and he was good at it; despite the tradition of martial courage among the Osage, war meant the disruption of his lazy life. Hence, his reaction to the truce his elders had just made. A truce just meant peace and quiet, no interruption to his pursuit of the women of his clan. And perhaps the Chickasaw men had brought some women along and while they were all off on the hunt, perhaps he would have a chance at them too.

Grandmother Spider unwound faster, and the scene changed to a view of a Chickasaw camp. And that was where Jennie got her first surprise, because this was not a camp, it was a settlement.

It was in a clearing among the trees and it looked a great deal more substantial than the ring of bark lodges that the Osage favored. A palisade of straight tree trunks had been driven into the earth in a still-incomplete ring around the settlement. There were "Summer Houses" already erected inside. Strong, straight trunks of pine, honey locust, and sassafras were driven upright into the ground to form the walls, and a pitched roof made of more trunks would last for decades. Summer Houses were rectangular and even a white man would have recognized them as a "proper house." They were meant to hold up against an attack, and had clay-filled arrow ports that could be opened up and shot out of as needed.

But Summer Houses were not the thing that told Jennie this was a settlement. The corn houses and fowl houses were one clue, but what clinched it was the sight of Winter Houses in the process of being constructed. These were round structures with peaked roofs, made of logs plastered over with clay and withered grass daub. The roofs were made of grass thatch and bark over white oak splints, cane or hickory and honey locust posts, protection against the worst winter weather. Winter Houses meant that these Chickasaw were here to stay.

They were also building a Mountain House, made of the same construction materials as the Winter Houses but square, in which to conduct their clan business.

Outside the palisade were fields not unlike the ones the Osage farmed; corn, squash, and beans. Women were tending the plants and harvesting the beans.

Although Jennie had known the Chickasaw came this far west to hunt before the Europeans turned up, she'd had no idea that any of the clans had tried to settle here. She'd assumed that the girl in the legend had just been someone brought to help tend camp for a far-roving band of hunters. It was a sensible thing to do; bring women who were not burdened with children to take care of butchering, smoking the meat, and tanning the hides. Old women might have a hard time keeping up; young ones would not.

Except that this wasn't a hunting party.

That might go a long way toward explaining why they were eager to make a truce. Not just for hunting, but to prevent conflict while they were still establishing themselves. Even with a truce, young warriors would still do their level best to count coup on each other. But it would mostly remain "bloodless," confined to weaponless fighting and the theft or winning of the feathers worn in the hair roaches sported by both nations, which represented their honor. The truce wouldn't hold forever, but while it did, this Chickasaw band would cement their position in this territory and establish their defenses to the point where it would be very difficult indeed to dislodge them.

Jennie's sharp eyes, made even sharper by being in the form of Kestrel, spotted the young Osage warrior lying belly-down under cover in a good vantage point. A moment later she saw what he was looking at.

A woman, of course. And the Chickasaw girl he was eyeing with greed was . . . well, nothing short of stunning. Even by modern standards she was fashion model or movie star material. Her body was as slender and graceful as a willow in the wind; her hair sleek and shining in the sun. She could have been the original of every cloyingly beautiful painting of an "Indian Maiden." And it was also obvious that, handsome as he was, the young Osage was no competition for the young man that she was standing beside. Probably her husband, in fact, though she didn't look older than fifteen or sixteen. They didn't touch, but from the way they were standing, staring into each other's faces as they spoke, they might as well have been. He was just as stunning as she was. The look of shining devotion in his eyes was almost painful to see.

And that was when it dawned on Jennie. This wasn't a sentimental "Indian legend." This was a story of real tragedy.

Because once she had been stolen away, this young creature would have known that if her clan or even her husband came to get her back, it would be war with the Osage. And it would be a war the Chickasaw were not ready for.

And he *would* come for her. More than his honor would demand it, his love would not let him leave her in enemy hands.

If she'd been human, Jennie would have sworn quite nastily enough to turn the air blue. As it was, what came out of her beak was an angry chitter.

Grandmother Spider stopped unwinding and looked at her with all eight eyes. "And so," she said, "you see."

"I think so, Grandmother," Jennie said carefully. "When the young man stole the girl, she killed herself, not only because she had been stolen from her love, but because she knew that at the very least all the young Chicka-saw warriors would come after her, led by her man. And that would be war, war that would end with all of them dead or captive. The women and children would be Osage slaves, and the men would all be dead. And she would have been the cause of it. She could not bear that thought, probably could not bear the thought of being the death of her beloved."

"Indeed," Grandmother Spider said, bobbing approvingly in her web. "And this is the rest. The one who became *mi-ah-lushka* was not very good at anything but being beautiful. He left a trail a blind man could see, and the young Chickasaw warriors, led by her husband, were already near when the girl flung herself over the bluff. In fact, they saw her do it. He had not told anyone in his village where he was going, and certainly had not told anyone what he was going to do. So when the Chickasaw caught and killed him, stripped him of everything and threw his body in the river, so far as his people were concerned, he simply vanished. None of the Osage had any reason to think the Chickasaw had done away with him and the Chickasaw held his death a secret."

Jennie pondered all of this. The thing that kept returning to her, over and over, was the hungry look in the Osage girl's face. "And the one who loved him?" she asked.

"Also died, of a summer fever." The spider made a kind of shrugging motion. "So it is said."

Jennie blinked. She could almost hear Grandfather's voice in her head, something he had told her long ago. *"The only thing as strong as a powerful ghost is another powerful ghost."*

And she had absolutely no doubt in her mind that the Osage girl would go through the Christian Hell five times over to get her man back.

"Thank you, Grandmother Spider," Jennie said fervently.

"Ah, so you have your answer then. It is well." The spider reached out with one long leg and touched her on the "forehead," above her beak, just past her nares. "Then it is time to go."

And with that, Jennie was catapulted abruptly out of the spirit world and back to her own.

It had been dancing that had brought the *mi-ah-lushka*. If Jennie was right, it would be through dancing that she would find the way to pull the snake's fangs.

But it had taken a lot of persuasion to get Caroline to cooperate, and even now, she was eyeing the garments that Jennie had brought very dubiously. This was not the trade-cloth dress with ribbonwork and silver brooches that she usually wore to dance. This was something much, much older. Jennie had worked feverishly with a Chickasaw tribal historian and her own mother to put this outfit together. It was the smoke-and-brain-tanned buckskin dress, leggings, and turtle shell ankle rattles of a woman of the time she had seen in her vision. She was grateful that her mother had been able to *find* that much traditionally worked buckskin and that many small turtle shells. The rattles were incredibly important, the most important part of a Chickasaw woman's dancing gear of that time. It was said that the great spirits themselves had given them to the Chickasaw women, so that they could keep perfect time in their dancing.

Jennie was wearing the same outfit. The only modern thing she had was her own dancing shawl, one that had a phenomenal amount of Medicine poured into it.

"Are you sure this will work?" Caroline asked plaintively.

"No," Jennie said bluntly. "And if it doesn't, Grandfather is going to get you out of here and put you on a plane to Albuquerque, while I work to find another way of draining the spirit's power." There was so much more riding on this than just Caroline—she'd explained that, but she still wasn't sure Caroline really understood.

One thing that Jennie did know—if this didn't work, the *mi-ah-lushka* was going to be incredibly angry at her. The beating she'd gotten at his hands before was nothing to what he'd do to her. Or try, anyway.

That was why David wasn't here. He had some idea of his own, something to keep the spirit from taking out his anger on her, and maybe something to help her with her plan. He hadn't wanted to tell her; he'd asked her to trust him. "I'm going to get you musicians," he'd told her. "This needs real special musicians."

"Special?" She had furrowed her brows at him. "The tape worked before—"

"Now, who's the magician and who's the musician?" he interrupted. "You Osage know how to dance, all right, but I never heard you produced any great musicians. Seriously. I don't know if I can do this," he said, holding her hands and giving her a pleading look. "I don't want you to count on something that doesn't happen. And I think I'm going to be working right up to the last second to *get* this help, if it will come at all. So trust me? And if I can't— well, I promise you'll get *me*, for whatever good that does."

Control. That was always her big stumbling block. She'd always hated to give up control of anything. And yet . . . in order to grow, she had to. That had been made clear in the past, and it was just as clear now.

So David wasn't here, only Grandfather, laying out the boundaries of a sacred dancing ground. She would trust in David, in Grandfather, in Grandmother Spider.

And in her own good reasoning.

"Time to go," she said firmly, picking up the boom box, which held a very different tape than it had before. She would play it on endless repeat, because she had no idea how long this was going to take. Just in case David didn't manage his own magic and bring that mysterious help.

When she and Caroline got to the dancing ground, it

was almost dark. Grandfather had already set up the four arbors in the four corners and finished smudging the area; the fire was burning in the east and David was nowhere in sight. She gave Grandfather a questioning look and he shrugged. She sighed and put down the boom box. Looked like it was a good thing she'd brought it.

Then she heard a little rustle of leaves, the cracking of a single twig, and David and two more men stepped out through the brush.

Both of the strangers were Indian, though she couldn't have said what tribe. The one carrying a beautifully made drum had a craggy, good-natured face, a veritable bush of hair, and an expression of amusement in his eyes. The other had a sharp face and extremely bright eyes that seemed to see everything. Both were wearing ordinary jeans, plaid shirts, and battered black felt hats. The second had a feather in his hatband.

"We hear you need musicians," said the drummer with the flash of a grin and his yellow eyes.

She forcibly kept herself from staring as the other man—obviously the singer—nodded. Yellow eyes? But—

"Your friend asked us for help, and your Grandmother sent us," the drummer added, with a wink.

My Grandmother . . . Jennie realized that he meant Grandmother Spider.

"A special dance needs special musicians, Honored Ones," she replied, suspecting that the drummer was Coyote and the singer, some other spirit.

The feather in the second stranger's hat might be a clue. Mockingbird, maybe. He'd be a logical choice. A lot of good Medicine, but not so much that he'd frighten away the ghost. Coyote was the supreme Trickster and could probably hide his identity from just about anything, so it was unlikely the ghost would take alarm from him.

"Oh, we are not that special," the drummer replied as they set up to play. "But we know some clever tricks."

Well, that pretty much cemented it.

Jennie looked at Caroline, who seemed bewildered. "Ready?"

Caroline nodded, then went to stand next to the singer. Jennie, Caroline, and the singer faced east. She yelled four times; the singer, the drummer, Jennie, Grandfather, and David answered her. The singer began the song, the drummer followed him, and all six of them joined hands, alternating male and female as much as possible, as he led them in the four directions of the circle. When they had completed the circle, Jennie, David, and Grandfather fell back, and the singer and Caroline began a stomp dance.

The boundaries of the dancing ground began to haze.

It was something like a fog—but it rose up out of the earth, blurring the trees and brush on the other side of that invisible boundary. The light changed too; instead of coming from the fire alone, some light came from that strange fog.

Jennie shivered as she realized that they weren't in the waking world anymore.

This was what having Coyote and Mockingbird as the drum circle meant. The dancing ground was in the middle place, halfway between the spirit world and the waking world. Medicine People and *mi-ah-lushka* would square off with only the power—and the wits—they brought with them.

As Caroline and the singer danced, a shadow formed in the north, a shadow that took on form and substance until the *mi-ah-lushka* stood there. Before he could move, Jennie danced out to Caroline, and in a move that had never been in any traditional dance that she had ever seen, she circled Caroline and the singer, then cut between them. The singer retired to the side of the circle, still singing, while she and Caroline danced.

Jennie flipped her shawl off her shoulders and held it by two corners in front of her. She flipped one of the corners to Caroline, who caught it. They continued to dance with the shawl held between them, then Jennie danced around in back of Caroline, draping the shawl over her shoulders. Then Jennie let go and danced back to the sidelines, while Caroline danced alone.

If Jennie had done her job right, Caroline now looked exactly like that long-lost Chickasaw woman to the *mi-ah-lushka*.

When she looked over at the spirit, she knew the trick had worked. The *mi-ah-lushka* stared at Caroline as if mesmerized; then, moving to the drumbeat, he came onto the dancing ground.

Now . . . now she had him. He was in the trap.

They danced together, the spirit staring down at Caroline with a terrible possessiveness, while the singer chanted and the drum held steady, the bright eyes of Coyote glaring with a wild glee from under the rim of his hat. But Caroline wasn't enthralled, not this time. The Medicine in Jennie's shawl was keeping her safe from the spirit's power. As long as she wore it, he wouldn't be able to control her and he wouldn't be able to drain her either.

Right now, it didn't look as if he noticed or cared. This was the object he had obsessed over for centuries. He had this woman right where he wanted her.

Or so he thought.

Jennie nodded to David and they moved out onto the dancing ground, joining the other two. Side by side, the two couples moved to the same rhythm, until the beat began to speed up and the words changed. Caroline pulled the shawl from her shoulders and held it out as Jennie had before. Puzzlement crept into the spirit's gaze, but they gave him no time to think.

Caroline flipped one corner of the shawl to Jennie as the beat sped up more.

The singer yelled.

At the same moment, Jennie spun, pulling the shawl over her own shoulders and stepping between the *mi-ah-lushka* and Caroline. As she momentarily blocked the spirit's view, David darted toward Caroline, grabbed her hand, and pulled her off to one side.

Now it was Jennie who was the focus of the spirit's fierce attention. The singer's voice took on a wild intensity and the drumbeat increased until it was the same pace as a shawl-dance.

Jennie gave up all pretense of performing a traditional Chickasaw dance. Instead she hopped and pranced, kicked and spun, in a shawl-dance worthy of a competition. The point was to get every bit of the spirit's attention on *her* and keep it there. The fire leapt higher, casting flickering light over both of them as she circled around and around him, sunwise, binding him up in the magic she was dancing. He'd likely never seen anything like this before. With any luck, he never would again.

Now if Grandfather just managed his part—

She couldn't think about that right now. Right now she had to dance right *on* the song, every step exactly in time with the drumbeat. As she spun, the fringe of her shawl flung straight out, she caught Coyote's eyes. He was grinning like a mad thing, his yellow eyes blazing.

One song led straight into the next, like a competition; there was no time to breathe, no time to think. She had to keep the *mi-ah-lushka* here. Had to make him see nothing but her. Had to make him forget about power and fighting and anything except what he *thought* he saw in front of him.

And then, as the song came around for the third time, and she spun a little away from him, she saw it—

Saw *her*.

The slight, sad spirit of the Osage woman who had been left behind, with Grandfather at her side.

Use that silver tongue, Little Old Man—

Jennie spun away again, keeping the spirit facing away from the woman. She didn't want him to see her just yet.

With little trotting steps, the singer and the drummer moved over to Grandfather and the woman-ghost. As Grandfather continued to speak in her ear, the singer's voice took on an edge of mockery.

She knew what goad Grandfather was using on the woman. *Are you a woman or a timid mouse? Are you a sparrow? Do you let your man be witched away from you like this? Stand up for yourself! Are you just going to give up like you did before? Too bad, this time you can't die! If you want him—take him back!*

Jennie watched with hidden glee as the woman's posture changed, her back straightened, and her mouth took on a stubborn set. Her eyes flashed, and she became more solid, more real, until at last she looked ready to fight.

That was when David—though it was *supposed* to have been Grandfather!—took her hand and danced her into the circle. Jennie spun, keeping the *mi-ah-lushka* mesmerized, then flipped her shawl over her shoulders and held it out before her again.

With a deft half turn, she faced the woman-ghost and flipped the corner of the shawl to her.

This was where it could all fall apart. Though she made no sound, in her mind, Jennie was screaming as she threw the bit of cloth. *Take it! Take it!*

There was a flash of surprise in the woman-ghost's eyes, but her hand snaked out and she seized the corner of the shawl.

Now the two of them danced with the shawl held between them. The *mi-ah-lushka* danced, looking bewildered, as his gaze went from Jennie to the woman and back again. The drumbeats slowed. Jennie made the transition back to a more traditional dance, though there was no traditional dance that featured two women, a shawl, and a bemused man, a dance where the women took turns curling into the shawl's embrace and out of it again, where they wrapped the man for a moment in the shawl's wings and then let him go.

The magic worked on him, dazzling him, until at last, Jennie spun the woman-ghost into the shawl for the last time and released the corner. David took Jennie's hand, leaving the two ghosts dancing slowly, deliberately, in the center of the circle. The *mi-ah-lushka*'s eyes never left the ghost-woman's. What he saw there, Jennie couldn't begin to guess. What the woman thought, though, was plain as plain. In her eyes was the same heat, the same adoration, that Jennie had seen in Grandmother Spider's vision. Jennie recognized the song; it was a Cherokee love song. Mockingbird added his own sort of magic to the mix, drawing the two together.

Finally, as the drum slowed to the pace of a steady heartbeat, the singer ended his song, though the drum continued. Slowly, the woman reached out and took the *mi-ah-lushka*'s hand. Slowly, she danced backwards, away from the fire, into the west, drawing him after her. He followed, obedient as a dog. They passed under the arbor, into the shadows.

And then they were gone.

The drummer ended the song. At the edges of the circle, the fog lifted and the waking world returned. Jennie felt her knees go weak and was very, very glad that David was there to steady her.

The drummer and singer crossed the circle and the drummer tipped his hat to her.

"That was some performance, Elder Brothers," Jennie said, still trying to catch her breath.

"We might say the same, Little Sister," Coyote retorted, grinning. Mockingbird nodded.

"I might make a song on it one day," Mockingbird added, the first time he'd opened his mouth except to sing.

"I believe you dropped your tobacco pouches, cousins," Grandfather called out, tossing a pair of fat leather pouches at the two, who deftly caught them out of the air. Coyote's eyes twinkled.

"I believe you are right, cousin," he replied with another tip of his hat. "Now, my friend and I should be on our way. But call on us again, if you reckon to stir up a bit of fun like this."

Grandfather laughed. Behind him, Nathan Begay finally stepped into the circle and Caroline practically glued herself to him.

"I think it's safe to leave these two now," Grandfather said, sounding a good deal more chipper than he had any right to, seeing how much Medicine he must have poured out to summon the spirit of the *mi-ah-lushka*'s lover from the Other Country.

"I want a gallon of lemonade, a steak, and another gallon of lemonade, in that order," Jennie said faintly. "Little Old Man, I will even share it with you. But you"—she turned to look at David—"you get whatever you want, up to and including half a buffalo. How did you *do* that?"

"Only half?" He laughed. "How, well . . . partly let's say I'm a good student, partly let's say it's my charm and devastating wit. There's only one thing I feel bad about."

Jennie blinked. "What's there to feel bad about? We solved this without anyone getting hurt!"

"But you lost your shawl." David grimaced a little. "That was your competition shawl."

"I can get another," she replied. "When you think what the alternative could have been—"

David glanced back at Begay and Caroline, outlined by the firelight. "Hmm. Good answer." He put his arm around her. "Let's go get that lemonade."

"You're buying!" yelled Grandfather, already three yards ahead of them on the trail.

Ghost in the
Machine

Welcome back to the present day, and a different sort of sorcery where magic and cyberspace intersect. Thanks to War Witch and Dark Watcher, devs at NCsoft/Paragon Studios, for vetting this for me!

Tom Bishop stared morosely at the sea of code on his computer screen. Every gamer thought that achieving the life of a dev—a game developer—was the Holy Grail. And yeah, you had to love games to work on them, because if you didn't you'd probably throw yourself out a window in the first three months. Mostly, being a game programmer meant a lot of long hours, a lot of cold pizza dinners, and if you were married, you needed a really, really understanding spouse. Girlfriends tended to leave after the first run-up to a release. Boyfriends—well, he wasn't sure about that. Gamer Grrlz tended to have gamer boyfriends, or at least, ones that were in software themselves and knew what schedules looked like. But Murphy's Law being what it was, probably the gals had almost as many problems in their love lives as the guys did.

Now, this wasn't prerelease, it was post. And under

normal circumstances, he wouldn't even have been here. Most of the floor was dark, cubicles lit only by the glow of screen savers. You could shoot a cannon through the office and not kill anyone; that was how it was this late at night, and doubly so right after an issue update once the catastrophic bugs and the hot patches to fix them were in. That the issue had gone live just before Christmas was an added bonus for the staff; it meant that, for a change, some of them would be free to travel to visit family over the holiday. The air held that curiously sterile smell of new offices, faintly scented by someone's fruity air freshener in some nearby cube. The only sounds came from some of those screen savers, and, now and then, his own typing.

Not that he was typing in the window that held the code he was trying to debug. No, he was answering IMs from friends who weren't stuck trying to figure out why Dark Valley was a whole lot darker than it should have been—and why PCs—player characters—were faceplanting a lot more than they should have been in there. Ah, the glamorous life of a dev. Tom chugged back a slug of Mountain Dew and kept staring and typing. Overhead, festive Christmas decorations moved in the currents of air from the vents they were strung on.

Tom worked on Many Worlds Online, one of the most popular multiplayer online games on the planet, and most of the time it was fun. He loved coding. He actually enjoyed debugging; he had the kind of patient aptitude for sleuthing that was perfectly suited to debugging. And while the life was far from glamorous, how many people actually got to make a living at something they loved these days? Oh, there were drawbacks. The long hours were a lot more wearing than they had been when he'd been in college. Sometimes the bugs drove him up a wall. And now and then he got a little tired of the players posting on the forums whining and bitching, but of course, there was a solution to that—he could choose not to read the forums. Mostly that was what he did—ignored the forums and the moaning and Drama Llamas, except when someone e-mailed or IMed him with something particularly funny.

But otherwise, this was a dream job. He loved games. He lived games. He loved and lived code. Not even forum trolls could spoil that for him.

Tom was a Gaming Geek and proud of it. He even had a Gamer Grrrl girlfriend who "got" being a code head. She had her own thing, first-person shooters, and her own real job, also coding, but for Web pages. There was nothing serious between them yet but . . . there was potential. So far neither of them had discovered anything about the other one that would drive a stake into the heart of the budding relationship. And now he was old and wise enough to look at the word "relationship" and not run away, to look forward to the possibility, in fact.

Most days, most weeks, he was happy to come to work, happy to stay late, happy to delve into the bits and bytes and figure just what had gone wrong where. It was something he was good at. He had a logical mind, and he had always been a puzzle solver, and a darned good one.

Except now. Why were so many characters dying so often in Dark Valley? Granted, Dark Valley was a whole new horror-themed zone, just implemented amid much fanfare and hoopla, and until they got the hang of the new quirks, mobs, and architecture, even experienced players planted a lot when a new zone was opened. There were always complaints, accusations that powers had been nerfed, that the mobs were tuned too high. Usually that stuff got worked out in beta test. But this time—there were complaints from some of the really experienced players who had been in beta and knew what to expect, and there were a lot of them. Way more than usual.

He stared at the AI code, and it still didn't make any sense to him. It was the same as in every zone. Enemies here shouldn't be defeating player characters at three times the rate they did in the other zones.

His message window chimed, and he checked it. *Still there?* asked jquest77. This was a player he'd gotten to know in beta test on the zone; levelheaded, not a troll, not a fanboy, an adult with a wife and two kids. Jquest77 never pestered him, but was more than happy to put together a fun team of friends for Tom when he got out on his personal avatars. He'd never asked Tom to do anything "special" for him, so Tom had added the guy to his IM list. Then again, jquest77's day job was also as a code head, so there was the sympathy and camaraderie of fellow coders at work. Another plus was that jquest77 typed in real words and full sentences, not l33t txtsp34k.

Yeah. The AI is fine, I've checked the tables so many times I could see them in my sleep, I even went in the test server and it runs normally in there. It's only a problem on the live servers.

He went back to checking the difficulty tweaking. Could he have mistaken a decimal point somewhere?

Not that he hadn't already checked this twenty times since this morning. *Hell, maybe I'm hoping that as I look at the numbers some illusion will suddenly wear off and I'll be looking at the real numbers.*

The main mob enemies in this zone were zombies, werewolves, and ghosts. The solo enemies were vampires. There was a Boss Monster that spawned randomly, something he had been told was a fairly accurate interpretation of the Native American Wendigo. They all ran the same basic AI, with tweaks for different powers. They all used the same tables.

Except in Dark Valley, everything was spawning weirdly. Mobs were spawning in greater numbers or at higher levels than they should. Solos weren't just spawning, they were sneaking up on the player characters and ambushing them. Ambushing them! Spawning right behind them—from the player point of view, out of nowhere! Which would have been fine, and hell, they could advertise that as a new feature ("It's not a bug, it's a feature!"), if the monsters weren't also spawning three or four levels higher than they were supposed to, which made it pretty hard on the poor players, who were faced with an enemy that could drop them in one shot. And the Wendigo was spawning at places it definitely shouldn't, like in the safe zones around the Trading Outposts and the Passage Gates that allowed player characters to move from one zone to another.

It was almost as if this zone was *trying* to kill the players. And that made no sense.

His IM pinged again. *Have you considered that there might be something in there that you never coded?*

His mouth went dry. A hack? That was a game writer's worst nightmare—that a hack would get in there and—

But that was also the parent company's worst nightmare, and the amount of ice and firewall they had on their servers was phenomenal . . .

Another coder here at the office? A patch? But that would show up in the code he was staring at, because he was looking at the raw code, the real stuff, and not the hard copy program copies of what was "supposed" to be there. *I don't know how a hacker would have gotten in there,* he replied. *And besides, it's on all the servers but Test. Dude, that is a lot of servers.*

Not a hack, came the reply. *And not a patch. Something else. Something that crawled in between the lines of code.*

Now, any other time, that would probably have made him laugh his ass off. It was like a line from a bad horror movie. But it was 3:00 A.M. and the offices were dark, except for the lights in his cube and the weird glows and weirder sound effects from dozens of disparate machines . . .

So that message made the hair on the back of Tom's neck stand straight up.

He shook it off and checked on the bug petitions and calls for help. Maybe he'd catch a pattern. As usual, even at this hour, there were plenty of them from Dark Valley; the one that caught his eye was that the Wendigo had spawned near the Passage Gate again on the Azure server. It occurred to him then that it wouldn't be a bad idea to have a look at this firsthand while he despawned the thing. He logged himself as accepting the petition and signed in as his god-mode avatar. He watched as the loading bar crept to the right, heard the zone in cue, and prepared to deal with the—

There was just enough time for the screen to register the safe zone at the Passage Gate, and the presence of the Wendigo inside the safe zone, when the screen filled with light and red numbers, the words "Critical Hit," and—

Tom stared at his prone avatar in shock. "He critted me? He *critted* me?" he said out loud, aghast, his brain simply not accepting the fact. It shouldn't be possible. The avatar was in god-mode, with every power in the book and impossible to hit. The Wendigo, awesome as it was and tough as it was, should not have been able to lodge a pin-prick's worth of damage, much less faceplant him.

For a long moment he stared at his avatar in utter disbelief; then the Wendigo uttered its trademark raspy laugh and he tore his eyes away from his avatar.

As the latest of the Boss Monsters, the Wendigo was the showpiece of the zone. With a little bit of H. P. Lovecraft and a lot of Native American myth, the devs and design team had, at least according to the reviewers, outdone themselves. Take a fifty-foot-tall man. Starve him to emaciation and dehydrate him until his desiccated skin pulls tight over his bones. Give him the ashen pallor of death and push his eyes back into their sockets, then light them with a feral red glow. Cover him with sores, and give him lips that were tattered and bloody.

The final touch was an endless appetite. That was the Wendigo. The mythic original, the Ojibwa legend, probably came out of some dreadful true story of a tribesman who had been forced to resort to cannibalism and had gone mad rather than face what he had done. According to the myth, some vile magic granted the Wendigo increasing power with every new victim, so that it grew larger and stronger with every human it ate.

In game terms, the Wendigo did something entirely new to MWO. Instead of simply reducing a player character's health and hit points by smacking him around with its war club until the players either defeated it or it defeated them, the Wendigo absorbed their health points, strengthening itself, healing itself, and growing a little bigger with every player character's defeat. That gave it the game analogy to the cannibalism of the myth. Of course, the mythic version would just keep getting bigger, while the game version was limited by the size tables, but it was still an innovation that the reviewers liked.

That was what it did according to the code.

The code didn't give it the ability to take sadistic pleasure in what it did.

The ugly thing laughed again.

Then it *looked right at him.*

Tom found himself frozen in his chair. The Wendigo was looking right at him. Not the avatar facedown on the "ground" in front of it. *Him.* The guy on the other side of the computer screen. The malevolent glare at the back of those almost-empty eye sockets was directed at *him.*

As if it knew he was there. He stared into that red gaze, mesmerized by it. It didn't matter that he knew it was nothing more than a bunch of pixels, designed by Erik in the cubicle across from his, rendered by the server as directed by the platform code. None of that mattered. Because what that smoldering crimson glow said to his gut was this—

Bring it on, code monkey. You can despawn me now, but wait. One of these days, you won't be able to. Then I will reach through that screen, and I will be coming for you. Personally.

He broke the thing's hold on his mind with a smothered gasp, revived his avatar, and despawned the damned thing. It laughed at him as it died.

He was shaking so hard that it took him a moment to

realize that his avatar wasn't alone in the zone. Jquest77's favorite character, an Amazonian warrior named Hippolyta, had spawned in time to see the Wendigo vanish. Hippolyta was why he'd singled out jquest77 in the first place in test when he put together a team to try out some of the new quests. Unlike most of the females-played-by-males, she was a fairly accurate rendition of a Grecian Amazon. She was fully and modestly clothed, and her cups weren't runnething over. The mere look of the avatar had told him that the player behind her was a sensible guy, which was borne out by his initial interactions with character *and* player.

"Something is seriously wrong here." That jquest77 was as disturbed by what he had seen as Tom was showed in the fact that the player had fallen out of character. Jquest was a role-player, and even at the most stressed of times, Hippolyta would have been speaking forsoothly. "I thought you couldn't get planted in god-mode."

"Looks like the Wendigo thought different." He wasn't usually this abrupt with a friend but—dammit, he felt shaken to his toes. "Gotta log." He hit the *Exit* button, exiting straight to the desktop.

Jquest77 wants to share a file, said his IM program. He hesitated a moment, then hit *Okay.*

The file was a tiny jpeg. No harm in opening it.

It was a business card.

Ellen McBride, techno-shaman, it said, with an address,

e-mail, Web site, and a phone number. The IM program pinged again.

If you've ever trusted me, trust me now, said jquest77. *You're not imagining this. Dark Valley's trying to kill us. The Wendigo is more than just code. Ell can find out why.*

Tom stared up at the old brick apartment building, one of many similar buildings in a modest neighborhood. He wasn't sure of the vintage; pre-1950s, he thought. Maybe 1930ish. It was only four stories tall and had huge screened-in porches on the front, less like balconies and more like sunrooms. This was where the so-called techno-shaman lived. Whatever a techno-shaman was. It seemed an odd choice of living space for anyone calling themselves techno-anything; he would have expected glass and steel, or maybe something futuristic. Four flights of stairs later, it seemed an even odder choice, unless the person in question really needed a lot of exercise. On the plus side, the apartment he wanted was the first door off the landing.

He'd had to buzz to get access to the building, so Ellen McBride was waiting for him at the door. He had a chance to get a real good look at her as he trudged up the last half-flight of stairs.

He hadn't been expecting the red hair. She had a wild, exuberantly curly mop of it, currently threatening to explode from the jaws of a banana clip. Then there were the freckles scattered across the bridge of her nose. And green eyes, just now looking at him with a suggestion of laughter. From the floor up, no-name running shoes, jeans, and a T-shirt that said I'M ONLY HERE BECAUSE THE SERVER IS DOWN.

"You must be—"

"Quiet Knight, yeah," he said, taking the hand she had extended and giving the name of the signature character he played when he was doing something public in the game.

"I was gonna say 'Bob.'" She grinned, giving him a good firm, dry handshake. "I don't play MWO. I'm more of an action-adventure, puzzle-game kind of gal." Her eyes twinkled. "Although classic Doom still has a lot to be said for it. Besides, playing in your MMORPG would be too much like going to work. I prefer something not fantasy, and something that has so little mind of its own that there is no way you can get a 'ghost in the machine.'"

"The which-what? Isn't there an anime with that name?" he asked as she waved him in the door.

"That would be *Ghost in the Shell*. No, the 'ghost in the machine' is from René Descartes." At his blank look, she elaborated. "'I think, therefore I am'? Which brings to mind a great joke—never mind, I'll get back to that." She ushered him to a seat in what probably would have been a living room in anyone else's house, but was a three-workstation office in hers. And the workstations—they were at least as good as Tom's office computers. Which was saying a lot. His mind kind of boggled as it added up the cost of what he was looking at. The center station, which had three screens that were twenty-one inchers, was the kind of thing a gamer would buy if he'd won the lottery. "Anyway, Decartes was the formulator of the theory of mind-body dualism—the mind is a separate thing from the body, making it the 'ghost' in the corporeal 'machine.' The phrase comes from a critic of his, who wrote a book by the same title. Anyway, that applies here, where according to the fellow you know as jquest77, we seem to have a ghost, or the beginnings of one, in your machine." She sat down in a comfortable-looking office chair, and whirled on its wheels to face him. "So. *Is* that your problem?"

Unwilling to launch straight into his problem, Tom dodged the conversational bullet. "How do you know—"

"Milton? He's one of my tabletoppers." She grinned. "Every other weekend, Saturday from ten to whenever we start to pass out. It's a nasty little habit I picked up in college. The wives are okay with this, because we all explained to them that it is better to have spent twenty bucks and fallen off the low-cholesterol diet twice a month than to have lost the mortgage payment in a poker game and indulged in way too much beer. MMORPGs just don't give me the same kick. I'm the Game Master and I like to see them suffer."

That surprised a bark of a laugh out of him.

"Now as for what I do"—she leaned back in her chair

and steepled her fingers, looking for all the world as if she was only a white cat and a tuxedo short of being a Bond villain—"I solve the problems that happen when mind intersects with machine and stuff crops up that was never coded for. You folks with your carefully crafted worlds, inhabited by thousands of avatars, each one with a brain and a spirit behind it, created more than you guess."

"I'm not sure I follow," Tom said carefully.

She nodded. "I'm not surprised. This sort of thing never occurs to coders. It's just too fantastic. But it does happen, and I will explain, but first I want you to accept—for the moment anyway—something that will sound completely ridiculous."

"Which is?"

"Magic is a real force." She looked at him penetratingly, as if daring him to laugh. He almost did, but stopped himself at the last minute.

She nodded. "Suspend your disbelief and accept it, just for the moment. Remember Occam's Razor; the simplest explanation is always the best, and when you eliminate the impossible, the merely improbable starts to look pretty good. Now, magic has never been a powerful force, except when someone with aptitude, training, and will manages to figure out how to use it. Even then, the results are not always predictable. And it tends to operate on the quantum level, so the smaller the thing you ask it to do, the more likely it is that it will get done. Think you can force the bouncing balls to spell out *your* lottery ticket number?

Won't happen. Especially not when at least a dozen other trained mages are trying to get it to do the same thing, not to mention the thousands who aren't trained but have the talent and the will and are wishing with everything they can drag up on the night. Planning to look into the future to predict what numbers you should pick? Maybe that will work, and maybe not. But there is no such thing as fate and destiny, and the future is infinitely flexible; you're looking into *a* future, one of many, and there is no guarantee that you've picked the right one, where the numbers will match what will come up where *you* are."

Tom snorted. "What good is magic, then," he demanded, "if it can't actually do anything?"

"You're thinking macro. Think micro." She leaned back and waited. He shook his head.

"That which we call 'luck,' my friend, is magic. The deliberate manipulation of tiny actions to bring about the desired goal. The successful mage devotes every day of his life, and every waking minute of every day, to finding the optimal path from where he is to where he wants to be. In short, the goal of his existence is to find the place to put his lever so he can move the world. Micromanagement at its finest. And it doesn't operate well under stress, which is why you won't find any magicians at the World Series of Poker." She grinned at him. He scowled. She laughed and waved a hand at the room around them. "Doubt all you want, my Thomas, but it got me here, and I live a very comfortable lifestyle where I have just enough of everything I want to be happy and just enough of a challenge to keep me sharp."

"So what do you *do* exactly?" he demanded.

She leaned forward. "I find the ghosts in the machines," she said in a sepulchral voice that, despite his annoyance, put goose bumps on his arms. She leaned back again. "There are all kinds of them. Actually, to be honest, I do a lot of other work too—garden-variety ghostbusting, bailing people out of magical situations they can't handle. But what puts the *fromage* on the table and the *pâté* on the *pain*, is, yes, finding stuff that crept into the machine and is lurking outside the code."

Now he did laugh. "Haunted computers? Yeah, right. Okay, so long—" He began to rise to his feet.

She nailed him back into his chair with a look. "Remember what I said about magic being micromanagement? Can you get any more *micro* than electrons? A magician can make those electrons dance for him. The last job I did was for Parks Winterhouse."

His mouth fell open. "The brokerage firm?"

She nodded. "Suppose, just suppose, you could make, not the whole stock market, but just one big board show a stock at a tiny bit higher than what it actually was trading at everywhere else? Then everybody looking at that big board would trade that stock at that higher price. And meanwhile, you're buying the stock elsewhere, or have already bought it, and you've done so at that lower price.

Then you wait for the buyers. And *then*, because one market starts trading the stock at that higher price, pretty soon the entire world just upped the price of the stock."

He nodded slowly. "You'd make a killing."

"No," she corrected. "I would make a profit. A small one. Smart magicians don't draw attention to themselves by making fortunes, at least not all at once. And no one is likely to catch that first artificial price increase because at the end of the day, that number *is* what the stock is really trading at. But sometimes someone notices, knows something about mages, and decides to call in a hired gun, which would be me." She jabbed a thumb at her chest.

"Did you catch him?" Tom asked.

She shook her head. "Magic is harder to trace than a properly spoofed IM running through three dozen proxy servers. So I did the next best thing. I put up magical firewalls. All Parks Winterhouse cared about was that it stopped." He thought he saw annoyance in her eyes as she shrugged. "And after all, even if I caught him, what could they do about it? Go to the board of trade or the SEC and say 'this guy did stock fraud with magic'?"

Tom opened his mouth, then closed it again. "Okay. But how did he do it?"

The muscles around her eyes relaxed a little. "A good question. And one I can answer pretty easily, if you are willing to make the assumption that magic is an energy that can be manipulated by will, and *perhaps* by other things. I say *perhaps* because at the moment, no one in the magic business is entirely sure if the various spells, incantations, and recipes are another way to manipulate the energy, or if they simply serve as tools that allow the magician to hone his concentration to a razor edge. That energy is—fantasy movies notwithstanding—weak, just as I keep telling you. You can't even flip a pair of dice with it. Now, if you got a thousand magicians all trying to do the same thing for the common good, which is a very rare thing indeed, you might be able to pull off something impressive in the real world. It's been done. The storm that wrecked the Spanish Armada, for instance. But it's rare.

"Now tell me, my friend, just what *is* a bit? Forget programming. Think real world. What is it?"

He floundered for a moment. He was so used to thinking in terms of *code* that for a moment the most fundamental definition of programming eluded him. "It's a—state," he said finally. "Kind of a switch in the memory, it's either on or it's off. Either way, that is how information is stored."

"Now think about this. How hard is it to alter that state?" She nodded encouragingly as he felt his eyes widen. "Remember when I told you to think micro? Magic may be weak, but it's strong enough to get in there and flip bit switches very easily. So, now we are in the computer age; important things hinge on a very, very small and weak thing, a bit, a collection of bits, inside something that operates on a quantum level itself. And all those magicians and sorcerers and witches and what have you have discovered that, and they are now trying to figure out the killer app that will put them on easy street."

"And you aren't?" He raised an eyebrow.

"*This* is my killer app." She chuckled and spread her hands to indicate her surroundings. "So far I am the only sheriff on a very wild frontier. As such, the pay is very nice. Now let's get down to business. Since you have come to me, and I am pitching my service, the explanation and initial consultation are free. Actually helping you, however, is not."

He blanched at the thought of trying to explain that sort of expense to upstairs, and blanched again at the idea of trying to pay for it himself. She regarded him with some sympathy.

"Relax, this isn't my first rodeo." She snaked her arm to a folder nestled in beside one terminal and handed it to him. "Here's my CV, tailored to the problem at hand. You'll note I have worked for several of your rivals—all of whom will stoutly deny that I did anything that had the faintest whiff of magic."

He scanned it quickly, with mounting relief. "Ah—what did you do for Worlds of Wonder?"

She laughed. "I made it harder for Chinese gold farmers to use magic."

Every game had a little economy of its own, since there were always rewards to be gained and people who were willing to pay real-world money to get those rewards without having to work for them. So a lucrative business had sprung up in the Far East, comprised of barrackslike buildings full of (mostly) young men who did nothing but play the games all day, eating and sleeping in dormitories owned by the company. In the real world, these players earned a pittance of a wage that was, nevertheless, much more than they could earn at most other jobs. These were the Chinese gold farmers and gaming clans, and they could be absolutely single- and bloody-minded about what they did to get the best loot. Hence, most game companies did what they could to shut the farmers down.

He did a double take. "Ah—wha—?"

"Think micro. The tables you guys use are a lot like the ones that slot machines use to decide the percentage of loot dropped over time. How and when it drops is random. The gold farmers used magic on those tables and skewed when the drops happened—when they were in zone—and the level of the mobs—barely high enough to drop loot. They'd exhaust the zone and move on, and no one would get anything until the time period rotated through . . . and then the Chinese would move in again like a swarm of locusts. In real-world equivalent, they made themselves insanely lucky."

He felt his jaw dropping. "And how did you—"

Ellen's smile turned cruel. "This sheriff doesn't like having the candy taken away from the kids and then sold back to them at inflated prices. And unlike my stocktrader, these guys left a bread-crumb trail I could follow. I put a curse on anyone from a Chinese ISP trying the same trick."

He blinked. "A curse?" How could you—

"In real-world terms, I left a ghost of my own in the machine, a magical watchdog, a permanent thing that waits for their 'scent.' It reverses their parameters, 'poisons' their magic, and makes them insanely *unlucky*. No matter what they try, they get the opposite result from what they want. Instead of getting a ton of loot, they end up on the other end of the bell curve and get nothing, and the mobs spawn as high as possible for the zone, so they're doing twice the work for no reward." She chuckled.

"They weren't very good at sussing out what I did; if they had been, they'd have tried to make themselves unlucky to beat the logic loop. Oh, they tried fifty ways to break the curse without knowing what the curse was or how it worked, then gave up and went back to gold farming the old-fashioned way. Now Worlds of Wonder can deal with them the way it always has." Her smile turned satisfied and lazy—a little like the smile on the face of a sated lioness sitting on what was left of her prey.

"Well, Tom, without actually looking into your setup, that is all I can give you for now. In my professional opinion, you have a problem. I don't know what specifically caused it—yet—so I can't tell you how to fix it. A single player or a group of players might be trying to sabotage you or it might be something entirely different. Taking the servers down for a reboot won't clear it. For free, I'll tell you that you might try to change the Wendigo code. I think all your problems center on it. Also for free, I'll tell you that I don't think it will let you, because to me all of this points to something that isn't player interference."

"And if I can't change the code?" Despite all the weird shit she had thrown at him, Ellen seemed to know her stuff, and . . . if you suspended disbelief and added "magic" to all the quantum forces there were out there, well . . . it would make sense that something could be mucking around with Dark Valley by skewing tables in a way Tom couldn't see because he wasn't looking at them at the time they were being skewed, in real time, he was looking at them the way they had been programmed. . . .

And how reverse Schrödinger's Cat was that? The act of looking at the tables in real time meant that they would not be changed. . . .

"If you are still in trouble, then find a way to bring me in as a consultant." Again, her eyes twinkled. "If you need to, get Milton to round up his buddies to avalanche bug reports. Nothing the management likes less than more justifiable complaints than they can clear." She got up then, and in response, Tom pushed himself up out of his chair, which reacted with a sigh of its pneumatic shocks. It wasn't just an ordinary office chair, it was a top-of-the-line office chair, and that was just for the visitors. He considered the cost of everything in this one room alone, not just the computer hardware, and sucked on his lower lip.

Either she was a world-class fraud who had pulled the wool over the eyes of some pretty smart people or—

Or she could do what she said she could do.

No way to tell for sure. People paid good money to be defrauded all the time. Computer and business professionals were not immune to being hoodwinked.

He trudged back down the stairs. By the time he reached the bottom, he had decided that he was going to try her suggestion first. Change the code on the Wendigo. He could justify that easily enough, given that it was spawning in safe zones. Maybe the Wendigo code, with its new powers, was interacting with the AI in an unpredictable way.

And if it wasn't?

Right now, that wasn't something he wanted to think about.

"Well, mistress, do you think he will be back?"

Ell quirked an eyebrow at her AIBO, that charming and quirky little robot dog that was the hot adult toy so many years back. This one was the honey-colored version, which she had hacked extensively and given a voder that she'd programmed to sound like the robot dog in the Doctor Who series. All this so that her familiar could move into it. What, after all, was a witch without a familiar?

Familiars were a power source for really expert magicians, since they could tap into arcane energies that were to ordinary magic power what a power station was to a triple A battery. Traditionally, a familiar inhabited the body of a live animal—anything from a toad to a lion, though usually a cat. But Ell was allergic to fur, and besides, she was a techno-shaman, so she had set Tobermarle (Toby for short) up in the AIBO.

But she wasn't going to tell Quiet Knight she had exactly that kind of bang-stick at her disposal. She had no intentions of telling any client any more than she needed to. Because ninety-nine times out of a hundred, when someone was mucking with the bits, you weren't going to be dealing with an adept with a familiar, you were going to be dealing with some slacker who had the talent for magic and enough code savvy to get clever.

"I think that by now, he's decided that his suspension of disbelief has run out, and he's going to try to forget everything I told him. He's going to try to reprogram the Wendigo, and that's either going to work or not. If not, he'll piss it off. And if he pisses it off, it will probably do something so egregious that even the big guns at his firm will notice." She turned to her keyboard and monitor and did a quick-and-dirty search to find out just who was who at MWO. "The really big gun would be Mark Taylor, the CEO, who pretty much invented this game. Huh, nice to see the initial developer still in the driver's seat. That'll make things easier when they call me in desperation."

"Shall I run a probability analysis on that, mistress?" Toby's cute little robot head went up and down eagerly.

"Yeah, and factor in any magical traces you can find on the game servers." She Wi-Fi-beamed him the server addresses and waited while Toby did his thing. He didn't rely on his own processors, of course. He was Wi-Fi-linked to her server, and thus to every Wi-Fi-capable machine in the flat. "I want to know if it's players or something really alive in the code." She went back to pruning her stock portfolio.

"Oh, dear."

That got her attention, the way a smoke alarm going off got her attention. "That's a little like hearing a surgeon say 'oops,' Toby."

"There is extensive magical activity on the servers, mistress. And . . ." Toby paused. "And the sort of trace associated with an attempt to manifest. It is not outside interference, mistress. I believe you would be wise to research the mythological attributes of the Wendigo. I calculate the likelihood of you being called back at ninety-eight point nine percent."

Ellen blinked. "And the probability of manifestation?"

Toby made a distressed noise. "Sixty-seven point two and rising."

"Rats. I'm on it." This called for the hard copy library, the things you just did not put on a computer because of the danger of someone somehow accessing what you put there. There really *were* some things man was not meant to know— or at least, things that were best only in the hands and heads of the (relatively) pure of heart and intention. Although she did have every book she owned backed up in image files on a hard drive and DVDs in three different bank vaults. Just in case. Because in her line of work, there was always the chance you'd be jumping out of your own window with your familiar tucked under your arm one day.

She just hoped that day wasn't looming on the horizon.

Tom faced his fellow devs—the four that hadn't left for the holidays—and prepared to tell them he was going to castrate their baby. "I've got good news and bad news," he said, the classic opener. "The good news is, I brought donuts. The bad news is I'm gonna have to nerf the Wendigo."

Tom listened to the groans around the informal conference table with sympathy. His baby in this zone—some of the door quests—were running as expected, given the slight glitches that always showed up with new maps. But these four had all worked on the Wendigo, and now—

"Look, I understand," he told them. "And I'm not taking it down. I'm just nerfing it. I'm no-oping the hunger code."

"Ah, bugger that, Tom!" Sean was from the UK, London, a West Ender, and it showed. When there was no one around who mattered he dressed like the punk rocker he'd been before he became a code head. "Come *on*, the hunger code is what makes the Wendigo the Wendigo! Nerf that and it's just another Boss!"

"That's the point, the hunger code is the only thing about it that's new, and it's not acting up on Test." He ran his hand over the top of his head nervously. "It has to be the hunger code acting unpredictably with the increased load on the game servers. I can no-op the code and have it ready to load with the regular outage tomorrow." He didn't mention that he already had the go from management, who were not happy with triple the justifiable complaints from the shiny new zone.

Sean groaned. The other three shrugged. "We can put it back in later," Tom promised.

"Yer makin' it so damn easy to defeat it's gonna be an exploit," Sean said bitterly. "And what's the bloody point of that?"

"So I take it out of the rare treasure table. At least until I put the hunger code back in."

"Sounds fair to me," said Kathy, who was in charge of landscape architecture. The other two nodded. Sean moaned, but did not make any further protests. Tom left them with the box of donuts and hustled off to load the nerf on Test and make sure it didn't break anything else. And to write patch notes for the rare folks that actually *read* the damned things, making it clear that this was a temporary situation and that as soon as possible the Wendigo would be back to its old slaughtering self.

By the time he left for home that night, he was positive that the nerf wasn't going to break anything, and reasonably convinced that this was the solution to the Wendigo's unreasonable behavior. Maybe even to the problem with the rest of the zone; sometimes code interacted strangely, sometimes there was a runaway process that went trampling all over other code. Usually that just crashed the zone, but—

Well, it still made more sense than some "spook in the server." When he headed for the office in the morning he was completely convinced that this "techno-shaman" was off her rocker and somehow pulling a scam on everyone gullible enough to believe her. He waited for the end of the normal downtime impatiently, and the moment the first server was up for final checks, he logged in his god-mode avatar at the Trading Post, figuring he would wait for the Wendigo to spawn—

And found himself staring up at the Wendigo's ugly face.

Inside the Trading Post safe zone.

It grinned at him, stomped his avatar flat, sucked all the health out of him, and left him planted on the ground, as it lumbered away in search of more victims.

The nerf wasn't in.

Except that it was. According to the code, it was. According to the Wendigo, it wasn't.

By midmorning, everyone knew. There was the kind of silence in the place that you usually only got at funerals— the kind of funeral where at least half of those attending are pretty sure the corpse is going to jump out of the coffin and start eating brains in the next fifteen minutes.

By lunchtime the entire team was sweating, because everyone had tried nerfing the Wendigo. The server went down. The patch went in. The server came up. The patch was gone.

The servers still weren't up. The natives were getting restless, complaints flooding the boards. The forum trolls were, as Sean put it, "going for the gold in whinging." As the Wendigo once again bypassed every god-mode protection and stomped Tom's avatar into a thin film on its filthy sole for the umpteenth time while the crowd around him watched, things suddenly went *that kind* of quiet.

Slowly, Tom turned around. Mark Taylor was watching, face unreadable, arms crossed over his chest.

"Servers are still down," he said in a neutral tone.

Tom nodded.

"Players aren't happy."

Again Tom nodded.

"If we bring them up without the nerf are things going to be any worse than they were yesterday?" he asked, coming straight to the point.

Tom shook his head.

"Fine. Write new stuff for the patch notes and the forums. Tell people that the new zone is unexpectedly dangerous and that until we tweak it, there's going to be a lot of planting. Then let them play." He looked around at his dev and design team, or those bits of it that weren't off getting whatever version of Christmas spirit floated their boats. "There are thirty-six zones in this game that aren't acting like this. If people still want to go into the thirty-seventh after being cautioned, that's their privilege." He rubbed the side of his face wearily, and it occurred to Tom that he must have been aware all along of how bad the problem was. And that he—Mark Taylor, CEO, signature character Johnny Worldwalker—had been burning as much midnight oil as Tom had. "What the hell, it'll give some of those hard-asses who are always complaining that the game's too easy something to smack their heads against. Bring 'em up. Bring 'em all up. You"—he pointed to Sean—"go write the patch notes. You"—this time it was Kathy—"go throw the forum trolls their meat. And you, Tom—"

Tom winced.

"I had a look at the CV for that consultant you were talking to. And I made some calls. Go down to Personnel, pick up the contract for her—it's already signed—and hand deliver it. Then escort her here."

Tom blinked at him, certain he hadn't heard what he *thought* he had just heard.

"Chop-chop!" Mark Taylor said sharply. Tom jumped to his feet and hit the ground running. He hadn't heard that tone in Mark's voice since the day some idiot with a backhoe on the East Coast cut through one of the major fiber-optic Net trunks and left the East Coast servers virtually unreachable for most of the player base.

Oh, my God, was all he could think, over and over again. *Oh, my God. Mark hired a loony. Or Mark hired a witch. And I don't know which it is. What's next, a voodoo doctor?*

Maybe, he thought, as he headed for his car in the parking garage, contract and NDA safely in the briefcase that Laura in Personnel had helpfully supplied him with, *I had better lay in a supply of chickens and goats*. . . .

The loony—or witch—brought an overnight bag with her. Tom was impressed with her dedication. At least she was serious. She was prepared to pull at least one all-nighter.

He mentioned that in the car on the way back. She gave him an opaque look out of those changeable sea-green eyes. "Of course I'm serious. This is your livelihood, the livelihood of—how many people? From the mailroom to server maintenance to Mark Taylor. Best-case scenario, this is something I can track down and nail down fast, so that no one is aware of anything more than a long maintenance outage. Players don't bitch and moan any more than usual, and nothing affects your income."

"You know what this is?" he asked hopefully.

She shrugged. "I have some theories. I'll brief your team when we get there. We'll be doing a lot of stuff on one or more of the live servers. I promise not to crash it."

"Worse-case scenario?" He looked at the street straight ahead of him.

"I have some theories. And some plans. And I hope that I don't have to tell you about them. If I do, it means things will have gone astonishingly pear-shaped, and we'll be worrying about something more than a loss of income stream."

Uh, that was reassuring.

"Taylor—"

"Already scheduled as soon as I get there. I will spend one hour with Taylor, no more. Then I meet with you devs and designers and him. And you think I'm a loony, don't you?" He didn't take his eyes off the road, but her bluntness startled him, and he caught the edge of her sardonic smile from the corner of his eye. "I had you convinced while you were in my office, and the moment you walked away, that started eroding. Don't worry about it, it's perfectly normal and the usual reaction. You won't believe again until you see what I do in action. And you will see—provided you can give me a real-time trace on your Wendigo." She paused. "It knows you're aware of it now. I don't think you'll be seeing it despawn on its own anymore."

Tom bit back his first response, which was that it had to, it was written in the code that it despawn after a certain period of time. But it wasn't behaving the way the code said it would. And—

"It's aware of us? You don't mean it's self-aware?" He shook his head. "Okay, you *are* loony, that's just not possible—"

"It's not possible for mere code," she corrected patiently. "But what you have is only shaped by the code, it's not confined by the code anymore. It's—but I'm getting ahead of myself. I want all of you to hear this, so I don't have to repeat myself." At that moment, he turned into the parking garage and, frustratingly, she clammed up.

Ell vanished into Taylor's office for a bit more than the hour she had predicted. Meanwhile, Tom was busy explaining what it was she supposedly did, and laying out what of her theory that he could remember. Which wasn't as much as he thought, and he was making a muddle of it when he and his team were summoned to the big conference room.

He half expected Mark Taylor to be in there alone. And he wasn't sure just what Mark's reaction was going to be to all this *X Files* stuff. But there Ellen was, in the chair at Taylor's right, looking like Wolf the Fixer from *Pulp Fiction*, and with that same air of being able to get the job done. They both waited while the other five filed in, then Ellen got up and shut the door.

She turned to face them with a disarming smile. Today the wild mane of red curls was pulled back into a ponytail, and she wore what looked like a standard business suit—but it was made of denim and there was a tank top underneath the suit jacket.

Taylor folded his hands atop a stack of papers. "I'll warn you all, this is going to sound delusional. But every time you start to think about locking us up, think back to what the Wendigo is doing and ask yourself if there is a so-called sane and rational explanation for *that*."

He said "us." So he believes her . . . holy guacamole.

295

With that for an introduction, Ellen went into her song and dance routine. But this time either Tom paid more attention, or she added some detail, because it all started to make even more sense than it had the first time.

"I've had a look at your bible for this zone," she said at last. She looked pained. "On the one hand, I have to say, well done when it comes to doing your research. But on the other . . . *oy*. I wish you guys had been a little less thorough."

"What do you mean?" Kathy asked, looking puzzled.

"Because you were thorough and very accurate, you have tapped into some ancient archetypes, which means . . . which means, in a very Jungian sense, that the whole is far, far more than the sum of its parts. You took the architecture of the zone from extant buildings, with terrain and landscape you re-created from real places. And as for your enemies—" Her brow creased as she thought before she said anything else. "Well . . . our buddy the Wendigo, for instance. You've basically built a mythago there, because you adhered so faithfully to the Native American descriptions."

"What's a 'mythago'?" Tom asked.

"It's a term invented by Robert Holdstock to describe idealized mythic images come to life." She shook her head. "In retrospect, I should have guessed this day was going to come. The more realistic you make games, the more people believe in them as they play them. If any of your players have untapped magical ability, the more they believe, the more of that gets invested in the reality of the game. You have a huge game; even a tiny percentage adds up to a lot of actual players that have magical ability. It's a positive feedback thing. You'll see it in people who are insanely lucky in the game; they believe in their character, believe it is unstoppable, and to an extent, especially when there are no other players around with conflicting beliefs, they influence the game in their favor. Remember, it's all bit switches, and those are easy if you have the talent for magic. Even if you don't know that you have it, or that you're doing it." She started to run her hand through her hair, then stopped. "So when you devs add things into the game that lots of people have believed in, not only in the here and now but in the past, all that magical pressure keeps things tweaked in that direction. And then, when you code in something that people believed in for centuries . . . you get a mythago."

"Belief can be very powerful," Taylor said unexpectedly. "Powerful enough to create things in the real world. I'm not surprised it can create something in cyberspace."

Ell nodded. "Now I *think*—I hope—that the reason your patches haven't taken and the thing keeps resetting is because it is a mythago and not"—she hesitated, then said—"not something else. It's being reset by the collective belief in it, embedded in the matrix of accurate description. In essence, because of that pressure of belief, you've made self-repairing code. It can't not be cannibalistic, it can't lose that game power, because that's what a Wendigo *is*, and making it otherwise would be making it into something that was not a Wendigo. Like memory plastic always returns to the shape it was cast in. Does that make sense?"

Erik, the dev who designed the Wendigo, sighed. "As much as anything does about this situation."

Ellen turned her attention back to Tom. "So, now I have a question. Just how defeatable is the Wendigo, right this minute?"

He shrugged. "It can be done . . . it just takes a lot of people. I think you'll need five full teams at least, eight for sure, and about half an hour. Most people aren't willing to invest that much time and effort in defeating a Boss. You can do a quest in the same time for a lot more loot."

"So let's make it worth their time." She turned her attention back to Mark Taylor. "How terrible would it be to your game economy to make it really worth defeating this thing? Make sure that until we get this solved everyone on every team that takes down one of the manifestations gets a really sweet drop? Much gold, much experience, and everybody gets a goody."

Taylor made his "thinking" face. "If it's short term . . . the problem is that the gold farmers and the power gamers will be on it like white on rice . . ."

"And for once, is this a bad thing?" she retorted. "Let them be useful for a change. While they're swarming it, it won't be bothering your regular players. And we want to make sure that the reward compensates them for the inevitable faceplants."

"She has a point," Kathy agreed.

"The loot is not an intrinsic part of the mythago, so I am pretty sure it won't reset every time you try to load it with the enhanced tables." Ell patted the zone bible. "Meanwhile I can look at what you did in detail, so I can figure out what is going on with the rest of the zone as well as how to un-mythago it." She paused and looked at Tom. "And I may ask you to log in an avatar in god-mode so I can do a real-time trace or a code capture on it when it squashes you."

He winced. The way the thing looked past his avatar and straight at the screen still gave him the creeps, and he wasn't too happy about having that experience again. "Why me?"

"I thought it was obvious." When he shook his head, she shrugged. "Simple. We won't have to wait around for it to spawn; when you log in, it will spawn right then and there. It recognizes you the same way that a cat recognizes the shape of a snake, on an instinctive level. It knows you for an enemy. It's watching for you; it'll spawn on top of you. Because it hates you."

"Why are we doing this again?" Tom looked unhappy about logging in Quiet Knight, and to be honest, Ell couldn't blame him. There was a reason why the Wendigo responded to him. He didn't know it, but he was magic sensitive. Whether or not he actually could use magic was another question, but he had pegged the Wendigo from the moment he logged in to look at it as something that was not operating by the rules he expected, and somehow the Wendigo recognized that. Maybe it too was sensitive to magic and magicians.

The real question here was this—was the Wendigo reacting the way a "normal" mythago would, like an invertebrate that has a crude ability to "learn" but has no real brain? Was it *only* that it was sensitive to magic and reacted accordingly? That was what she hoped. Because the alternative could be very nasty indeed. If it actually was able to think . . .

"We're doing this so I can take snapshots of the Wendigo code and compare it to what it's supposed to be," she replied patiently. "You haven't done a real-time trace or a live capture yet. You haven't *got* real-time trace on your live servers, so I am going to have to depend on captures. Some of the things the Wendigo is doing are not in the code or the mythos, like critting you in god-mode. I want to see how it's doing that." She very much wanted to see that, in fact. Nothing in the myths suggested that the Wendigo had that sort of ability to neutralize another's powers. This one had been coded pretty faithfully from the Ojibwa version of the myth, in which all of its abilities were strictly those of any gigantic creature—immense strength, the power of sheer size, and the game equivalent of "devouring" what it "killed."

Tom nodded, but he was looking a bit green.

"Look, all you need to do is let it plant you, then just log out or rez back in the town and log. The player mobs will pounce it as soon as someone broadcasts that it's spawned." She patted his shoulder; in his shoes she would be just as reluctant. He was feeling every bit of the thing's malevolence, didn't understand why, and the bottom had fallen out of his universe. Poor fellow. His world had been rational and run by numbers up until this moment. She wished there was time to have him talk to Jin Lee. Jin had been a code monkey first and only came into magic later. Maybe she should do that when this was all over.

Nah. He'll probably want to forget all about it. On the other hand, if he didn't . . . yeah. Take him to Lee.

"Okay. Here goes nothing . . ." He selected his avatar and logged in—she began taking captures as fast as she could mash the macro button that allowed her to take a hundred "snapshots" in the time it would take a human to grab one. You could never do this with most gaming machines, the buffers would fill up before you could store to memory. But this was as good as her machine at home. It was a good thing she was using that level of machine and macro too, because the Wendigo spawned inhumanely fast, and she only had time for one set of captures as it spawned, one set of captures as it planted Quiet Knight, absorbing his hit points and health as it did so, and one set as it shambled off.

"Bastard," Tom muttered, and looked on grimly as swarms of gold farmers and power gamers descended so fast you would have thought someone had yelled "free beer" in the parking lot of a football stadium on game day. Then again, in a sense, someone had. Even people who don't normally read patch notes are going to sit up and take notice when you announce you've superbuffed a reward instead of nerfing it.

Ellen claimed her dumps, then remote accessed her own computers and IMed Toby. Fortunately she had cleared this beforehand with Mark Taylor, saying merely that she had a code analyst back in her office. He didn't have to know what Toby was, after all—and she was rather certain that hauling in an AIBO that sounded like K-9 was not going to win her sanity points. There was such a thing as suspension of disbelief—and there was such a thing as hanging it by the neck until it was dead.

Yes, mistress? came the reply in the chat box. Toby could plug in via a USB port and "talk" directly into chat and documents.

Isolate the Wendigo and Quiet Knight from the dumps, then run comparison in time. Message me if you find anything.

Yes, mistress! She uploaded the dumps to her server and went back to work, looking at the background of the zone in detail. Because the thing was, if this was something more than a mythago, it was going to be doing more than keeping itself intact and acting out the mythic tales. It was going to have desires and it was going to act on them. And there would be something it might very well want.

Out.

There was a pressure of unbelief in magic as well as a pressure of belief. That was why you didn't see a lot of real magic operating in the modern world, even from people like her, who had familiars and access to a lot more oomph than your average talent. The counterpressure was simple; far more people disbelieved in it than believed, and an equal percentage of talents were disbelievers. That was why the old gods and spirits rarely appeared anymore; how could they, when the greater numbers of the talented disbelieved in them so strongly?

But allowing a mythago to appear in an online game changed all that. Now the Wendigo had a huge audience that were being made to believe in him, an audience that invested all of its time and concentration in living through this game while they were in it. Even the power gamers who were only interested in beating the game as fast as possible and getting the most loot on the way "lived" in it to a certain extent. There was a piece of the subconscious that believed, strongly, in the reality of what was on the monitor. Perhaps for the power gamers that was even more true, because they would spend every free hour in that game. In a month, they might be on to another game, but while they were here, they ate, slept, and breathed MWO. What the Wendigo was doing now was reinforcing this . . . and if he could find a way, and the energy, to free himself from the computer, he would have that to empower him. . . .

She put the brakes on her imagination. Best not to hatchet that count before it had chickened. Look through the world book first.

Unfortunately, looking through the world book and comparing it side by side to her own research did not make her any happier.

The design team had chosen the most powerful and dangerous of the Wendigo descriptions and had been absolutely faithful to it. This Wendigo could move faster than any human; it was able to seize its prey before the hapless victim was even aware it was there. That tallied with it being able to spawn in without warning to plant someone. The more it devoured, the more powerful it became; that was certainly happening, although as yet the limitations of the game itself were keeping it from going completely out of control. There was only so much processing power that a Boss could take up, and that was partly what was saving it from growing until it hit the zone "ceiling" and wiping everything in the zone.

Hmm. There was another idea. Could they put a further limiter on it? It would have to be something not in the Wendigo code, but imposed from outside. Limit the processing cycles on all Bosses? No, that didn't seem practical . . .

All right; according to the world book, it's coded so that it loses what it absorbs over time. The myth kind of implies the same, since the Ojibwa Wendigo never turns into Attack of the

Fifty Foot Zombie. *So we can limit it by limiting how much it can absorb from the victims. But that will have to be imposed from outside . . .*

Back she went to her own research, this time into Ojibwa magic. *Got it.* This had to be fast and dirty, but it was solid, should be easy to code and fit the myth.

Who handled Temp Powers? She checked the world book again. Kevin. She left the workstation she'd taken over from some lucky, lucky vacationing coder and went in search of Kevin.

She found him studying the world book himself, with a window open on a view of Dark Valley on one of his monitors and a worried look on his face. He looked up when he heard her footstep.

"How long will it take you to design up and load a Temp Power?" she asked. "Autogive it to everyone who zones in, take it away when they zone out. Blocks the Wendigo from absorbing their health and hit points. Make it look like a cowrie shell, and *call* it an Ojibwa cowrie." She thought a little more. "Think you can give me an NPC that looks like a Native American and call him Ojibwa Medicine Man? Have him 'give' the cowrie to the players?"

"Uh—" Kevin began, obviously caught flat-footed by her questions.

"As fast as you can," she said, as her phone chimed with the *Stargate* theme—she was being texted, and that could only be Toby. She checked.

Results, mistress.

She sprinted back to her workstation. Behind her, Kevin reached for his keyboard.

"All right, folks, gather 'round," Ellen said. It was close to midnight and the pile of empty pizza boxes by the trash can testified that none of them had gone home yet. Even Mark Taylor was there; he was sitting in the back, and staying quiet, but the fact that the boss was still in the trenches was heartening to the whole team. She had a projector in demo-mode hooked to her notebook computer. "Code monkeys to the front, I want you to see this. Here are my snapshots of the code. Here's Tom"—she pointed to the right-hand section of the side-by-side capture—"and Wendigo on the left. Now, this highlighted section is Tom's god-mode powers. This snapshot is where the Wendigo first spawned. And here it is a moment later. Tom and the Wendigo."

"Haven't you got that reversed?" asked Kathy, looking at where the highlighted code suddenly appeared on the left-hand stack.

Ellen shook her head, and waited for them to grasp what had just happened.

Tom got it first. "He *stole my code?*" he sputtered in a tone of complete outrage.

Ellen nodded. "He snatched it off you, just like taking

your knife or club away from you. Now here's the next difference. Toby tells me that this"—she indicated a section
that had been highlighted in another color—"means your
powers were no-oped, nulled out. Which is why Wendigo
could crit you. In effect, he stole your club and whacked
you unconscious, then kicked the bejeezus out of you. And
here is the last snapshot, after you were planted." The
god-mode code was back where it belonged, on Tom's
Quiet Knight, and his powers were turned back on again.
"And if we hadn't been taking millisecond by millisecond
captures of the code, we would never have seen it happen."

"How can—this thing is—" Kathy's voice faded. Ellen
knew what she wanted to say, *How can it do that? It's just
a piece of code.* If Mark Taylor was Fox Mulder in this
little scenario, Kathy was definitely Dana Scully. But she
couldn't argue with her own eyes. The god-mode code
had jumped from Quiet Knight to the Wendigo and back
again. It was there in black and white.

There was silence. It was one thing for her to talk
about magic acting to flip bit switches. It was quite another for them to see the evidence in a form they couldn't
argue with. "But why didn't it keep the code?" Kathy said
finally.

"Because, thank the god or goddess of your choice, it
can't. The mythic Wendigo can't absorb powers, it only
gets *strength* and *size* from the people it eats. The mythago
is coded essentially the same way. To try and keep a power
it steals would be violating its coding *and* its own mythos,

and that could destroy it." She pulled her hair out of the clip and ran her hands through it. "Makes me very, very grateful for that limiter. Kevin, how's the dingus coming?"

"Already on the test server and working fine. It'll go in on the morning outage." Kevin beamed at her.

"Well done. Now, my second question. Have you lot been watching the Wendigo? Paying attention to what it's doing?"

They all nodded. Ellen took a deep breath of pizza-flavored air. "And?"

The exchange of glances around the table told the tale. None of them wanted to say it out loud, but . . .

"It's learning." Tom broke the silence. "More than the AI should be able to, that is. It learns who is the most dangerous to it, and the next time, it zeroes right in on that person and tries to plant him first."

She nodded. "Hence, Kevin's dingus—it's a Temp Power that will at least keep it from absorbing the strength of the people it plants. Your own code and the myth will make it lose that power over time. We can't starve it out, because it still has its basic strength no matter what, you already know we can't weaken it because it won't take a patch, but we can keep it from getting any stronger. And that will buy us some time." She rubbed her sore eyes. "As for the rest of the zone, Toby is still looking things over. My thought, though, is that the mythago is operating not only when it spawns, but when it's despawned too, by altering the spawn-tables for the other zone monsters, making them harder than they should be to defeat. I don't know why it's doing that—but we are dead certain this is what is happening."

Mark Taylor let out his breath; until then, none of them had been aware he was holding it. "All right, Ellen. Can we do anything else before the morning outage?"

She shook her head.

"All right then." He looked around the table. "All of you, go home. You've gone above and beyond and there is nothing we can do for now. Get some rest while you can."

She saw the relief on their faces. They had been expecting to pull an all-nighter.

Well, that still might happen, but right now . . . she needed more research. And it was not the sort of thing she could explain to any of these people.

"I'll see you all in the morning" was all she said.

On the one hand, Tom would have liked to stay. He hated leaving problems unsolved.

On the other hand, he knew a campaign when he saw one, and this had just been the opening skirmish. Though he'd had one hell of a jolt when Mark Taylor had called the consultant by her first name. Mark didn't do that with anyone he didn't consider to be a peer.

Damn. Now he wished he'd been the proverbial fly on the wall for *that* conversation.

That had been nearly as much of a jolt as when he'd seen with his own eyes how ownership of the god-mode code had flipped from Quiet Knight to Wendigo and back again. No matter how much she'd babbled about flipping bit switches, it hadn't been *real* to him until that moment.

"Skynet became self-aware at 2:14 A.M. EDT August 29, 1997," he thought to himself, as he headed for his car, and felt a chill running down the back of his neck. Okay, so the thing in there probably wasn't self-aware at all, just doing a convincing simulation. And even if it *was* self-aware, it was—what had she called it?—a mythago, a spirit thing . . .

He realized he was glad, *damned* glad, they hadn't built that animatronic Wendigo for the trade shows. Somewhere in the dim, dark recesses of his memory stirred vague images of a sci-fi thing, maybe a made-for-TV movie, about an evil sentient AI that jumped into someone's animatronic monster, and he shuddered.

Okay, it would have been tethered by an umbilical of cables five inches around, but still . . .

It's not an AI, it's not an AI, he kept reminding himself. *It's not self-aware. No code is self-aware.* No, it was something else, some malevolent haunt that was using their code to write itself a new life. Something that had invaded their servers from outside. They just had to find a way to exorcise it.

He wondered, was it a bunch of mini-Wendigos, separate mythagos, or was it a single entity spread out across all the servers? If it was the former, they could take it out server by server, but if it was the latter, they'd have to eradicate it across all of them at the same time. There wasn't supposed to be a connection across all the servers, but technically there was. The global chat system let players talk across servers to their friends and the bug reporting system also linked all the servers. If the Wendigo was a kind of ghost spread out in pieces across the servers, it could communicate through either of those systems without a lot of trouble. And that meant it could probably find a way to hide itself somewhere they wouldn't think to look for it when they started taking it out. He worried at the problem all the way back to his apartment, where he logged onto chat just long enough to catch Bev and let her know the vague outline of Major Problem at Work.

Heard the new zone was giving you fits, came the reply. Bless Bev, bless her for typing articulate sentences. Having to deal with l33tkidz who texted everything, leaving him to try to decipher what the hell the trouble log was about, made him deeply appreciate anyone who knew how to string nouns and verbs together properly. *No worries. When you put the baby to bed, I'll claim a steak dinner off you.*

He grinned, despite the current worries. *With all the trimmings,* he replied. *Night, babe.*

Her icon went inactive and he was about to log off when jquest77 pinged him. *Thought you might want to know, there's a couple of Chinese gaming clans getting waxed by the Wendigo over on Topaz server. Did you hire Ellen?*

He blinked. *Yeah, why?*

Good. We're not just gaming buddies, Ell and me.

No duh. There was no chance jquest77 *(and I know your real name, Milton!)* could have known just what Ellen did for a living if they were "just" gaming buddies. But now he was curious, so he asked the leading question. *Really? How so?*

I work for the DoD.

For a moment, he thought jquest77 had typed D *and* D, for the game . . . but no. Jquest77 was a precise guy and rarely mistyped. DoD. Department of Defense? Tom blinked again. What—

We go back a long ways, college, in fact, and I was just as skeptical as you when she first told me what she does. Then— well, let's just say that it's a good thing there's a black budget for things like this, or Congress would be having litters of kittens right now. When this is over, I'll tell you the story of how she exorcized a stealth fighter. Right now, get some sleep. You're gonna need it.

Jquest77's icon went inactive.

Tom stared at the screen for a long time before finally flagging himself as inactive. It was not going to be an easy night.

"Mistress, this could be very dangerous." Toby's prim little voice did not properly reflect the amount of anxiety the familiar was feeling right now. Ell didn't blame him. She was feeling a fair amount of stress herself.

"I know it is, but this is the only way to get the information firsthand," she replied. "Magic traces are not going to show up in the machine the way they will truly be acting in the game world. And our ugly friend is investing himself in the game world right now. I need a first person viewpoint."

The AIBO pawed at its ear. "I do not like it, I do not like it at all. But I concur, mistress. Please be careful."

Careful; oh yes, she was going to be careful. She'd done this with animals before but never with something that only lived inside a computer. And she was going to be helpless here, Toby was going to be the puppet master. For this run, anyway. If she needed to do this again, she'd find a way to be more than just a passenger.

Tom had set her up with an endgame character, as high as you could go, with all of the bells and whistles, just short of actually having god-mode. She'd had him leave it outside the portal into Dark Valley. Best to get used to this in a safe zone first.

Here goes nothing.

She logged in her avatar; an elfy-looking chick armed with sword and dagger, chest as flat as you could get it in the character generator and still be female, and costumed to have the least amount of skin showing. The last thing she needed right now was hormonal teenyboppers hitting on her avatar. Tom had also set her up with some temporary weapons, the sort of loot that would only last a few days or a bunch of uses. Hers were all distance weapons; properly run, this little flower was lethality on two legs.

She'd asked Tom to program the avatar so that its combat moves autofired if anything unfriendly got within range. If anything got close, barring the Wendigo, of course, it would be coleslaw. You weren't supposed to automate more than one move, but that's what devs are for, right?

She'd told him it was because she wasn't used to hack and slash, but she'd lied—in the real world she'd been doing reenactment and stage fighting since she was in her teens. It was so that all Toby had to do was steer; AIBO paws were not good for mashing buttons.

Note to self; hack the little shite some hands.

All right, there was Stevie the Elf and here she was, and it was showtime.

Ellen drew on Toby's energy and murmured the mnemonic for spirit transfer at the same time that she sketched the pattern in the air with the special new twist that should send her—

She found herself sitting on her very shapely ass, looking up at a flat blue sky with painterly clouds scudding across it. It looked less real than a ceiling painting, especially because she was seeing it in a kind of double vision. Ghosted under the sky was . . . code. Machine language, which meant it would take her a while to decipher, but she had a good idea what it was she was looking at—the code that specified what the sky was, what the ceiling was (so a flying character didn't find himself outside the zone), how the clouds moved and in what directions, what color everything was . . .

In short . . . the sky.

She was fairly relieved that she didn't actually *feel* anything other than enough to give her a kinesthetic sense of where her limbs were. That was good. If something started shooting at her, she really did not want to be feeling pain. . . .

In fact, she felt a curious disconnect. She felt no weight, felt no pressure of any sort on her skin. Every moment of every day, a human being was aware, if not consciously, of all the little adjustments that had to be made, the feedback from skin and gut and muscle and nerve, things that registered wellness or illness, the downward pressure of gravity. Everything had a scent, and though your conscious might not register it, your subconscious did.

But not now. Ell felt nothing. Nothing had an odor. There was no taste of anything in her mouth. There was none of that. She had done sensory deprivation once, and even that was not like this. She had sight and hearing and body sense.

Hmm.

Suddenly, without warning, her body leapt to its feet and spun around in a deadly circle of steel. She didn't register that something was attacking her until her two blades had already marked the attacker and deflected a knife. *Black clothing, head wrap, Oriental eyes, and katana. Great. Why are the game ninjas after me?*

Even while she was thinking this, her body was moving in on the NPC, a ninja that was probably something generated by the computer to make her life exciting.

All right, there's no two ways about this, she thought, as her body executed the patterns in the macros as mechanically as the ninja was executing its own macros. Which was fine going against something the AI was running, but the Wendigo was not in the AI. *I am going to have to have full in-game control next time I do this. If I go up against a living Wendigo, or the blasted Wendigo figures out how to flip the Player versus Player switches to let the hypercaffeinated crowd into Dark Valley, I would be in deep kim—*

OW!

The ninja's attack "got through"—that is, the computer had added up his ability to hit with her ability to defend, with a skew on the ninja's side to allow for chance, and she had been found wanting. And it *hurt!* This might be a Rated-T-For-Teen game, with no gore allowed, but the character reacted with animation indicating pain, and she by deity *felt* it.

Crap crap crap crap . . . that's not supposed to happen!

It hurt *badly,* the way an inch-deep katana swipe would hurt in the real world. Instead of blood, she was bleeding health, more bits being flipped in the code, but if she could have screamed, she would have, and for a moment the pain blinded her. She hadn't signed on for this . . .

Too late. She was signed on, and anyway, this wasn't one she could just walk away from. Not if things got out of hand here. She didn't dare walk out and take the chance that they wouldn't.

Fortunately two things happened. One, Toby managed to figure out how to access her self-healing spell, so the invisible (No gore! This game is rated T for Teen!) gash across her arm stopped hurting and she stopped leaking health. Two, the macros finally beat the ninja; he collapsed like a rag doll at her feet and a moment later faded away into that never-never land where all defeated things went.

It was a heckuva way to be introduced to life-in-the-game-world.

"All right, Toby, let's zone into Dark Valley. And remember to toggle invisibility cloak when we get there." She spoke out loud, but of course she heard nothing but the sound effects from this zone. What she said would appear in the onscreen chat box. What other people said would appear over their heads in cartoon balloons, as well as in the chat box. Unfortunately this meant that Toby couldn't actually talk back to her.

But her body moved to the portal and she had a disorienting and frighteningly long moment of blankness as the tangle of code that was her avatar got passed from one part of the virtual world to another. It went on just long enough for her to start to worry, and not long enough for her to panic.

When she could see again, she was in Dark Valley, and immediately she felt a peculiar sensation, as if something had brushed every nerve ending in her body at once. When she looked down, she could only see the faintest shadow of herself. The invisibility cloak was in place. The Ojibwa Medicine Man had autodispensed her a cowrie shell that appeared as an active icon in her powers inventory.

It was showtime. But she was at a distinct disadvantage—unless she was standing right next to someone who was saying something on the general broadcast channel, she would not know what was being "shouted" across the whole zone. And there were shouts she needed to hear—like where the Wendigo had spawned. Toby knew this, though, and presumably he got some directions, because suddenly her body lifted into the air (she had chosen "flying" as her means of transportation) and headed off game-east. She knew it was game-east because the sun was heading toward setting behind her.

The melee was easy to spot from up here. The Wendigo towered head and shoulders above the trees, and those trees were not small. It looked as if he was playing host to a small army of Far Eastern martial artists, while less uniformly clad people stood around and watched. She winced and looked away from one fellow who looked like he was wearing a cow that had died in a collision with a paint truck.

She recognized the Wendigo's attackers from numberless articles in online gaming forums. *Chinese gaming clans. Literally cutthroat. If they think they can get away with it, they'll kill your avatar, steal your stuff before you come back from revival, and bugger off with it to sell on eBay.* It was virtual loot of course, it didn't exist in any form except here, but there were a lot of people who would pay real-world money for some presumed advantage in the game. It made no sense to her, except in the abstract: work equals money, and if someone has worked to get something, it should be worth money.

Still, she could admire their finesse and their sheer dogged tenacity. Blades flashed, feet and fists thudded, the Wendigo bawled its outrage. It surprised her at first that so many people were simply standing around watching, until she caught a speech balloon over the head of one of the attackers in the gray-on-white of broadcast speech, warning everyone in the zone that this Wendigo had been claimed by the Red Lotus Clan and interlopers were not welcome.

Despite being the biggest, baddest thing around, the Wendigo was having a hard time against this bunch. It couldn't grab god-mode to turn the tables on them, because no one around here was in god-mode. It could heal itself, but not as fast as it was used to doing, because the entire Red Lotus clan was wearing their talismanic cowrie shells, preventing it from using their health to heal. They were whittling it down, bit by bit, and it did not like that at all.

There was grumbling in local speech about the selfishness of the Red Lotus Clan—after all, this was a rare case where everyone who laid any damage on the thing was going to get juicy loot! But no one moved in on the Wendigo. Finally, a brass-bikini-clad wench with breasts so enormous that in the real world she'd be falling over from the sheer weight of them pushed her way through the onlookers. What she said was pretty much indecipherable texting-based leet-speak, but the gist of it was that she was going to go beat on the Wendigo too, this wasn't a Player versus Player zone, so what could the clan do to her?

"Dude, chill," came the reply from a seven-foot-tall, blue-skinned trollish-looking thing. "They can herd a hundred zombies on ya and loot the corpse."

The wench typed an explicative-laden reply, most of which was bleeped out by the profanity filter, but no longer made any moves toward joining the melee.

Through this all, the faint ghosting of the code was over everything, like an arcane sort of filter. Not like that famous business in *The Matrix* with the streaming numbers. No, the numbers didn't move—but they did change. There was her real-time trace, if only she knew machine code well enough to read it.

But she was here for another purpose, and while the Wendigo was busy with what looked like the casts of twelve kung fu movies, it was time for Ellen to do her thing.

"Now, Toby," she said, and felt a tingle as somewhere out there in the real world, Toby hot-keyed her spells.

Through study, research, and what she suspected was an instinctive grasp of how magic interfaced with technology, Ell could create a process—which was, in essence, what a spell really was. She had the world book for this game; she had access to whatever crafting items existed in this virtual world. She could find the equivalents to real-world items and she could use them to help create a process that would take her energy and send it into the machine to do her bidding.

In other words, in this world of pixels and bits, she could combine virtual eye of newt and imaginary tongue of frog and give herself the power of mage-sight, which would let her see just how magic was flowing. She hadn't done it until now because she wanted to be very certain that the Wendigo was fully concentrating on its attackers. Using real magic here would light her up like a Christmas tree to the eyes of something that could see magic too.

Oh, now this is an interesting side effect. . . . She hadn't expected to feel anything, given that the only sensory feedback she was getting was pain. But she felt her whole body start to tingle as a faint and subtle shimmer washed over her. Fortunately, in this crowd full of people with rainbow-effect auras demonstrating their powers and abilities, it passed completely unnoticed.

She closed her eyes and counted to three as the tingle intensified, then looked.

And yes . . . there was a third layer of reality now. The machine code, the visuals, and . . .

The power map.

She could see how the energy that was magic was flowing within this place. The Wendigo was lit up with so many kinds and flavors of power that if she had been using her real eyes she would have been blinded. And the second she saw that—her heart plummeted.

Because this could only mean one thing.

This Wendigo was not a mythago.

This Wendigo was the real thing.

Self-aware? Oh my, yes. And if he hadn't had all his attention concentrated on squashing the ninja hordes, if he'd caught sight of *her*, all lit up with similar power, she would have been in very dire straits.

It was very strange, being grabbed by sheer terror while inhabiting Stevie the Elf. There was no corresponding physical reaction, no tightening of the throat, no cold sweats, no shaking. That made it easier to do what she generally did when she was scared shitless. She went entirely cold and analytical, her mind working much faster than normal. She dictated everything she saw to Toby, with one eye on the Wendigo. Because if it noticed her—

She saw power passing along what she knew must represent the communication channel that cut across all the servers, but it was power that was actually part of the Wendigo. That told her that all the Wendigos were actually one Wendigo. Its essence, its soul, was shared out across the entire game system. Which made sense, since this was the real thing. That would have ramifications, but she would think about it later. Right now, she was eyes and a mouth.

Power was flowing from the avatars around it to the Wendigo as well—not just from the ones it was fighting, but from the onlookers, and even from PCs beyond the onlookers. It wasn't much, the merest thread from each— but a hundred thousand threads can be spun into a very strong rope. . . .

The sight was startling. This wasn't the in-game health that the Wendigo had been mostly blocked from absorbing. This was something else entirely. It was as if every person logged into the game was somehow feeding the Wendigo. No, more than that—it looked as if the Wendigo was feeding *on* them, magically.

And then it dawned on her; that was exactly what was happening.

And she knew why.

It was, in fact, her worst-case scenario.

"Toby, log me out," she said quickly—because the Wendigo must not be allowed to know that there was a real magician here, someone who could do what the monster *wanted* to do. If it flipped the code switches on *her* . . .

She felt her "body" freeze and there was a moment of blackness.

Ellen opened her eyes, staring up at the ceiling of her computer room, flat on her back in her zero-g recliner. Her body, her real body this time, broke into a cold sweat.

But now was not the time for paralysis, because time itself was against them.

The Wendigo wanted out of the computers and into the real world.

And it had a plan to get there.

The phone woke Tom before the alarm did. Because of the weird hours he sometimes worked, blackout blinds weren't good enough for his bedroom; he had silvered bubble insulation, the kind they wrapped around hot-water tanks, carefully taped over all the glass in the windows, and heavy curtains over that. So his bedroom was pitch-black and very peaceful, until that peace was shattered by the shrill ring of the phone.

Fortunately the thing lit up when it rang, or he would never have been able to find it in the dark.

"I know I woke you, and I'm sorry." The voice on the other end of the line was female and unfamiliar. His sleep-fogged brain couldn't even come up with a shadow of an ID before the caller identified herself. "This is Ell. Remember when I told you there could be a worst-case scenario?"

He didn't, but she took his vague mumble as assent.

"It's the worst-case scenario."

That woke him up like a bucket of cold water in his face. "How worst case is worst case?"

"Imagine the Wendigo in the real world."

Oh, God. Oh, God.

"Meet me at the offices. I need to pick your brains. We're running out of time."

He blinked at that. Yesterday she had said that it wouldn't make much difference one way or the other if they sat on this for a few days or weeks.

"What changed?" he demanded harshly, phone clutched in a hand gone suddenly sweaty. "Yesterday you said we had time—"

"Yesterday I didn't know it had another way of feeding."

"What?"

"It's feeding on belief, Tom. On your players' belief. The more they believe in the world, the more real the game feels to them, the more they feed the Wendigo. It was one thing when that belief was just passively allowing it to be there. Now it's active feeding; the Wendigo is sucking it all in. That is real, in the real-world real, it happens 24/7 and it isn't something we can block with code. Meet me at your offices."

There was a click, followed by the dial tone. Tom stared at the softly glowing phone for a moment before gently replacing it in the cradle. Then he threw himself out of bed and grabbed clean clothing out of the laundry he'd just done.

His mind was racing so hard he drove on automatic; he didn't even realize he was at the garage until he found himself turning into his usual parking space. As he climbed out of the car and looked around, a little dazedly, he saw by the scattered vehicles in the otherwise empty space that the rest of the team had been called in too.

It wasn't just instinct that took him to the conference room, it was the smell of fresh donuts and coffee. A very grim-faced Ell, eyes showing the lack of sleep, was presiding over both. The rest of his team were slumped into chairs around the table, fueling up.

"Good, that's the last of you," Ell said with a nod to Tom. "Now . . . I hate to do this to you, but we are in a world of trouble here. So I need to know something and I need to know it now. Do you guys believe that I know what I'm talking about? Because if you don't . . ." She shook her head. "Let's just say I need absolute trust from you, because if you thought what I said before was crazy, you're going to send for the nut-wagon before I'm done now. And we don't have time for that. So. Anyone?"

She looked around the table. So did Tom. Kathy bit her lip. "Um . . . last night . . . the rest of us decided we were going to check the Wendigo out ourselves, on some of the other servers." Kathy looked very pale. "It . . . it did things we never coded it to do. And . . ." Her voice faltered and died for a moment and she looked down at her hands. When she looked back up again, there was real fear in her eyes. "Let's just say we all compared notes and . . . whatever you say, I think we'd believe."

Ell's lips twitched. "Scared you, did it? Good enough.

All right, here's the skinny. We have the worst possible scenario going. It's not a mythago. It's the real thing. It's intelligent and self-aware; it's learning more every second your servers are up because it can access whatever is on those servers. It knows very well it's not in the real world, and it wants out." Again, she looked around the table. Tom noted that although Erik and Kathy looked shocked, no one looked as if they disagreed with Ellen's assessment. "I've been pounding away at the world book for the last couple hours, and I think I know how it happened. In Ojibwa myth, a human becomes a Wendigo when he resorts to cannibalism. So tell me something, Erik—what, exactly, did you code the Wendigo *from?* Did you make him from scratch or did you mod something that already existed?"

Erik looked as if he had swallowed something very sharp and painful. "I . . . I tested out the health and power absorbing powers first. I used an old avatar I already had rather than roll something up, I just revised him for a Boss Monster, went into the beta costume generator and the devs-only art to add the code for the new look and tested it on him, tested the powers the same way, the size-increasing business as he fed . . ."

Ell closed her eyes. "The game equivalent of a human getting into cannibalism. That'd do it, all right. If you have a cannibalistic avatar, you already have the Wendigo in concept, and that's how you guys invoked him. This"—she put her hand on the world book—"this was the equivalent

327

of a summoning spell. The only reason he's taken this long to figure out that where he found himself is not where he wants to be, is because he's stretched across all of your servers. He literally was scatterbrained until he learned how to talk to himself on the chat channel."

"Oh, God," Erik moaned.

"Look, you couldn't have known." Ell was very quick to say that, for which Tom was grateful. But then she added, "Unfortunately, after looking through your world book, I figured out that it's only a matter of time before he gets what he wants."

The shocked looks around the table, and the silence that met those words, were the only answer they could give her. Finally it was Tom who spoke. "I thought you said that magic could only affect little things—"

"I said it could only affect little things given the level of power that most magicians have access to. But belief is power, and you have thousands and thousands of gamers believing, somewhere inside themselves, in the Wendigo. I bet a percentage of them dream about fighting him every night. That belief, that power, is trickling into him as long as the servers are up."

She tapped the world book. "The last thing he needs to transition—to manifest—in the real world, is in here too. You guys have a crafting system, and a game system that dumps out a lot of loot. The little descriptors define what that loot would be if it was in the real world, so each of these things is a kind of magical equivalent of the real thing. Magic works on symbols and words. One of the things that makes me a techno-shaman is that I am good at figuring out how to make modern objects stand in for the ancient equivalents—and you've coded the ancient equivalents right here.

"Put them all together on a single avatar, in the right order, and bingo, you have a working spell. I know this because I've done it myself, to assemble a collection of objects that gave me the equivalent of what I would need to work a traditional magic spell."

Tom blinked at her. "You mean, one that worked in the game?"

"Several, actually." She nodded. "And I had another look at the snapshot of the Wendigo code that we took. He's doing the same thing. You guys managed, somehow, to create exactly the right objects for a manifestation spell. He needs two things: power, which he is getting, and certain objects, of which he has all but one or two. He's been stealing the objects he needs from the avatars he defeats, just like someone looting a body."

Erik looked at her with his mouth open. "But—how?" he blurted. "He's a Boss Monster! He doesn't have loot slots . . ." Suddenly, he went white. "He does," Erik said softly.

Ell nodded. "Because you coded him out of an old avatar and you forgot to delete the loot slots."

"And when he fights people—"

"He can swap the ownership codes and take what he

needs from them." She rubbed the side of her hand nervously. "The only reason he can't get this stuff for himself is that he *is* a Boss Monster, so he can't go on quests. He can only spawn in and hope to get what he needs off his enemies. He's not more than a couple of pieces away from having that manifestation spell. Luckily, the world book says those items are ultrarare. But the Wendigo is on *all* the servers, so the odds are he's going to find what he's missing sooner rather than later."

The silence around the table felt like the silence when the boss comes in and tells you a project is canceled. Only more so. They looked at one another. The only noise was the air from the vents.

Erik looked hungover and had stubble. Kathy looked like she might have slept in her clothes. Tom knew what he looked like—just as bad. But the expression they all shared was pure fear.

"So what do we do?" Tom spoke for all of them.

"We could take those pieces of loot out of the game," Kathy suggested.

But Ell shook her head. "There's more than one manifestation spell, and he'll just switch to another. Besides, unless it's crafted into something, loot doesn't go away, and someone could still have the piece on his avatar. You can't track down every player and ask to go through his backpack. But the thing about spells is that they are tricky things and liable to reverse on you. The one thing I need to know is this—can you slip something into the game code, a change in the description of something, while the servers are still up?"

"Something like a description change? That doesn't affect game play and goes into a table?" Tom nodded. "Yeah. We don't like doing real-time patches and hot fixes, but it can be done."

Ell took a long breath. "In that case, I have a plan. And I need all of you to help with it."

The team was assembled, although Ell was the only one actually inhabiting the avatar. It wasn't Stevie the Elf this time, or at least, it wasn't the original Stevie. This had originally been what the devs called "a brick," a character made more as a meat-shield than a damage-dealer. Stevie looked the same, still elfin and slim, with a sword as big as she was, but now she could absorb punishment. Lots of punishment.

They'd done some dev tweaking on it, of course. It didn't quite have the fast response of the light little fighter, but Ell could whack things out of the park with that broadsword. And it would be *Ell* doing the moves now, not Toby and his key mashing. She had full control, within the code limits of the game itself.

And she was practically on fire with real magic. She had defense spells up like nothing anyone in this game would ever see again (she hoped); plus spells for luck, to skew the bits; spells for accuracy; and spells to increase her damage. If this had been in the real world, even with Toby's help, creating and maintaining all those spells would have left her as limp as overcooked linguine, but this wasn't the real world. In the game, she could keep this sort of thing up all day if she had to. She hoped she wouldn't have to.

Tom was on a Healer, a brown-robed, bearded Druid-type wielding a honking big wooden staff, with every long-distance fix-up power in the game. It was his job to stay out of the way and keep everyone from faceplanting. Kathy was on a big Nordic blonde in a fur bikini and a pair of shaggy boots, a light fighter like the original Stevie the Elf. Erik was on an emaciated, white-faced, black-clad, winged archer, standing back with Tom. Kathy and Erik would do the damage. Ell was there to keep the Wendigo's attention on her and hold it, like the red cape of the bullfighter.

They were about to run what Ell privately was thinking of as "Operation Briar Patch." Which sounded harmless enough, and the consequences for everyone but her if this didn't work were fairly minimal.

For her . . . well, she honestly did not know. She'd never ridden an avatar before. If an animal was killed while you were riding it, if you were experienced—which she was—you could get out safely. But this was unexplored territory, and the machine operated on micromilliseconds, not human reaction time.

Of course none of them had the slightest idea that she was doing this, that her "character" was the real Ellen. They thought she was just playing an avatar, as they were.

On the plus side, avatars didn't really "die"; they went down to zero health and fell over and couldn't move unless a friend restored their health and "resurrected" them. They could also resurrect in a Healing Shrine, but that cost, and some people preferred to wait for as long as it took for a friend to come along.

If you were in a zone that allowed players to defeat other players, it was definitely a winner-take-all situation. Lose in PvP and the victor got to "loot the body." That might be how the Wendigo was taking what it needed from the players it defeated—switching on the PvP code. Or it might simply be switching the ownership code of the objects, as she'd first surmised. She really hoped it was the second. If it could switch on PvP code, it could make things very uncomfortable and even more complicated for her and her team.

She wondered if the Wendigo really understood what it was doing and knew how to work the code, or if it was just a matter of "want-take," with the code manipulation a combination of magic and instinct. She really, really hoped it was the latter. Because a Wendigo that actually knew how to manipulate code could go anywhere and do anything. It could lock down an entire secure facility building full of people, make sure they couldn't escape, and feed at its leisure. Unrestricted by the game code it would grow, and grow . . .

The Ojibwa Wendigo was limited by the small numbers of people in the remote forests where it lurked. In the modern world . . . imagine it loose in New York City . . .

They waited for Tom to locate where it was now, because it was no longer despawning on its own. The only time it despawned now was when it got taken down by gaming clans.

"Got it," Tom said in the little cartoon balloon that appeared over his head. But now, thanks to another spell, she could hear them too. He sounded like Dr. Stephen Hawking. It was a good thing the avatars couldn't giggle.

"Are you shutting the servers down now?" she asked. The world flickered a little as her avatar tried to do something it couldn't—laugh hysterically. She sounded like Stephen Hawking too.

"Roger," Erik replied. "Mark's handling it himself. The first five-minute warning is going out on Emerald server now."

One by one, the game servers were going to be shut down. As that happened, more and more of the Wendigo's "self" would consolidate on the servers that were still up, until, finally, this would be the only server left, and all of the Wendigo would be here.

That would be the most dangerous moment of all.

Every bit of its consciousness would be *here*, and it would be concentrating entirely on them. And they had something it wanted very, very badly.

They had the last two pieces of loot that would allow it to manifest.

"There's some more Chinese gold farmers engaged with it," Erik said, reporting what one of the troubleshooting game masters was telling him in the real world. "Serge is ready to take them out of play as soon as we get there."

Serge was probably going to enjoy this. Most people who loved their games hated the gold farmers, likening them to cockroaches. And that was when they were feeling polite.

But the gold farmers had served their purpose against the Wendigo. They kept it occupied, kept it from roaming the zone and ambushing players. What was even better, they apparently kept its attention so fully occupied that it was not able to interfere with the AI to make the zone harder than it should be. As long as the Wendigo was spawning, the rest of the zone ran smoothly; the other problems vanished. Gold farmers never kept much loot on their own avatars, so the Wendigo never got a chance to pick up those precious couple of pieces of loot when it defeated them. And they kept other players, who *might* have had those bits of illusory treasure on them, from engaging the Wendigo themselves.

"Never thought I would be grateful to those greedy—" the

Hawkinglike voice sputtered unintelligibly and Ell realized she still had the profanity filter engaged on this avatar. Well, no way to flip it now.

"Showtime?" she asked. There was a chorus of yesses, and Erik spread a pair of sinister ebony wings and headed off for the location of the Wendigo, followed by the rest of the team.

"How's our countdown?" she asked as they all flew over the dusky countryside, a landscape so mist enshrouded that she had to strain to see the code underlying it.

"The servers are coming down now."

There were a lot of servers. It would take about thirty minutes to shut them all down. Ell and the devs were not going to engage the Wendigo themselves until it finished off the gold farmers. Which it would. She was pretty sure of that. The servers hadn't come down since the last attempt to patch the beast. No one had ever seen what the Wendigo could and would do if it had all of its consciousness in one place.

They joined the crowd around the fight to watch.

There were at least a hundred people engaged with the creature, and Ell was glad she was on something even better than her home rig with a big fat pipe and a lot of RAM, because she was pretty sure she would otherwise be suffering terminal lag what with all of the powers going off at once. It looked like a Las Vegas show. Fireballs, ice bolts, torrents of pure energy, all poured down on the Wendigo. Swords of metal, flame, and ice slashed at it. Arrows of a dozen styles arced toward it. In the real world, the landscape around the beast would have been utterly obliterated, but of course, nothing that the players did altered the terrain, so the bushes and trees the Wendigo stood among remained serenely and eerily green. The ground, which should have been pockmarked at best, merely demonstrated cracks and craters that lasted a few seconds and sprouted fires that did nothing to damage the "turf."

After so long studying the game and the Wendigo, it became apparent to Ell pretty quickly that her speculation was right. The more servers went down, the more of the Wendigo's "self" migrated here. And the more of that "self" there was, the more formidable it became.

It was catching even the gold farmers by surprise.

To coordinate, they generally used the open channel rather than their team channel, and it was usually only the leaders who "said" anything. Now, however, the air over their heads was full of balloons with indecipherable characters, generally followed by one or more exclamation points.

It would have been funny if it hadn't been so grim.

The Wendigo slammed its foot into the ground, knocking half of its attackers over, and a lot of them didn't get up again. Their healers scurried among the fallen, trying to revive them. The Wendigo, acting like an intelligent creature and not an AI creation, ignored the attempts of the bricks to engage its attention and flailed its club at the healers, felling those who were not fast enough to get out of the way. Someone shouted something in red and bold-face, and the fallen vanished, presumably back to a Healing Shrine, while the rest engaged again.

More avatars swarmed into the area as the Wendigo laughed and swung its club.

"Pleese!" came the shout in the local channel. *"Pleese! Everone to help!"*

There was a moment of shock when the onlookers realized that the gold farmers had gotten in so far over their heads that they were not going to be able to get out of this one without logging out. There was another moment as some people realized that there was something very, very wrong with this Wendigo.

Then there was a flurry of activity. About half of the avatars watching either fled to the Zone Portal or logged out in place. The rest waded in.

"Man," said Kathy, "I hope you guys are recording this."

If the fight had been epic before, it was of Hollywood proportions now. There must have been close to five hundred avatars piling onto the Wendigo, so many that a lot of them couldn't even get within close combat distance. Those that could fly took to the air and layered themselves above the ones on the ground. Within moments, there was literally not a pixel of the Wendigo to be seen; nothing but an enormous stack of avatars and powers.

And then, with a deafening roar, the stack burst apart

and avatars went flying in all directions, to land in twisted, unmoving tangles all around the beast.

The Wendigo was still standing.

None of the players were. Except Ell, Tom, Kathy, and Erik.

The Wendigo turned toward them as the gold farmers' avatars vanished—their accounts suspended for exploits and cheating. As for the rest of the PCs . . .

"Run!" The word sprouted in local chat balloons all over the field, like a blossoming of strange flowers over the greensward. Many avatars fled or disappeared.

Ell's team stepped forward.

The Wendigo laughed—and stopped abruptly as Ell triggered all of her combat spells and all of her game powers at once. The rest followed suit, except that they didn't have any real magic. They didn't need to. The real-world magic was serving its real purpose, which was to rivet the attention of the Wendigo on her. She looked like a walking fireworks display within the game and to anything that could see magic.

"Holy @#%$!" said someone nearby. "Devs!"

And the cheering began, at least among the real player avatars—interesting. This wasn't the real world. They didn't know this horror was a real threat. And yet they were acting as if this team had come to save them.

They're invested in the system. They believe. Intellectually they know that this is a game, but their guts tell them it's real.

*And belief is power . . . power we are taking away from it. The
ranger isn't gonna like that, Yogi.*

She stepped well in front of the rest, lit up like a Christmas tree with magic. For form's sake, she also shouted at it,
even though she knew very well that the code to grab the
thing's attention wouldn't work, and it wouldn't understand English. And she didn't know Ojibwa.

"Hey, you! Your father gets studied by proctologists,
and your mother took First Place at the Kennel Club
Show!"

There was a fair amount of "WTF?" behind her, which
her speech synthesizer rendered as "dubyou-tee-eff" until finally some bright boy a bit faster on the uptake than
the rest blurted, "She said its dad is an @$$40L3 and its
mother is 61TCH!" That gave rise to a veritable torrent of
LOL and LMAO and other acronyms the speech synthe-
sizer was sputtering on. But she was already moving, be-
cause the magic alone was enough to tell the Wendigo it
had a *real* enemy to face, and it was coming straight for
her.

As the huge club slammed into the ground half a foot
from her, she was terribly grateful that she was the one in
control now, and not Toby. Maybe the Wendigo couldn't
kill her in here—but it could certainly make her hurt.

She dashed sideways, spun, and slashed at the
Wendigo's legs. It howled and stomped a foot the size of a
Yugo, knocking them all backwards. For Ell, landing *hurt*.
She cursed, not caring who heard her and blowing the

Rated-T-For-Teen right out of the water. But she also got right back up again, feeling a wash of warmth as Tom hit her with a "healing spell"—the game kind, not the real-world kind. The pain disappeared.

Erik's arrows kept the thing busy swatting them away like pesky insects, while she got to her feet again.

This time she came at it from the rear, with a combination of an overhand slash followed by a sideways cut that also took her out of range again. The Wendigo howled and something utterly unexpected happened.

One of the nearby groups of NPCs, computer-generated citizens and nonadversarial characters, just—vanished. And the Wendigo's health indicator went back up to full.

This time it was Tom's turn to curse, though he did it in team-speak. "He can't *do* that!" Tom shouted, after a good polysyllabic spew.

"He did it," Erik pointed out. "We just have to keep him away from the personified objects."

"Ell, he's eating NPCs!" Kathy said. "I'll get someone to try and herd them—"

"No, don't!" That was Erik. "The only person who can herd NPCs is a game master or a dev, and—"

"No no no no, we do *not* want someone with god-mode in here!" Tom replied.

"I'll try to keep it away from the NPCs," Ell shouted back, rushing in for a fast double swipe and jumping away again. She had to get the Wendigo focused on her long enough to see what she was carrying.

That was going to take a while, because all the loot components she was carrying to create her actual spells would conceal the specific things the Wendigo was looking for, at least for a time

And that was the point. It had to think she had these two rare items by accident—part of a massive pile of loot she just happened to be carrying around. If it ever got the hint that this was a trap . . .

Ellen hurled another insult at it, while Kathy dashed in and out again, much faster than Ell was. Erik poured down withering covering fire. He and Kathy damaged the Wendigo exponentially more than Ellen could.

The Wendigo backhanded her, and for a moment, as her avatar went flying through the air, Ell herself was physically blinded with pain. But Tom was right on her with the heals. She felt another burst of pain as she hit, then Tom's fix went in and she got back up on her feet.

Suddenly, the Wendigo stopped moving. It stared at her.

She continued to behave as if it was about to attack her. She had to. She didn't want it to realize there was a person riding the avatar, rather than just pushing buttons on the other side of the screen.

It had to take the bait. It had to.

Tom first realized that there was something very odd about Ell's avatar when they all confronted the Wendigo.

342

At first, he couldn't put a finger on what bothered him; it just seemed that there was something different about it. He knew what it wasn't—it wasn't that it didn't have any effects auras, because they'd shut off the auras to keep their stations from lagging during the fight-to-come. And it wasn't anything about how the avatar looked—he'd seen far more outlandish creations in the time he'd been working on the game. But there was something about it that bothered him, down at the subconscious level.

It wasn't until he put his own avatar into a "forced rest position," because he hated how it fidgeted otherwise, that it dawned on him.

Her avatar wasn't fidgeting. But it wasn't in any of the "rest" positions, either.

This was something that every avatar, even the god-mode signature avatars, had coded right down at the most basic level. To keep the game from looking like a field of statues whenever characters "stood around" to talk about something, the avatars were coded to go through a repeating loop of five different positions. Left hand on hip, left foot forward. Hand down. Left foot back. Both hands on hips, right foot forward. Both hands down. He referred to it as "fidgeting"—most players got used to it, but it drove him mad. He always put his avatar into "default rest one," which was hands clasped thoughtfully behind the back. There were other rest positions, like feet wide apart with hand on sword hilt; he just happened to like that one.

Stevie the Elf wasn't posed like any other avatar. She

had her left arm crossed over her abdomen, her right elbow resting in her left hand, her right fist resting on her chin and mouth.

That had never been coded for.

Now, either Ellen McBride was the greatest game programmer *ever,* to get into the core character coding and add that—in which case, what did she need the rest of them for?—or there was something seriously bizarre going on.

He became even more convinced when she finally moved and began jeering at the Wendigo. The avatar didn't perform any of the standard taunting moves. Instead, she was waving both hands over her head, then blowing raspberries. Which was very funny and visually arresting, and certainly got the Wendigo's attention—but it was an alteration to the core programming.

When she finally moved out and started fighting the thing, Tom realized exactly what was going on. In college he'd had some friends in the fencing club, and some of *them* had a subgroup that went out sparring with real, Renaissance-style rapiers. They were careful, and they were very, very good, and a couple of them had gone on to careers in Hollywood as stunt sword fighters and coaches.

Ellen's avatar moved like that.

This stuff couldn't be coded for. The movements were just too subtle, the patterns too complicated. And yes, the devs had overridden the code for the two swordswomen,

reducing the recharge time for their powers to zero, beef-
ing up their reaction time to "as fast as you can mash
buttons," and seriously buffing the accuracy and damage.

But no avatar could possibly move like that.

Ell was outfighting Kathy, who had played this game
practically every day since they rolled out the first, buggy,
beta version. The only reason she wasn't doing more damage than Kathy was because of her inherent type—bricks
were coded to be slow and there was nothing to be done
about that. Kathy could get in a hit and a half for every hit
Ell made.

But.

But—

Ell was doing strikes and move combinations Tom had
never seen outside of a live, human fighter.

As crazy as it sounded, as impossible as it seemed,
there was only one possible conclusion.

Stevie wasn't an avatar. Somehow, that elf *was* Ellen
McBride.

Impossible.

Inconceivable.

Unbidden, his mind supplied the quote from *The
Princess Bride: "You keep using that word. I do not think it
means what you think it means."*

But if that was her—what was going to happen when the
Wendigo hit—

It hit.

And he didn't know how he knew, but he did. Red numbers exploded out of her—and pain. Real pain.

Tom yelped and mashed buttons, pouring healing energy recklessly into her as if he had bottomless wells to draw on—which he did; they'd overridden that too. It wasn't god-mode, it was all hard-coded, so it wasn't anything the Wendigo could steal with a flick of a bit switch. But getting the powers to work still depended on his reaction time, and—

And the damn thing was hurting her when it hit her. So it was up to him to fix it. Fast. As fast as possible.

Sweat began pouring down his face and he let Kathy and Erik get dangerously low a time or two while he concentrated on Ell. If they dropped, he could get them up again, but if Ell dropped, what would happen?

He didn't know. According to the world book, you weren't actually *dead* unless you abandoned the avatar to find someone to bring you back to life. So if she just stayed there until he got her up, she *should* be fine . . .

She'd better be fine. Because the plan . . .

In the real world, sweat was pouring down his face, as he unconsciously jinked his real body around to semi-match the movements of his avatar.

This was bad. This was very bad. The plan—

He saw it coming. Saw the Wendigo's eyes suddenly light up with greed, an expression that no sane person would ever have coded for, and felt a wash of real-world terror.

Watched Kathy, Erik, and Ell freeze as the Wendigo's fear weapon hit them right through all of their protections. Watched the Wendigo's giant club come up and sweep down and smash Ell's avatar into the turf.

Saw something that—again—had never been coded for: a burst of purple-black incandescence shot out of the Wendigo as it combined the bits of loot and prepared to step out of the game world and into the real one.

He didn't need the typed *"now!"* that Ell's avatar (thankgodthankgodthankgod!) screamed at him across the team channel. His finger was already mashed down on the revival spell so hard that he almost dislocated it.

Ell's avatar came to life with a wash of light so bright that he had to shade his eyes. Then as the light passed through his shading hand into his brain, he realized it wasn't the kind of light you could shield against.

WTF? He was seeing magic?

Never mind. This might be magic, but it needed energy, and her bar was dropping fast as she poured everything into her spells. Black energy warred with white as the Ell and the Wendigo stood frozen. Tom fed her, then ran his avatar over to hers to pass potions to her. This was all in the plan. The Wendigo had to believe that she was fighting it to the last moment—

Suddenly the white light went out, as if it had been blown out. The purple-black light flooded the screen, then vanished. And so did the Wendigo.

347

Now he mashed another button so fast and hard that he *did* dislocate a finger joint. The button that took down the last server.

Then he ran for the cube that Ell was in.

Her T-shirt was drenched with sweat, her hair looked like she had stuck her finger in a light socket, and the last time he'd seen anyone who looked that exhausted, it'd been the winner of a marathon race.

But she was grinning from ear to ear and cradling something in her hands. She held it up for him to see.

Inside the promotional snow globe from Many Worlds Online, a tiny, and very lively, Wendigo raged.

They all gathered at the incinerator solemnly, yet Ell sensed the suppressed manic grins behind their quiet faces.

"You know," she said, holding the snow globe carefully in its nest of bubble wrap, "I've never understood why, in all of the movies about terrible monsters and magical din-guses, nine times out of ten the heroes take the damned thing and *put it somewhere safe.* I mean, come on! Sink it in concrete, an earthquake rips the building up. Drop it in the ocean, a shark eats it and gets caught by a fisherman. Shoot it into orbit, it gets picked up by an astronaut. Shoot it *out* of orbit, it gets brought back by an alien!"

"They want sequels," Tom said helpfully.

"*Oy*. No sequels for us. I'm with Elrond. Destroy the Ring, baby." She eyeballed the open incinerator door, then shot the wrapped snow globe into the heart of the glow, sending her dissipation spell after it in a burst of power, fueled by Toby, that left her a little weak-kneed. "Get out of my universe," she said quickly, before any of the others could quip "Hasta la vista, baby," or "I'll be back."

Words had power.

She felt the Wendigo dissolve into atoms, into wisps, into smoke on the wind, and finally, into the vague and amorphous memory of a memory it had been before the gamers got hold of it. She let out a sigh of relief.

"Your patches will take now," she told the team.

"I've written some extensive descriptor changes on it too," Erik said. "That's going in with the code patch. I put in some self-contradictory stuff, and borrowed some Lovecraft but used the wrong Elder Gods. The OCD trolls will be all over it, but . . ."

"No buts. You guys never read the forums anyway," Kathy said scornfully, calling up a weak laugh from the rest of them.

Mark Taylor ran his hands through his thinning hair. "Go home," he ordered. "You've earned your rest. And you"—he looked pointedly at Ell, who cocked an eyebrow at him—"you've earned yourself a big fat check. And a lifetime account. If you want it."

"I'll admit, this game is growing on me." She grinned.

"Besides, I have a bud who's been bugging me to join since the beta rolled out. Guess I have no excuse now."

"Guess not. Stop by Accounting and get your check and your account key." Mark waved tiredly at Ell, then followed the others back up the stairs, presumably to head home himself.

All but Tom.

She cocked an eyebrow at *him.* "Something on your mind?"

"I saw your magic," he said flatly. "When you and the Wendigo duked it out and you planted that misdirection spell on him. I saw that."

"Do tell." Interesting. Very interesting.

"Does that mean I'm a witch?"

"Techno-shaman. And no, it just means you can see magic. Or maybe you always could, and you've just *allowed* yourself to see it now." She waited to see what he would make of that.

He mulled it over. "Could I be? Could you teach me?"

She scratched her head and answered both questions. "Maybe. Depends on how bad you want it."

He mulled that over too. "I'll think about it. Buy you a cup of coffee?"

She chuckled. From the look on his face, she didn't think he was going to ponder for too long. She knew his kind. She'd taught them before, like Jin Lee. They got hold of something and they couldn't let it go until they understood it. And then there would be one more good guy between the world and the bad things out there that wanted to break in. "Deal. And you can give me advice on the best archetype to roll up to start with in this game of yours."

"And you can tell me how you exorcise a stealth fighter."

She laughed. "I'll go one better. I'll tell you *why*."

Yep. One more good guy. Life was excellent.